Death of a Blue Hero

Death of a Blue Hero

A. C. Tassie

*To Patricia Mayne Ellis, fellow scribbler.
'A dear and good friend is the best
of all possessions.' — Xenophon*

A C Tassie
XI – II – MCMXCVI

Northwest Publishing, Inc.
Salt Lake City, Utah

Death of a Blue Hero

All rights reserved.
Copyright © 1995 Northwest Publishing, Inc.

Reproduction in any manner, in whole or in part,
in English or in other languages, or otherwise
without written permission of the publisher is prohibited.

This is a work of fiction.
Although none of the occurrences portrayed should be treated as factual,
some of the characters and events are based on actual history.

For information address: Northwest Publishing, Inc.
6906 South 300 West, Salt Lake City, Utah 84047
J. B. 12-12-95

PRINTING HISTORY
First Printing 1996

ISBN: 0-7610-0014-3

NPI books are published by Northwest Publishing, Incorporated,
6906 South 300 West, Salt Lake City, Utah 84047.
The name "NPI" and the "NPI" logo are trademarks belonging to
Northwest Publishing, Incorporated.

PRINTED IN THE UNITED STATES OF AMERICA.
10 9 8 7 6 5 4 3 2 1

For Irene Lea

uxor maxima

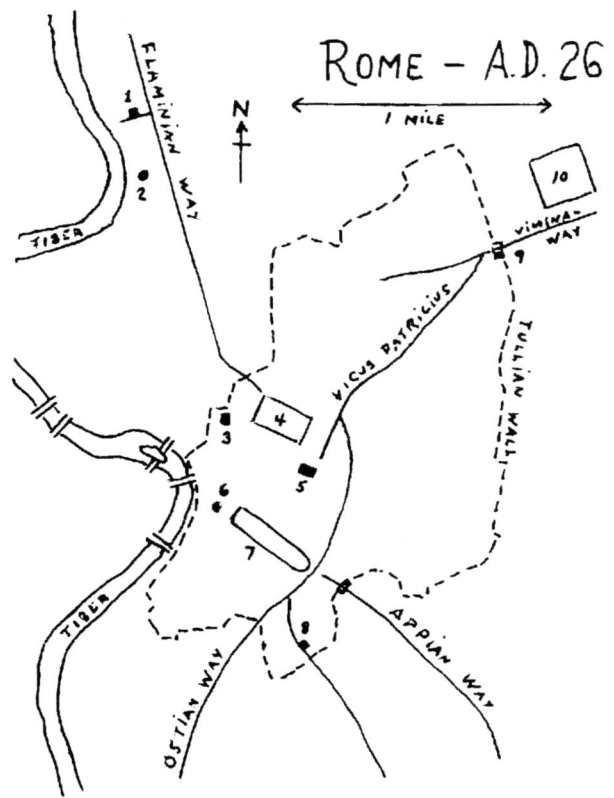

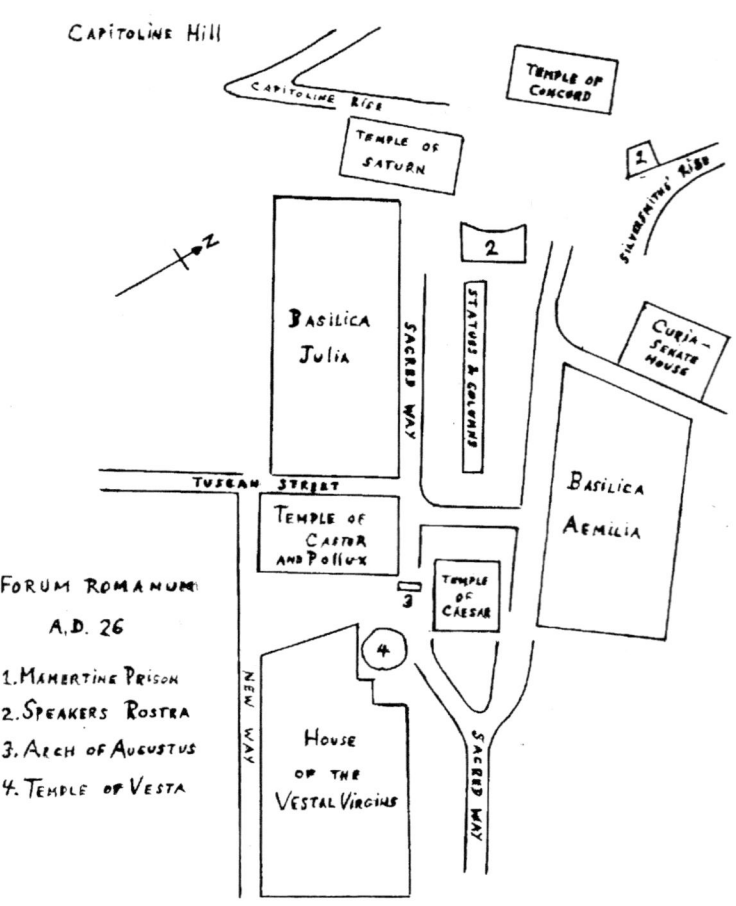

Prologue

It's almost six months since Vitalis Hesper was murdered. His two killers were given a spectacular public execution, for Vitalis Hesper had been the leading charioteer of the Blue Stable; his racing deeds acclaimed throughout the empire.

What the populace doesn't know is that the two men who were crucified and burnt alive for the athlete's murder were innocent of the crime. Oh, they were thugs all right—probably deserving execution for other reasons—but they hadn't killed the hero of the Blues as he lay half-drunk in a prostitute's bed.

I, Quintus Sutorius Anthus, know who murdered Vitalis Hesper. So do two other men, both in high position. They aren't aware of my existence, and I want it to stay that way. I want to stay alive.

Looking back, I wonder at my own brazen audacity in becoming involved in such a delicate situation. I, a slave, told a prefect of Rome that I was better qualified to investigate the murder of Vitalis Hesper than the police were!

Yes, I was a slave then; just plain "Anthus," not entitled to the three names of a freedman or the *toga* of a citizen. I was, as I still am, the household steward of Quintus Naevius Cordus Sutorius Macro, *praefectus vigilum* of Rome. My master commands the seven thousand *vigiles*, firefighters located throughout the fourteen city districts. As Prefect of the City Watch, Macro is a ranking public official, his position enhanced by additional responsibility as head of the *cohortes urbanae*, the city police force. The Urban Cohorts number four thousand men. Altogether, my master commands eleven thousand para-military troops—the equivalent of two legions.

So it was that the emperor, concerned about the mounting public outrage over the murder of their idol, directed Macro to find the killer—and quickly. Don't be too fussy, Macro was told by Tiberius Caesar, anyone will do. Just produce someone to satisfy the damned mob before it grows out of control.

And so it was that I discovered who the charioteer's killer was. It all seemed so easy at the outset, but I soon found myself in deep water. However, it ended well enough, for me. My *dominus*, Macro, gave me my freedom. But there were others involved who were much less fortunate.

There's an ironic twist, though—I never did tell Macro who murdered the charioteer. I couldn't, for Macro's own sake.

So I lied a little.

I

Flavius Merula absently rubbed the stump of his left wrist and sighed in satisfaction. Well, well—Tiberius Caesar had finally acknowledged the guild's offer with a personal letter. Nice of him to take notice, Merula thought, looking at the single piece of parchment on his table. A far cry from Augustus, that one. But the Claudians have a long-standing reputation for being aloof bastards, haven't they?

The thought of Augustus Caesar took him back to the day he'd lost his hand in a six-chariot pile up, a three-horse team race, it was. His hand had been mangled in the whirring wheel spokes of the wreckage, and a surgeon had removed what remained of it. Eighteen years since he'd lain in the *circus* infirmary, fighting the waves of agony from his shattered arm and broken ribs.

"Hero of the Reds, I was then," he said to himself. "Thirty-two years old and on top of the heap."

Merula's reverie was broken by the shrill staccato of women arguing in the street below. Annoyed, he looked down from the second-level arcade window to where, gathered around a street vendor's pushcart, two women in garish dress screamed at a third.

"Foreign bitches," he muttered, "why don't you all go back to Antioch, or whatever stinking place spawned you?" And that's another thing, he thought, all these babbling foreigners—Tiberius seems to care little how many of them infest the City. Augustus, now, he'd have done something about it!

Turning from the window, he went over to a large niche in the office wall in which stood a two foot bronze statue of Hercules. Resuming his reminiscence, he addressed the deity's image with the familiarity of one at ease with the god he'd served faithfully for many years.

"Hero of the Reds, yes, but a broken one when I looked up and saw Augustus Caesar standing beside my cot in the infirmary. He was at the games that day—had a good interest in racing, he did, unlike our present man—and had witnessed the accident. Put his hand on my shoulder, gentle like, he did, and said, 'Bad luck, Merula. But the surgeon says a tough nut like yourself will be around for some time yet.' Then he said something about me not worrying, the guild would take care of me."

Merula paused, then touched the statue's chin in respect, inclined his head and returned to the table.

And the guild did look after me, he reflected. Of course, the *imperator* was an honorary member and also patron of the athletes guild. A nudge and a wink from Augustus was, in effect, an imperial decree. So I became secretary to the guild and a few years later, president.

Augustus Caesar, master of the world, found time to visit an injured athlete, the son of a slave. Tiberius Caesar seems barely aware that we exist. Well, perhaps in his old age, Tiberius is mellowing toward the lower classes.

Merula read the letter again.

> *Tiberius Claudius Caesar Augustus Nero, pontifex maximus, holder of the tribunician power, consul; to Flavius Octavius Merula, President of the Traveling Athletes Guild Dedicated to Hercules, greeting. I endorse your Guild's offer of a gift to the mausoleum of the divine Augustus as a token of loyalty. It will please me to meet with your envoys, Severus Cerellius and Albino Vitalis Hesper on the seventeenth day of September, following the twelfth anniversary rites at the shrine of the divine Augustus. I consider it appropriate, in consideration of the occasion, to have my mother, Julia Augusta Livia, priestess of the shrine, present at our meeting. My nephew, Tiberius Claudius Drusus Nero Germanicus, will also attend. Farewell.*

• • •

Jostled by the crowd outside the imperial palace entrance, an old man peered through cataract clouded eyes toward the hubbub. "What's happening?" he whined to a boy standing beside him.

"It's Vitalis and Cerellius! They've just left their litters and are going into the palace!"

"Oooh," gasped the old man. He joined the crowd which had begun to chant "Vitalis! Vitalis! Cerellius! Cerellius!" He pictured the disbelief in his wife's face when he told her that he'd actually stood only a few feet from Vitalis and Cerellius. Relishing his good fortune, he wiped the drool from his chin and chanted the revered names as loudly as he could.

Four Praetorian guardsmen held the crowd back as two others escorted the charioteers toward the gate in the palace wall. The cheering admirers pressed forward, still chanting the names in unison. At the gate, Vitalis and Cerellius turned toward the milling crowd and raised their arms in a magnanimous gesture. Then each drew a handful of coins from the *sinus* of his tunic and flung them into the gathering.

Raising their arms again, in farewell, they entered the gate as the mob scrambled for the *sesterces* scattered by Vitalis, charioteer of the Blues, winner of 983 races and Cerellius, charioteer of the Whites, winner of 816 races.

They were escorted to a small colonnaded courtyard, bright in the afternoon sun but shaded by ivied trellises.

Their usher, a short swarthy man wearing a slave's tunic, bowed his graying, close-cropped head to the two men. "Caesar will arrive shortly. Please remain standing until you have been invited to sit. Do not speak until he has addressed you. When you do, refrain from any honorifics…merely call him 'Caesar.' Should you have occasion to address his mother, call her 'lady.' The emperor's nephew, should he speak to you, is to be called 'noble Claudius.'"

As the charioteers nodded their heads in acknowledgment, Vitalis spoke in Greek. "My friend and I thank you." The slave smiled thinly, replying in the same language, "My accent betrays my origins. And I know, of course, that the renowned Vitalis is from Corinthus."

Gesturing toward Cerellius, Vitalis said, "In deference to my Hispanic colleague, perhaps we should talk in Latin. What is your name?"

"Diocles, sir."

Vitalis handed him two coins. "Well, Diocles, here's two *denarii* for you…one for your courtesy and the other because us Greeks have to stick together, eh?"

At that moment another servant entered the courtyard,

drawing aside the entrance drapery. The athletes bowed their heads as Tiberius Caesar approached, followed by a handsome, elderly woman who supported herself with a cane, and a tall, blond, younger man with wide-set blue eyes.

Diocles spoke. "Caesar, the envoys of the Traveling Athlete's Guild, Severus Cerellius and Albino Vitalis Hesper." He bowed, retired to a corner of the courtyard and stood with his arms at his sides, staring straight ahead.

"Yes, yes. I welcome both of you," Caesar said abruptly, though his tone was friendly. "This is my mother, Julia Augusta Livia, and my nephew, Claudius."

The charioteers bent their heads first to the old woman, then to the young man, both of whom inclined theirs slightly in return.

So, this is Tiberius Caesar, Vitalis thought. At close quarters he's quite impressive. Strong build, tall, remarkably huge eyes—you'd never know he was sixty-seven, other than for a few lines on his face and his gray hair. I wonder why he wears his hair so long at the back, curling over his nape? He has an odd gait, walking stiffly with his head thrust forward. Family mannerisms, maybe? Livilla says that the Claudians are an eccentric bunch. She ought to know, being one herself. She says that Caesar's as randy as a goat and drinks like a fish. She should talk! And may Caesar never know that his niece and I have been sharing each other's beds in recent months.

"Now then, which one of you is Vitalis?"

Caesar's nephew stepped forward, lurching noticeably. "Oh, c-c-come now, uncle...everyone knows the f-f-famous Vitalis here," he stammered, indicating the taller of the two charioteers.

"Dammit, Claudius, maybe everyone else does, but *I* don't! You know I rarely attend the games...I have enough to do without sucking on a honey-cake in the *circus* at state expense like a baker's assistant."

"Y-y-yes, uncle, b-b-but…"

"Claudius, do be quiet," the old woman snapped. She looked at Vitalis. "True, my son has little time to attend the games, however I enjoy the races and recognize the celebrated charioteer of the Blue faction, Vitalis Hesper." She smiled at Cerellius, adding graciously, "And of course, the renowned Severus Cerellius from our Lusitanian Spanish province."

"Vitalis, the way I see it, you owe me about four million *sesterces*," Caesar said. "That's what I've lost betting on you in the recent games, even though I wasn't present. What have you to say to that?"

Vitalis spread his palms and shrugged. "Caesar, you mystify me. Of thirty-six races, I won twenty-three. Had you bet on each race, you would surely have more than doubled your wagers."

"Yes, yes. I suppose so," Caesar grunted, "but I didn't bet on every race…and that damned Armenian who does my horoscope will be looking for a new job soon. However, let's get on with business. And I think it's time we sat down."

At this, Diocles strode to the entrance, opened the drape and clapped his hands once. Three boy slaves, about ten years old, entered, each carrying a wide, cushioned, four-legged, backless chair. These they placed in a row a few feet apart, as Diocles laid two cushions on the stone bench which bordered the small fountain in the center of the courtyard. Caesar motioned his guests to sit on the bench as he sat on the middle chair, his mother and nephew to either side.

Now that formality was required, Caesar changed from brusque camaraderie to a more impersonal tone.

"My mother and I thank the Traveling Athlete's Guild Dedicated to Hercules for its generous gift of a bronze statue to be placed at the mausoleum of the divine Augustus. We approve your proposal that the statue be life-sized and that, in view of your guild paying the cost, the divine Augustus should be represented wearing the gladiatorial vestments. At the installation ceremony, which your guild suggests will be eight or nine months hence, my mother, Julia Augusta Livia, as priestess of the Augustan shrine, will preside over the rites. Convey to your guild our appreciation and assurance that I shall continue to support the privileges extended to you in the past by the divine Augustus. A transcript of this statement made in your presence shall be sent to the president of the Traveling Athlete's Guild."

The emperor nodded at the two men and relaxed, signifying conclusion of the brief formality. Diocles again walked to the entrance, clapped, and the three young slaves entered with wine and a tray of fruit and cakes.

"We thank you for your gracious reception, Caesar," Vitalis said, accepting a cup of wine from one of the boys.

Grunting in acknowledgment, Tiberius drained his cup with one swallow. While a boy replenished it, the emperor looked at Vitalis. "You seem to be the spokesman for your guild, eh?" He turned to the other charioteer. "How about you then, Cerellius? Are you the strong, silent type, or what?"

Cerellius' brown, scarred face creased in a smile. "Caesar, I'm neither a learned nor loquacious man, so I follow the maxim that if a fool holds his tongue, he will pass for a sage."

Pleased at the Lusitanian's reply, Tiberius threw his head back and laughed. Claudius spoke up.

"Th-that's Publilius Syrus."

Livia stared austerely at him. "Perhaps you'll be good enough to tell us what you're talking about, Claudius."

Claudius turned his head to her, jerking convulsively a couple of times. "P-Publilius Syrus, g-grandmother," he stammered. "The dramatist from Syria...he was once a slave and was honored by the div-div-divine Julius himself. Publilius wrote the maxim that Cerellius just quoted."

Livia sighed. "I'm sure that we're all impressed with your vast scholarship, Claudius."

Tiberius' face darkened at the exchange between his mother and his nephew. He put down his cup and arose, indicating that the audience was over.

The charioteers stood, bowed to their imperial hosts and thanked them for their courtesy. As they left the courtyard, escorted by Diocles, Tiberius suggested to Claudius that he accompany their guests to the entrance.

Alone with Livia, Tiberius snarled, "Dammit, mother, at times you infuriate me!"

"I'm well aware of that," she said, "ever since you were a small boy, in fact."

"Why do you always behave so miserably toward Claudius? He's a decent enough fellow and he's always treated you with respect!"

"Yes. And he'd better continue. He's a clumsy fool and we both know it."

Glaring in fury, Tiberius shouted, "Well, I won't stand for your belittling a family member in the presence of strangers! It's disgraceful."

She sipped her wine, looking at him over the rim of the cup. "What? A couple of sweaty athletes from the provinces? Neither of them Roman citizens. Do you honestly believe that I care a fig for what they might hear or think?"

"Mother, for your information, those sweaty athletes as you call them, probably made more money in the last few years than three-quarters of the senators and equestrians of Rome...and furthermore, throughout the empire, from Corduba to Damascus, millions of people have only vaguely heard of you and me, but they can no doubt recite in detail the racing history of Vitalis and his ilk, yes...and tell you the name of every horse they've ever driven!"

Livia gave an exaggerated sigh. "I wonder about you, Tiberius. You seem to be elevating such scum to the status of heroes."

Face mottled with anger, Tiberius stalked from the courtyard. At the entrance, he turned back to his mother, stabbing his finger at her. "No, dammit, I'm not! But in the public eye, they *are* heroes and—whether you like it or not—if one of them were to die, there'd be far more public grieving than ever there was for your husband, the late Augustus!"

II

Petronia, in one of her Slavic snits again, called me "King Anthus" and "your majesty."

Her latest ill-humor began yesterday when I called her my pretty *sucula*. "I'm not your 'little sow'!" she said in her thick Pannonian accent. She's only been in Rome four years and her Latin's shaky at the best of times. She usually ends up berating me in the incomprehensible gabble of Pannonia. And she can't get it through her head that *sucula* is a term of endearment.

Her birth name wasn't Petronia. When our mistress, Ennia, Macro's wife, brought her home from the slave market, Ennia assembled the household staff. "This is the new kitchen maid," she announced. "Her outlandish barbarian name is unpronounceable, so she shall be called Petronia."

Our mistress then informed me, "You, Anthus, have the task of teaching her Latin. I expect her to learn it passably well in three months. See to it."

"I'll do my best, *domina*," I assured her. And I meant it; one doesn't trifle with the mistress of the house of Macro.

Petronia wasn't exactly discoursing after the fashion of the late Marcus Tullius Cicero at the close of her instruction, but Ennia grudgingly granted her a pass in Latin.

As to Petronia's sneering use of "your majesty" and such, let me explain. I'm a Briton, born here in Rome in the year that the late Augustus Caesar was invested as consul for the twelfth time. That makes me thirty. My parents came from Britannia, with no choice in the matter. They had been slaves in the retinue of Tincommius, a British king.

Now don't get excited when I say "king." The Britons weren't too well organized back then and, in my mind, still aren't from what I hear in the market place. Kings are about two *sesterces* a dozen in Britannia, and each trying to outdo the others. King Tincommius probably held sway over a dozen or so hamlets and a few thousand people. Then, when a couple of other kings down the road hassled him, he headed for Rome to petition the emperor for help. Ever since the divine Julius invaded Britannia eighty years ago, for no good reason, the Brit kinglets have been pandering to Rome, hoping for foreign aid to assist them in clobbering one another.

When Tincommius arrived on the scene, Augustus Caesar had other things on his imperial mind, so he made vague promises, set Tincommius up with a small pension and a villa and forgot about him.

Soon after I was born, my father ran away and King Tincommius, good and just man that he was, vented his displeasure by having my mother flogged. We learned later that my *tata* had died in Moesia, near the Black Sea, while serving in Legion Five Macedonica. Come to think of it, my errant dad must have acquired false affidavits because only a Roman citizen can serve in the regular army.

But, whatever. When I was six, Tincommius sold my mother and me to a wealthy grain merchant, Julius Viator. Hoping to inflate our price, no doubt, the lying old *mentula* told the merchant that I was the bastard of Tincommius' son. And it was to our benefit, as our new master—impressed that one of his household servants was descended from royalty, albeit barbarian—treated us well.

He acknowledged my "noble" birth by sending me with his grandson to a private tutor, a humorless Greek *magister* who beat us regularly on general principle, but taught us well. By twelve I had a good grasp of mathematics, could read and write Latin fluently and was on my way to mastering Greek. At eighteen I became scribe and accountant to the Viator household.

Then my life was jarred by a double tragedy. My mother, wardrobe mistress to the merchant's wife, died of a fever that afflicted the city that winter. Shortly afterward, my master and mistress were taken by the same plague. The heirs to the estate had no need for a *scriptor amanuensis*. So I was sold, and for twelve years now have served Quintus Naevius Cordus Sutorius Macro.

But I was telling you why my Petronia gives me the mocking royal treatment when she's in a bad mood. Well, when Macro purchased me, the accompanying documents included an attestation by my former master that I was the grandson of a British king. Macro wasn't at all impressed by such nonsense, but when he introduced me to the household staff, he jokingly alluded to my alleged noble ancestry. The servants took this for what it was worth—"Big deal, but look at you now." But, all in all, they're an amiable bunch and any teasing they do isn't spiteful.

That's why my beloved snipes occasionally with her

royal allusions. Mostly, though, she's quite pleasant. No raving beauty, but she's handsome with black hair and dark brown eyes. The two of us are a good contrast, what with my blond hair and blue eyes. Her skin is darker than mine, which embarrasses her. Generally, patrician women value milky skin and avoid direct sunlight as much as possible. The lower orders, slaves included, emulate this and consider swarthiness unbecoming. Well, that's women for you, isn't it? Irrational about most things…there's no talking to them.

I haven't mentioned this to Petronia, yet, but I'd like us to be married. Of course, we'd need Macro's permission and even then the marriage wouldn't be recognized in law. Not while she and I are slaves.

But I don't intend to remain a slave forever.

III

    Vitalis traced a meandering pattern with his fingertip along the length of the woman's back. Face half-buried in a pillow, she sighed, squirming sensuously at his feathery touch. His fingers reached the crease of her buttocks, then moved slowly upward again toward her shoulders. Leaning on his left elbow, he studied her naked body. How old is she, he thought. Six, seven years older than me? At least that. Attractive, exciting, intelligent. She knows which way is up. So she should, Caesar's niece—and his son's widow—with all her background and opportunities. And she likes her men...made that clear from the start. Well, that makes her and me a good pair. I like my women.
    She also likes her wine. Too much so. I wonder, is her

tongue as loose in the presence of others as it is in mine when she's into the wine? I'd be wise to drift away from this situation. That won't be easy, knowing her. If she has a mind to, she can hurt me. Badly. She's arrogant and selfish—used to having things her own way. If I displease her, she could put an end to my career.

Yes, this Livilla could ruin me. Or worse. What if she wearies of me, or rather *when* she wearies of me—and she will, with her insatiable sexual appetite—she deems it prudent to ensure my silence, one way or the other? There's only one sure way, isn't there? A word to her uncle would be enough. The emperor would listen to her story over that of the likes of me. I may have wealth and be a hero to the mob, but Caesar and the aristocracy rule Rome. They wield power over life and death, make no mistake about that. And I, Vitalis Hesper, am not ready to die. Or if it must be, then let it be at the reins of a chariot with the applause of the spectators thundering in my ears.

Livilla wriggled onto her back, interrupting his speculation. "Bring me wine, my love," she said.

He brushed his lips against the tips of her breasts and kissed her throat. "You speak and I obey, my thrush."

"Yes," she whispered.

Arising, Vitalis pulled a loose tunic over his head and went to a sideboard, returning with a cup of wine.

"How long will you stay?" he asked.

"A few hours more. I have no engagements tonight. Last night, at Tiberius's decree, there was a party in honor of my mother's birthday. She's one of the few people he can get along with. Good luck to them. I can't get along with either." She drained the cup and held it out to him.

"The noble lady Antonia is one of the most respected people in Rome," Vitalis said, pouring her more wine. "Your mother is revered by all levels of society."

"Oh, yes," Livilla said peevishly, "and she never ceases reminding me that she's the daughter of Marc Antony."

"Rome may be the focus of an empire now, but many people honor its republican past and Antonius remains one of their great heroes," Vitalis said. "But that's not why your mother is admired—it's because she's set an example of good taste and matronly behavior for many years. The populace wouldn't admit it, but they need someone that they can look up to and respect. Tiberius doesn't fill their need as Augustus did—so it seems the void has been filled by the lady Antonia."

"What a long speech," she said archly. She sat naked on the edge of the couch and handed him her cup. "My virile charioteer is most philosophical today, isn't he? I'd never have thought that such lofty sentiments would be lodged in the mind of an athlete."

Annoyed at her condescension, Vitalis nonetheless affected a jaunty manner. "Come now, my pretty egg, you know I'm no moralist. I know full well what I am, a public performer who does his job well. I was merely observing that the lady Antonia is high in the public esteem."

"You also are esteemed by the populace."

"Well, yes," he agreed. "And the public delights in the antics of a theater comedian. But it reveres a gifted tragedian. Your mother and I are to be contrasted, not compared."

Livilla sighed in feigned boredom. "Venerate my mother, then, if you must. But I find her to be a quarrelsome old woman. And her behavior toward Claudius is downright outrageous." She mused a moment. "My grandmother, Livia, can barely tolerate Claudius, but my brother's a fool and deserves what he gets. Do you know, some years ago a seer prophesied that one day Claudius would be emperor? Now, that's one time my mother and I agreed on something. We both laughed in the prophet's face."

She glanced at her cup which he still held. "Fill it, Vitalis. Then remove that tunic and come to me. If Vitalis is nice to Livilla, she can be nice to him, too…"

This time he added extra water to her wine but she didn't seem to notice.

Later, lying drowsy in his arms, she sighed. "You're a real man—I'd like to marry you!"

Startled, he sat up. "What! Marry...me?"

She giggled. "Lie down, there's a good boy. *That* got your attention, didn't it? No, I don't really mean marry you so much as to have you around whenever I want you. You know very well that you could never marry a woman of my rank. Come to that, there are very few nobles who qualify."

If she interpreted his silence and blank expression as disappointment, she was wrong. His agile mind had seen in her words an avenue by which he might escape their relationship. Yes, the broken heart, he thought—the destitute lover, the torment of his soul to be so near the woman he knew could never be his—her destiny lit by the stars; his, at best, guided by a guttering lamp along some forgotten byway. Ah, no—they must part, but he would be braver than Orpheus and not look back; yet the pain would linger forever. And so on and so forth, with much swearing by the entire pantheon of the gods and vows of perpetual whatever. And a decent gift for her, of course.

Could he do it convincingly, he wondered. Yes, he thought so. Years of basking in public adulation had evoked a certain innate histrionic aptness which he'd refined and polished. Perhaps his forebears had been tragedians, who knows? He did know, however, that he was far from the low comedian he'd suggested earlier.

But now was not the time, he realized. It would be better to wait until he returned from the games at Neapolis in a few months—and with any luck, she might have forgotten him by then. In any case, it would give him time to think and plan.

He smiled with what he hoped would pass for brave acceptance of the bitter lot decreed him by the gods. "Yes, my queen of heaven," he said, "I realize that you can never be mine and that I am unworthy of you."

"But I can help my charioteer," she cooed. "Oh, yes—Livilla will look after her friends."

He looked at her questioningly.

"Gimme some more wine, that's my good boy. Then I'll tell you something."

He refilled her cup, again watering it well.

"You remember I told you I was sleeping with Sejanus? You remember that?"

He nodded. "Yes, I do."

"Well, he and I have been cozy for three, four years...oh, yes, quite cozy." She took a drink of wine, slopping some on the pillow. "In fact," she whispered conspiratorially, "he wants to marry me. Me, little old Livilla."

Vitalis pursed his lips reflectively. "He's a man of authority, a powerful man...and you're a widow of noble pedigree. Yes, it would be a very good match."

"Damn right I'm a widow," she smirked, wiping her mouth with the back of her hand. "Me and good old Sejanus, we arranged that, didn't we? You bet we did."

"Oh?" he said, curiosity overruling prudence.

"Lissen here...my husband was just like his father, Tiberius. No sense of humor. Nothing. Drusus spent all his time talking with bloody engineers and architects. Never talked to me. And he hated Sejanus. Said he was trying to get rid of Tiberius and take over. So that's when I got interested in Sejanus. Seduced him. He probably thinks he seduced me, but he's wrong. No matter. Anyway, I could see his power and ambition. A man who knows where he's going, Sejanus is." She closed her eyes and lay still.

"You were talking about Drusus," he said softly, after a pause.

Livilla opened her eyes and looked at him. "Oh, yes, I was. Well, Sejanus and I...we poisoned him."

"Oh. Oh, I see," Vitalis said.

"No, my beautiful athlete. No, I don't really think you see at all. Drusus had to go because he was probably going to succeed Tiberius. But that's what Sejanus is after. He's almost there already. Who do you think runs Rome, eh? Well, it sure isn't uncle Tiberius, even though he thinks he does. Sejanus is in charge and when he becomes emperor, I shall be his wife."

She smiled sleepily. "And when he's emperor, he's gonna have a twenty-five *denarii* gold piece minted with his likeness on one side and mine on the other."

"But surely there was curiosity over your husband's death," Vitalis prompted. "He wasn't very old, was he?"

"Thirty-five…he'd be thirty-eight if he was still alive. No. No curiosity. Half a million *sesterces* for the court physician saw to that. Yes, poor old Drusus died of a quotidian fever despite being treated with ass's blood."

She yawned and burrowed into the pillow. "Drusus would never have put my likeness on a coin. No, not him…" She slept.

Vitalis rose quietly from the couch and covered her. He put on his tunic, looking down at Livilla as she snored, her mouth slackly opened.

Now he knew beyond doubt that he had to free himself from this woman. How stupid I was, he thought, to become involved with her. She's depraved, evil.

Vitalis knew that the gods paid little heed to mortal petitions. They expected the honor due to them, but guaranteed nothing in return. But he knew also that the gods took note of their celebrants and might smile upon them in divine pleasure. Vitalis vowed to sacrifice a white ox at the temple of Hercules the Victor, patron deity of athletes, before he left for the games in the south.

She murdered her husband, he thought, still staring at the sleeping woman. She could have my life snuffed out just as easily.

IV

I'd hoped that Macro would take me with him to Ostia, but he didn't. He left a few days ago, on business, and comes home tomorrow night. I've always enjoyed it when occasionally he's let me accompany him on short trips away from the city.

I've never been to Ostia, even though it's only about twelve miles from Rome—a seaport at the mouth of the Tiber. From what I hear, it's not much of a place these days, what with the river clogged by silt and the docks long neglected.

The politicians talk forever about renovating Ostia's waterfront, but Tiberius Caesar is miserly with the public purse, so nothing much will be done while he's in charge.

So say Macro's friends. I overheard one of them say that almost all of Rome's imports are carted overland from the southern ports. He wasn't complaining, though, being an investor in the cartage business.

But, you know, the senate never asks for my opinion, so why should I worry? Never once has a herald arrived breathless at the door, crying, "Is this where the slave Anthus resides? Good! Put on your best tunic and come quickly, Anthus! The Conscript Fathers eagerly await your advice on matters of state. By the way, Caesar sends his best regards."

Nonetheless, the last few days have been pleasant. My delectable Petronia is over her ill spirits and behaving most affectionately. And our *domina* Ennia is in good humor. Yesterday she dispatched me on errands around the city, which took about three hours. It was a soft, balmy day, and I enjoyed mingling with the people and taking in the sights. Spending as much time as I do indoors, in a house on the city outskirts, I forget how busy the streets of Rome are.

They say Rome has close to a million inhabitants and most of them seem to peddle goods from roadside stands. Those that aren't hawking their wares are occupied in scribbling on the walls and sides of buildings. Except for temples and buildings watched over by guards, it seems that every wall in the city is covered with painted notices.

About half these inscriptions concern candidates for public office. Most are done in red paint so they'll stand out against the white-washed surfaces. Political life in Rome is quite spirited, judging from the wall writing. Here's one I remember: "The fruit dealers urge the election of Julius Polybius as *duovir*. He makes good bread."

The scribbling doesn't stop at politics, however, as witness this one: "Vettius, display some decency and take your lewd looks off another man's wife."

One that caught my fancy was done by someone who couldn't afford paint because he'd scratched his offering on a wall with a sharp stone or nail, what they call *graffito*. "I wonder, O Wall, that you have not fallen in ruins from supporting the stupidities of so many scribblers."

There was another bit of *graffito* on the same wall. An admirer had scratched, "Albino Vitalis Hesper of the Blue faction is the greatest charioteer of all." Some wag had scrawled beneath it, "Who wrote this? His father?" And a third had added, "Vitalis is great with the ladies also."

There's one thing I noticed particularly in the city: Statues of Sejanus—they're everywhere, it seems. Lucius Aelius Sejanus, he's the Praetorian Prefect, in command of the Praetorian Guard, the emperor's elite household troops. Sejanus isn't a patrician, but of the knightly class, the same as my master, Macro.

Somehow Sejanus has wormed his way into the emperor's confidence to the degree that he's virtually co-regent of the empire. They say that he has *delatores*, paid informers, everywhere. Barely a day passes that an aristocrat isn't charged with treason on some flimsy pretext. These are extremely perilous times for the upper classes, never knowing when some pimply shop-keeper's assistant may report them as having insulted the imperial family or criticized government policy.

And that reminds me, I recently found a small plaster bust of Sejanus in one of the servant's rooms. Knowing the scant regard that Macro holds for his fellow prefect, I confiscated the bust and delivered a brief lecture to its owner, one of our assistant gardeners who isn't too bright, but means well. It's difficult to get good help these days.

I bought a little wooden box from a street vendor, a gift for Petronia. It has a painting of Diana, goddess of hunting, on the lid.

Oh, yes! I met one of my old acquaintances when I was in the city on lady Ennia's business. Marcus Soter, he's a freedman who used to be a slave of a friend of my old master, the grain merchant.

He's married now and has two children. He works for a large catering business and says he's doing the same work he did as a slave, only getting paid for it. When we met, he was on his way to work as a wine attendant in the house of senator Valerius Aviola, I believe he said. Told me he'd be up 'til the small hours, helping the gentry get plastered. I know the scene.

His pay can't be all that good, though, because he also has a part-time job. He seemed reluctant to talk about it on the street but hinted that I might be interested in such work and suggested that we discuss it sometime soon. He said such work wouldn't interfere with my regular duties. Well, I'll wait and see.

V

"You've done an excellent job, Tiro." Aviola returned the two waxed tablets to his steward. "The menu, seating arrangement, entertainment—all most satisfactory. Thank you." He paused. "Now, the entertainers...an Egyptian troupe, you said?"

Tiro knew Aviola well. "Have no concern, master. I've spoken with the troupe manager. He knows that there's to be no nudity. The dancers will be suitably attired."

Aviola smiled affectionately at his steward and dismissed him. He reflected, as he often did, how fortunate he was to have such a capable and loyal major-domo as Tiro to manage his household.

• • •

Senator Aurelius Valerius Aviola had served the state faithfully. As a young man, he had performed his military service as a *quaestor*, a non-combatant job concerned with finance and administration. His participation in senate debate had been infrequent, and then usually an endorsement of some other's thinking. He was the first to admit that he had no special talent as a statesman, nor in the arts and sciences. But he had always done his duty willingly and to the best of his ability and he was liked well enough by most people.

His father had served with distinction under Octavian in the war with Marcus Antonius, a fact not forgotten by Octavian when he became the emperor Augustus. The patrician Valerius family, already wealthy, became even more so.

Now in his seventies, Aviola was rarely called upon to perform public duty. His two sons served the state in far off places, one in Egypt and the other in Spain. His only daughter had married into a wealthy and respected family although not of the patrician class. Aviola had been a widower for ten years.

Under such circumstances, men of his age might drift into loneliness and ennui but this wasn't his way. If the senate and his family no longer needed him, there were other things to fill his days. Without seeking public acclaim he quietly put his personal wealth to good use. Recently he had given a substantial donation toward the repair of the Temple of Minerva and, guided by an elderly scholar friend, was providing, anonymously, for the tuition and living expenses of several impecunious students of promise.

His good works, however, took little of his time and the remainder, to a large degree, was passed in attending the games and entertaining guests in his home. Unlike most of his peers, Aviola had never enjoyed the gladiatorial shows or the slaughter of wild animals but he was an enthusiastic supporter of the athletic contests...the foot races, pancratiasts, chariot races, everything. His favorite sport was chariot racing and his favorite faction was the Blue Stable, most of whose charioteers he knew personally.

He often visited the stables of the Blues, located on the outskirts of the city, savoring the sounds and smells of the sprawling establishment. He'd meander happily for hours, chatting with grooms, veterinarians, blacksmiths, even the stable cleaners at the bottom of the hierarchy. The stable workers in their turn enjoyed the old man's visits, not the least reason being that Aviola's attendant discreetly passed a *denarius* or two to each of them after the senator had chatted and strolled on.

Two or three times a month Aviola invited friends and acquaintances to dinner. A typical gathering might include four or five members of the patrician and equestrian classes with their wives, two or three representatives of the arts—perhaps a historian, a playwright and a physician; and usually one or two of the more renowned athletes. His dinners were excellent, with seven or eight courses, good wine and entertainment. On such occasions his household staff was augmented by cooks and dining room attendants provided by a caterer who dealt exclusively with the noble houses.

One evening in late September, Albino Vitalis Hesper reclined on a couch beside his host in Aviola's capacious dining room. A larger party than usual, thirty-six people, lay in varying positions on the scattered *triclinia* couches, several of them asleep, sated by food and wine. The meal was over and the Egyptian entertainers had departed. The plaintive melody of a flute was lost in the dissonance of conversation and laughter.

Vitalis had dined well but had imbibed more freely than usual. Like most top athletes, he avoided alcoholic excess but tonight had yielded to recent stress...the demanding preparation for the forthcoming games at Neapolis and his resolution to cut himself loose from Livilla.

Turning to his host, Vitalis grinned with sloppy contentment. "It was kind of you, sir, to invite my friends and me tonight. Good party, real good. Thank you, very kind of you." Aviola inclined his head, murmuring something lost in the buzz of surrounding conversation.

"Y'know," Vitalis continued, "I seem to move in high circles lately, yessir. Couple of days ago I was drinking wine with Caesar. Yes, Caesar himself. And his mother and his nephew, uh, the one who stutters…"

"Claudius." The senator smiled.

"Sure. Claudius. That's him. Hey, I know his sister, too."

"Livilla? You know her?" Aviola asked.

Vitalis, leaning closer, winked. "Hey, do I know her? Oh, yes, I sure know her…yessir, you could say that." He hiccupped and drained his cup. An attendant appeared at once and refilled it, then stepped back a couple of paces.

Taking another swallow, he looked at Aviola. "Senator, you're a good fellow…decent sort, yessir…so just between you and me, I've been having a little fling with Livilla. Sure have. She likes athletes, I guess, but…" he took another sip, "I'm gonna break it off. Real soon. Fun while it lasted, but she's too much for me. And I sure don't wanna get mixed up in her messy affairs. Nossir."

Aviola cautiously asked, "Messy? How so?"

The wine server filled the cup of a matron close by and resumed his position, this time a little closer to the charioteer.

"Senator, that woman poisoned her husband, the emperor's son…she told me so…sure, her and her boy friend Sejanus."

His face turned pale, Aviola gaped at him. "Sejanus! You're not serious!"

"Dammit, Senator, I'm only telling you what she said…and she said a lot more, too. Like Sejanus is really in charge of things and is gonna become emperor and she's gonna marry him…and when he's emperor he's gonna…"

"Vitalis!" the old man snapped. "Enough! Say nothing more. This is dangerous talk…see me later if you wish, but say no more here."

Aviola turned to the nearby matron and spoke to her graciously.

The unobtrusive wine server deferentially filled the guests' cups.

• • •

Caepio listened with interest to his visitor's story. He smiled and nodded his head in self-satisfaction. "Yes," he purred, "a most intriguing piece of information. And you say this happened last night in the house of Valerius Aviola? My friend, you've done well."

He gave the wine server the equivalent of two month's of his normal earnings with the caterer.

• • •

"Your man is quite certain that nobody overheard the conversation, is he?"

"So he says, Sejanus," Caepio said. "And he has been a most reliable in the past. Yes, if he says so, I believe him." After a pause, he added, "His position with the caterer provides him frequent entry into the houses of the aristocracy…a most convenient situation for those of us who think of ourselves as, shall we say, the guardians of the constitution?"

Sejanus returned Caepio's ingratiating smile with a cold stare. "Very well. If your man is reliable, then we have a clear case of violation of the law of *maiestes*—both the charioteer and Aviola have soiled the imperial honor. I care nothing for myself…I am only a servant of the state…but

I will not tolerate such vicious stories to be spread in abuse of a member of the imperial family."

"You believe the senator is guilty of treason? But it was the charioteer who made the remark and Aviola only…"

"The senator," Sejanus interrupted, "is guilty of complicity because he has failed to inform me of the charioteer's disloyalty. If you have had time to do so, then most certainly he has."

Caepio pondered this. "True, but perhaps Aviola has gone direct to Caesar. He has such privilege, surely?"

Sejanus smiled humorlessly. "No, Caepio, he hasn't seen the emperor. All appointments with Caesar, be they with governors or plebian petitioners, must be approved by me. It has so been decreed by Caesar."

"All appointments…" repeated Caepio.

"All. Save those with members of the imperial family, of course."

"Oh, of course," said Caepio. And the most prominent member of the imperial family—other than Caesar, himself—is Caesar's mother, the lady Julia Augusta Livia, with whom I have an appointment today, he added silently.

• • •

Aviola stared in disbelief. "How dare you suggest that a member of the Valerian family is disloyal to the state and to Caesar who is its embodiment!" The usually soft-spoken senator hissed the words in rage.

Sejanus returned the senator's outburst with icy calm. "Yes, Aviola…and your next comment will be about how your people were building the foundations of Rome while mine were nothing but swineherds. I've heard it all before from others…including your late friend, Cremutius Cordus, last year. You were present, as I recall, so you'll remember that neither the emperor nor senate were impressed with his rantings during the trial."

"Yes, I remember well. I remember Cordus, a loyal and gifted scholar." Aviola's voice shook. "Cordus, who took his own life before the senate could pass sentence."

"And after his death," Sejanus said coldly, "the senate ordered his books to be burned publicly. Perhaps, Aviola, you were one of those who voted for the act?"

Standing erectly in his formal vestments, tunic with a broad purple band running vertically from the neckline, and white toga, Aviola took a step toward the table and stared down at Sejanus.

"I know that I have never distinguished myself in senate debate or other matters of executive nature...but I know this also, Aelius Sejanus, I have never conducted myself in a dishonorable manner either within the senate or outside of it. And I was one of the nine senators who voted against the degrading act of burning a scholar's lifetime work...even though Caesar himself attended the trial and no doubt took note of those who sided with Cordus."

Sejanus arose and held up the document which had been lying before him on the table. "This, senator, is a warrant for your arrest."

"By whose authority!" Aviola exploded.

"Mine."

"I demand to see Caesar! As a member of..."

"No, senator. You shall *not* see Caesar," Sejanus interrupted. "Unless, of course, he chooses to attend your trial before the senate. That is his decision to make."

His voice quiet now, Aviola shook his head. "No, Sejanus, that is your decision, not his. Do you know, when that fool, Vitalis Hesper, told me his story last night I attributed it to his drunkenness, a thing I deplore in my guests, but which I cannot always control. Yes, I was disgusted by his monstrous statement, and told him so later. But in the light of your statements of the last few minutes, I begin to see things more clearly. The charioteer is too simple a man to have concocted such a tale as he told me, and I now believe that he spoke truly, that he is indeed the lady Livilla's lover and that you are another and using her to enhance your position." Aviola coughed and, eyes fixed on the prefect, took a cloth piece from his tunic and wiped his lips.

"You referred earlier to your ancestors. If indeed they were swineherds, that at least is an honest occupation. But you, their descendant, have brought disgrace to the ashes of your fathers by becoming what you are today."

Sejanus now spoke through gritted teeth. "The warrant for your arrest will be taken to your house at this time tomorrow. You have three children. In the event of your being tried, found guilty and executed, your will would be invalid and your entire estate would revert to the state. But you know all that already. And I believe that you take my meaning. Now you will be taken to your house and will remain there until the warrant arrives tomorrow."

Sejanus strode to the door and called out. Two officers of the Praetorian Guard entered, saluted and stood at attention.

"You are to escort the senator to his house. Take one squad of men and post guard there until further notice. Nobody is to be given access or allowed to leave without my personal permission. Go now."

Aviola looked into Sejanus's eyes one last time. "Remember always, *praefectus praetorio*, the ashes of your fathers." He turned and faced the two soldiers, one of whom placed his hand lightly on Aviola's arm.

"Do not touch me, please, centurion. I am Aurelius Felix Valerius Aviola, a Conscript Father of Rome and a member of the College of the Arval Brethren."

The centurion removed his hand. "Sir," he said respectfully. Aviola smiled at him and inclined his head courteously, then walked from the chamber with dignity.

Late that night Aviola's slaves found him in his bath, the water bloodied from the opened veins in his legs and arms.

They wept as they lifted the frail, white-haired old man's body from the bath and laid it gently on his couch.

A few days later the slaves of the house of Aviola wept again when they learned that under the terms of his will, all of them were freed and each had been left a substantial bequest of money.

• • •

As though addressing a dull-witted servant, Livia contemplated her son with weary resignation. "Yes, Tiberius," she said. "I know exactly what I'm saying. I'm telling you that my granddaughter, your niece and daughter-in-law, is reported to have told the charioteer Vitalis Hesper that she and Aelius Sejanus poisoned your son three years ago."

"This is monstrous!" Tiberius shouted. "At the time of Drusus' death I had the matter fully investigated. There was no suggestion whatever that..."

"Oh, do grow up, Tiberius. You're a reasonably capable administrator—nothing close to Augustus, but you perform well enough. However, in other matters you're a complete fool. No," she said as he started to speak, "let me finish what I have to say. Now, the alleged statement by Livilla is, I agree, pure hearsay. But, it comes to me from an extremely reliable informant. And I believe that it's high time you faced the fact that Livilla has been behaving like a tart for years, even before her husband's death. I'm quite willing to accept that she's been sleeping with that athlete—and probably others of his breed—and babbling family confidences to them."

Tiberius sank onto a couch. In a voice now quiet but trembling with anger, he said, "And that damned charioteer had the impertinence to present himself here as a delegate of his guild and accept our hospitality..."

"Yes," she mused. "Yes, my son. And he was no doubt laughing up his sleeve the entire time, thinking 'What would Caesar say if he knew I was his niece's lover?' Well, Tiberius, there it is. And as for your friend the Praetorian Prefect, yes, he's been sleeping with little Livilla for several years. I haven't the slightest doubt as to his ambitions, which you're helping generously by granting him so much authority. Really, Tiberius, you're so obtuse, not to see what's happening."

"I'm not as stupid as you believe, mother," he said, his rage now controlled. "I'm well aware that Sejanus hungers after power and I'm aware that I've been wrong to delegate him the authority I have. But no more. It may interest you to know that Sejanus has already asked permission to marry Livilla. Which I refused."

"Well, praise to all the gods for that, at least," she sighed. "Perhaps I've misjudged you, Tiberius. But what are you going to do about Sejanus?"

Tiberius stood and paced slowly about the room. "Nothing. Nothing for the time being. It would be poor strategy to move against him at present. Apart from the executive authority he holds, he commands his own personal army of four thousand men, quartered right here in the city."

"Soldiers who are supposed to be Caesar's personal guard," she sniffed. "Now isn't that a nice touch of irony for you? You fear your own bodyguard. I'll tell you this, it wouldn't have happened in Augustus' time."

He glared at her. "Don't start again about the glories of Augustus! And remember, too, that it was *his* administration that set the stage for the power that the prefects now hold in Rome. Let's stick to the business at hand and forget the accomplishments of my late stepfather. I lived in his shadow long enough while he was alive and I'm damned if I'll continue to do so now that he's been dead for twelve years."

He sat again, opposite her, and leaned forward. "And now, mother, I have some news for you. Your informant told you that the charioteer made his comments about

Livilla and Sejanus to Valerius Aviola—in Aviola's house?"

"Yes, Aviola, a harmless enough old fool. But I've always rather liked him. And Augustus was a very close friend of his father."

"Last night Aviola took his own life. He opened his veins in his bath."

"What!"

"Yes, Aviola committed suicide late last night, mother. And I suggest we can attribute it to Sejanus. My informant—who is equally as reliable as yours—says that Sejanus sent for Aviola earlier in the day. Later he had him escorted home by a detachment of guards who remained on duty outside his house."

"In short," she said, puzzled, "Sejanus placed Aviola under house arrest."

"Exactly. And somehow convinced Aviola that he should commit suicide. But why? Why?"

They sat silent a moment, then Livia said, "Well, it's quite obvious, really. Sejanus had to get rid of Aviola because Aviola knew that Livilla and Sejanus had murdered your son. There can't be any other answer."

Tiberius sat alone, pondering the matter, for a long time after Livia had left. Aviola is dead, he reflected, because he'd been told that my son was murdered by his wife and her lover. But Aviola was a man of honor who would never have passed along such information to others. He may have been a bumbler but he was an honest, decent man. His conduct during the trial of Cremutius Cordus illustrated that. One of the nine men who openly defied the imperial will, while hundreds of others eagerly wagged their senatorial tails at my bidding. But why didn't Aviola come to me with what he had heard? Not, surely, because he was afraid of me; I know that. There was some other reason. True, I've given Sejanus authority to screen my petitioners, but that doesn't include the senior senators of Rome. No, I'm sure that Aviola would have come to me if he could have. Surely he's one of the last men who'd have been disloyal to me. I'm certain that he would have tried to caution me that such a story was being passed. He could only have been prevented by the house arrest.

Aviola is dead, yet the charioteer still lives. Sejanus must see Vitalis as a greater threat to him than Aviola. Does that mean the charioteer's days are numbered also? Sejanus can't afford such accusations being made against him.

On the other hand, Tiberius thought, I don't want an issue made of it right now. Not yet. If Sejanus thinks that I suspect him of killing my son, he might panic and try to seize power by force. Something he could accomplish with that damned guard of his. Oh, I'll avenge Drusus' death if indeed he was murdered by those two, but later. Better to let Sejanus remain confident for now. His time will come.

And, what is to be done about Livilla? I believe it's time I had a talk with her mother. Antonia will have good advice, I'm sure. She's one family member I can rely upon.

VI

"I daresay, Anthus—damn your alien hide—that you've been robbing me blind in my absence, eh?"

It was good to have my master back from Ostia. And from his remarks I knew that he was in good spirits. He damns my 'alien hide' frequently, along with allegations of embezzlement and various assorted criminal behaviors. But only when he's in excellent humor.

Yes, although I'd enjoyed an easy time while he was away, I was pleased at his return. Life's more interesting when Macro's around. He bullies me something terrible to the tune of outraged cries, cursing, sighs of despair and much imploring of the gods. But it's all an act and we both know it. My role is to pay solemn heed to his proclamations, express my admiration of his sagacity, then continue doing things my own way. It keeps both of us happy.

Now, Macro—he's a strange man in some ways, but an intelligent, perceptive man behind his public mask of a gregarious extrovert. I suspect that very few people really know him. But I do, after twelve years of being his scribe. I've become more than that, now. Three years ago when his household steward died, I took over the duties temporarily, then was given the permanent job.

Macro paid thirty thousand *sesterces* for me. That's about ten years earnings for the average artisan or household administrator, which is my present status. Now that I'm thirty, the legal age after which slaves may be freed, I hope that he'll consider *manumitto* for me soon. Or permit me to purchase my freedom, not that I have near enough money saved for that. Macro gives me occasional gifts, around a hundred *denarii* or so every few months. And his *clientes*—he has a large number of hangers-on, like any man in his position—they like to keep in the good graces of their patron's major-domo. A *denarius* here and there from them, it all adds up.

But I was talking of Macro. He's been *praefectus vigilum* a few years now. When he completed his military service with Legion Twenty-One Rapax, he became known to the imperial family through the renowned general, Germanicus, the nephew of Tiberius Caesar. The emperor was obviously impressed with Macro to have appointed him to the prefecture. I believe I mentioned that my master commands not only the City Watch, the firefighters; but also the Urban Cohorts, which makes him head of Rome's police force. Normally, you see, the Cohorts come under the City Prefect, an elderly senator. But, because of the old man's failing health, Macro has been temporarily given the duties.

I said that I know my master...yes, and I know that he has his eye on the Praetorian Guard. He wants the praetorian post all right, but he's in no rush. Macro is a political animal and I'm sure that he's waiting patiently to see if the Sejanus star will wane. He can afford to wait. He's a knight and holds an influential position. And he's privately wealthy. Very. I should know; I'm his accountant.

Macro will achieve his goal, I'm sure. That's why I wish to remain with him, be it as slave or freedman. I'm with a winner.

And while Macro is biding his time, he's cultivating the right social and political connections. Here, I'll give an example.

A few years ago Macro's old army commander, Germanicus, died in Syria, leaving a widow and several children. The youngest is Gaius, now fourteen and a frequent house guest of Macro and his lady. Macro first met the boy when he was a child in his father's legionary camps in the provinces. His nickname is Caligula, "little boot"…the soldiers called him that because his mother dressed him in a tiny legionary uniform, complete with little army boots. The name has stayed with him. His full name is Gaius Julius Caesar Augustus Germanicus.

I know why Macro cultivates friendship with the boy. Caligula is descended on both sides from the Julian and Claudian families. One great grandfather was Marcus Antonius and another was Augustus Caesar…and a grandfather was Marcus Agrippa, for a time co-regent of the empire with Augustus. So the boy's pedigree makes him someone to be reckoned with and he could well be on his way to wearing the imperial *toga*. Hopefully, he'll acquire some manners before then. He's spoiled rotten and has an evil disposition.

But Macro believes that grooming a relationship with him is time well spent.

You could say that my *dominus* worships the rising sun rather than the setting one.

VII

The officer dismounted his gray mare and led her to the stable a few hundred feet distant from the white-washed villa. After turning the horse over to a young stable slave, he removed his helmet and cape and washed the grime from his face and arms at a water trough.

He shook the dust from his cape and was brushing his helmet when he noticed someone approaching, a middle-aged man wearing a loose blue tunic, work boots and a wide-brimmed straw hat. An estate worker, the officer thought; but when the man drew close, he recognized him at once.

"Sir!" The officer stood at attention, helmet held formally against his left breast. "I was making myself presentable before looking for you. I have brought you a letter from Rome, sir." From the leather pouch secured to his waist, he removed a scroll container and passed it to the knight.

"I know you, *primus pilus*," the knight said. "Forgive my poor memory—where did we serve together?"

"Vindelicia and Pannonia, sir. I was…"

"Wait." The knight held up a silencing hand. "You were *aquilifer* of the Twentieth. And, your name is Priscus."

The old soldier grinned. "Titus Serapio Priscus, sir. Yes, I was eagle standard bearer of the Conquering Valerians. I am honored that you should remember." With the confidence of an old hand who knows to whom he's speaking, he added, "Most senior officers today don't know the names of their juniors even when serving with them, never mind twenty years later."

"And now you're a chief centurion; the man before whom even the legion commander quails, eh?"

"Hardly that, sir. I'm happy as long as the junior officers and troops are terrified of me," Priscus replied. "And you, sir, how have you been employed since completing your time in the legions?"

"I held a few minor judicial posts in the city and then spent a few years on the administrative staff of the imperial palace. I left the palace last year when my wife inherited this estate. We felt that we should be here to attend to its operation. Now we both realize that the overseers run it efficiently without our interference. All that's expected of us is to nod understandingly and express approval at the appropriate times." He sighed. "In all truth, Priscus, I find myself bored in the role of gentleman farmer."

Now the two men strolled in a small garden to one side of the large two-storied villa, the soldier's cape and helmet having been placed on a stone bench.

"How long were you on the road, Priscus?"

"Five hours, sir. I left Rome at first light."

"You traveled swiftly, considering the Via Valeria's wretched condition this far east of Rome. I trust your horse is being attended to?"

"I asked one of your stable hands to feed and water her and rub her down. I'll pay, of course, sir."

"Oh, no," the knight replied. "You won't. The deities of this household would be affronted at the thought of a guest being charged for his horse's oats."

As they walked, the knight held the dark blue, tubular letter container in his right hand, slapping it absently into his left palm. "I take it that you're no longer serving in a regular legion."

"I'm awaiting discharge, sir. Thirty-two years in. I'll be released in a matter of days. Until then I'm attached to the third Praetorian cohort. General staff duties, not a command job."

The knight raised his eyebrows at the slighting tone of the centurion's words. "I take it that the Praetorian Guard leaves you unimpressed."

"Those pretty boys with their plumes and capes couldn't fight through a wall of papyrus, sir," Priscus snorted. "When was the last time the so-called elite guard saw battle—other than in a tavern on a public feast day? No, sir, I'm not happy about ending my military career alongside that bunch."

"I appreciate your sentiment, old friend, but try not to express it publicly. The Praetorians are a powerful force these days and…well, I needn't say more."

"I haven't lasted this long, sir, without knowing when to hold my tongue. I tell you because you were always a soldier's officer, not a perfumed dandy from the senatorials doing token military service. And there's plenty like me who'd agree."

The knight stopped and looked into the veteran's crinkled eyes. "Thank you, Chief Centurion Serapio Priscus. That means more to me than the silver standard awarded me when we campaigned together years ago."

He looked at the letter container he had been holding. "So, Priscus, you've brought me a message from Rome. We'll go inside and I'll read it. Are you to take a reply back to the city?"

"I was told that there would be a reply or that you would return to the city with me, sir."

Inside the house, Priscus was given over to the ministrations of a young male house slave. "After you've bathed and I've read this, we'll discuss the matter over a cup of wine," the knight said. Seated at a table in his private suite, he broke the outer seal and removed a rolled sheet of parchment. His eyebrows rose when he noted the *sigilla* embossed on its seal.

A few minutes later, at the door to his wife's chamber a short, sturdy middle-aged woman barred his way. "Sir, my lady is having her afternoon rest."

"Satia, for more years than I remember you've taken excellent care of your mistress...and it is appreciated. But I must see her now on an important matter."

"My lady will be annoyed with me, sir." She stood her ground, arms folded.

He looked down at her patiently. He had commanded battle-hardened soldiers with confidence but had never mastered dealing with this tenacious little woman whom he knew would give her life for her mistress.

She returned his gaze steadily a moment, then said reluctantly, "Very well, sir. I'll inform my lady that you insist on seeing her. Wait here." She opened the door, entered and closed it behind her.

He rolled his eyes heavenward. "Juno," he muttered, "protectress of women, your servant Satia continues to prove her fidelity. But couldn't you have a word with her sometime?"

Satia returned, leaving the chamber door open. "My lady will see you, sir," she stated disapprovingly.

As he entered, his wife smiled sleepily at him, holding out a hand. "Satia is most distressed, my love. You've upset her routine, I fear."

"As long as you're not displeased, Procula." He sat on the edge of her couch and handed her the letter.

After glancing at the broken seal, she looked at him briefly, then read the letter. "Do you know why he wishes to see you, Ponto?"

"No idea whatsoever," the knight said.

"When will you leave?"

"First hour in the morning. The messenger is a *primus pilus* who once served with me. I'll go back with him. He's a rough and ready specimen but worth ten of most men. He'll be our guest at supper." He thought a moment. "I believe he'd planned on returning today—a night ride would be nothing to him—so he won't have a change of clothing. I'll loan him one of my tunics."

He smiled. "Yes, one of my dress tunics will be appropriate. He retires from the army soon and as a chief centurion is qualified for promotion to the equestrian order, should he so choose. Tonight he can experience wearing the purple stripe of a knight."

• • •

The knight and the centurion departed for Rome at daybreak and arrived at the Viminal Gate just before midday. A few hundred feet before the gate Priscus gestured off to the right. "The Praetorian camp, sir," he said bitterly. "All four thousand of them garrisoned in the city now."

"Remember what I told you, Priscus," the knight cautioned. "Don't say too much. You have only a short time before retirement."

The centurion stopped his horse when they had passed through the gate. "And now, sir, I must leave you. My orders were to accompany you to the city gate and then return to the camp. The message container had no cypher on the outer seal, so I don't know your destination. Obviously that's the way it was intended."

"I thank you, Priscus. I've enjoyed your company. May we meet again."

"I hope so, sir. My thanks to your gracious lady and yourself for your hospitality." The centurion raised his clenched right fist to his breast in salute. "Farewell, sir."

"Farewell, Chief Centurion Serapio Priscus." The knight raised his right hand toward the soldier, then clucked gently to his horse, nudging it with his knees into a walk.

The centurion watched as the knight proceeded slowly along the Viminal Way, then lost sight of him when he turned off to the left and entered into the Vicus Patricius.

• • •

The knight stared absently at a large decorative urn in the corner of the room, giving thought to the matter. The other man waited patiently.

"Well, a thorny situation," the knight said. "This man is certainly an affront to the established order. I've long deplored the extreme adulation given these athletes by the population, including the patrician and knightly classes. They're even more at fault because they should have better sense. This is a good example of a public performer whose sense of social station has been corrupted by hero worship."

"Precisely," the other said. "It would be a simple matter to charge him formally and dispose of him publicly. But then he'd become a martyr. There'll be a public outcry in any event, but it's not in the state's best interest to proceed legally."

"I agree." The knight hesitated, then added, "Why have you asked me?"

"I can trust you, Ponto. We've known one another many years, long before I achieved my present position. Your family has served the state well and your own contribution is beyond reproach. There are others I could ask, but it's you I prefer."

A moment's silence, then the other spoke again.

"Your talents are lying fallow. I believe it's time you put them to use again." He smiled at the knight's puzzled stare.

"Oh, I know that a man like you doesn't seek reward or favor. You're not being bribed, in any sense of the word. However, I can think of a position, one worthy of your ability. I would send for you, say a month or so after the charioteer has been dealt with and forgotten by the crowd, as he will be."

After a brief silence, the knight responded, "I'll do it. Perhaps you could provide me with a weapon. A military short sword, honed to perfection. One you can afford to lose; I've no wish to be encumbered by it after I've used it."

The other leaned across the table and took the knight's hand. "Thank you. My debt to you will be honored. Now I'll brief you on what my informer—a reliable man, a groom in the charioteer's immediate circle—has learned. He reports that Vitalis Hesper and his friends will celebrate their departure for the games in Neapolis three nights from now. They'll be spending the night at…"

• • •

Two days before Vitalis and his entourage were to depart the city, the charioteer and half a dozen of his colleagues were dining noisily in a private room in the house of Jucunda. The brothel catered chiefly to wealthy plebians, but its clientele included members of the noble class.

While the charioteers reveled, the knight talked to Jucunda, freedwoman and proprietor of the establishment.

She listened attentively, pulse quickening at his words. In the dim light of the oil lamp which illuminated her small office, his features were indistinct within his *paenula's* hood.

When he had finished, she nodded apprehensively and he handed her a small leather bag. She emptied the contents on the table. The gold coins gleamed dully in the lamplight, and after a glance at him, she counted them. Forty. One thousand *denarii*.

Not a fortune, Jucunda said to herself, but a very respectable sum. I wouldn't betray a friend for such. No. But I'll betray the charioteer. I don't seem to have any choice in the matter, do I?

She spoke. "I will arrange it, sir. As you have described."

"Jucunda, it's almost sunset," the knight said quietly. "Do you enjoy watching an autumn sunset?"

"Well, yes," she answered, perplexed. "Not that I have much time for such pleasures."

"Perhaps, madam, you should watch tonight's," he said. "Because if during the police investigation, which is sure to follow, you should refer to my presence here, it will be the last sunset you'll ever see."

• • •

Vitalis Hesper ascended the stairs to the second floor, his arm draped around the shoulders of a small, dark-haired girl whose ornate make-up made her look older than her seventeen years. She led him to her *cubiculum* halfway along a narrow passageway. Inside, she closed the door and submitted to the tall charioteer's fumbling embrace. Her face resting against his chest, she could smell wine and garlic on his breath as he kissed the top of her head.

"My little Dorcas is quiet this evening," he said, fondling her buttocks.

She stepped back, looking up at him. "But only because

her valiant Vitalis is going away and leaving her," she whispered, touching his lips with her finger. She took his large hand and led him to the wide couch that was placed parallel to the wall opposite the entrance. She knelt and removed his sandals, then arose and loosened his short tunic, helping him to remove it, then his under-tunic and lastly, his loincloth.

She pushed him gently onto the *cubile*. "Lie down, I'll return in a moment. I have wine and fruit to bring from the kitchen. Enough to last us until dawn, my hero." She bent over him and kissed his forehead, then silently left the room, closing the door behind her.

Vitalis sighed in contentment, rolling onto his side to face the wall.

When Dorcas knocked softly on the door, Jucunda opened it at once, beckoning the girl to enter. The hooded man looked at her. "Well?"

"He is there, sir," the girl said, voice trembling. "Alone. I left him lying on the couch."

"Which room, girl?"

"The third door on the right from the top of the stairs," the girl whispered, eyes downcast. "The floor above this."

"Both of you remain here. Let no one else enter. I shall return shortly." He left.

Vitalis yawned noisily. He heard the door open gently and, without turning, said, "Ah, my Dorcas has returned."

When the girl didn't reply, he rolled onto his back to smile up at her. The blade sliced halfway through his throat. Vitalis convulsed violently then lay still as the second and third strokes severed his head.

The knight laid the bloodied sword beside the body, placing the charioteer's right hand on the sword hilt. Stepping back, he looked at his own hands. The right one was splattered with blood. He went to a small stand in the corner of the room on which rested a ewer of water, a bowl, and towels.

He washed his hands.

"It is done," he told the two women. "In one hour you will send for the police."

He handed four gold coins to the ashen-faced girl. "After I've left, your mistress will tell you something concerning the sunset." He looked at Jucunda and she nodded.

When the door closed behind him, Dorcas dropped the coins to the floor and sobbed in the older woman's arms. Later, when Dorcas had ceased weeping, Jucunda wiped the smeared, black, teary stains from the girl's face with a towel.

"I have prepared the story we must tell the Urban Cohort men," Jucunda said. "But first, I'll tell you what he meant about the sunset."

• • •

"Three women knew of my presence in the brothel," the knight said. "Two know that I killed the charioteer."

The other man silently waited for him to continue.

"The proprietor, the freedwoman Jucunda, I'm sure I can trust her to say nothing. She seemed intelligent. Knows that a word to the wise is sufficient. The word I gave was that she'd join the charioteer, should she be indiscreet. I gave her one thousand *denarii* in gold coin. She knew it was recompense for my having disrupted her establishment and not a bribe."

The knight fell silent, staring into the flames of the three-branched bronze candelabrum on the table.

"I told her what I wished her to do and she sent for the girl in whose room the charioteer had arranged to stay the night. Dorcas, a slave prostitute. Young, sixteen or seventeen, I'd guess."

He doesn't say "Vitalis," the other man thought. He says "the charioteer." Perhaps his way of putting the event at arm's length, distancing himself?

"It was obvious that Dorcas was frightened. But her mistress assured me that she'd follow directions. And she did. I felt sorry for her, although I'd have slain her on the spot if she'd done anything foolish. Before I left I gave her four gold pieces. Small coin to you and me, but probably the largest sum she's ever had or ever will have. Her mistress could take the money for herself, of course, but I feel that Jucunda will allow the girl to keep it."

The other spoke now. "You said that three women saw you. Who was the third?"

"The one who opened the door for me. A young woman, a cheerful sort, who took me to her mistress's office. Jucunda called her Emmachia. I didn't see her after I'd dealt with the charioteer."

"Do you think, Ponto," the other asked, "that they would recognize you again?"

"No," the knight said. "No, I wore my cloak with the hood pulled well forward, and the interior of the house was dimly lit. It wasn't yet sunset, but the windows were covered with heavy drapes. I suppose that's the custom in a brothel, although I must admit it's the first time I was ever in one."

"Can't say the same for myself," the other said. "So you're quite certain they wouldn't know you?"

"Yes."

"And you left the sword in the girl's room?"

"I did. Beside the body."

"Ah, well. No doubt the Urban Cohort detachment will draw lots for it," the other said. "And you're sure that you weren't followed when you left the house?"

"Yes, certain. The streets were still crowded and I returned by a meandering route," the knight replied. He paused. "But I did stop once to talk with someone. Not far from the brothel a hot chestnut vendor offered me his wares. I recognized him as an old soldier I'd served with years ago in the Rhineland. He didn't know me. I was still wearing my hood up and he'd lost an eye, with poor vision in his remaining one. Lost an arm, too. I was there when it happened. A German axeman got him. When I recognized him, I was compelled to stop as though it was an omen of some kind, this pathetic man from my past. Another man was with him, probably a customer. He was off to one side and couldn't see my face. We talked only a moment or two, then I gave the vendor a coin and left. He didn't remember me, of that I'm certain."

"And you remembered him after so many years? Better than I could do. Did you remember his name?"

"Ignatius Carbo. A brave soldier, I can testify to that."

"And now the poor fellow's a chestnut seller…where was it that you talked to him?"

"At the corner where the lane the brothel is on meets the Flaminian Way."

After a moment the other spoke. "I said before that I'm indebted to you, Ponto. I will ask you to return in a month or so, when this matter has been resolved."

"I ask for nothing," the knight said. "What I did was my duty to the state. There is something, though. The chief centurion who escorted me to the city, Serapio Priscus… he's a good man and about to retire from the army. Should his name ever come to your attention, you might remember that I vouch for his integrity."

"I'll not forget," the other replied.

The knight smiled wryly. "It's been an eventful day for me and I'd like to retire now. I'll depart in the first hour in the morning."

They said goodnight, and when the knight had left, the other man sat down again. "So," he mused, "Jucunda, Dorcas and Emmachia. And Ignatius Carbo…"

VIII

All Rome is buzzing with the news. Last night, Vitalis Hesper was murdered—Vitalis, hero of the Blues!

I heard all about it from Horio the greengrocer when he came to the house with a delivery of melons and vegetables. He burst into my office early this morning, raised his eyes and arms to the ceiling and cried, "Anthus! Oh, Anthus—the world as we know it has come to an end!"

Having delivered himself of this timeworn remark, he sank into a chair and sobbed like a child.

Horio's piteous condition left me unmoved. You see, he's a Neapolitan, therefore prone to violent passions and richly embroidered speech. I endured his weeping and moaning for a moment, then asked the reason for his grief.

"What!" he exclaimed, streaming eyes wide in disbelief. "You haven't heard? Anthus—we are punished by the gods! Truly, great Jove himself is angry at us for our mortal transgressions—to pluck from our midst the bright beacon of our hopes, the flower of Roman manhood in his..."

"Horio," I sighed, sated with his inept metaphors. "*What* has happened?"

"Vitalis Hesper is dead," he whispered tragically, clasping his forehead in despair.

Now, I've heard of Vitalis, as I suppose most people have, but I can't get wrought up over his demise. Those of my status aren't privileged to attend the games, so we don't become too emotional over athletic heroes. However, I made some appropriate expression of condolence to satisfy the distraught fellow.

Horio happily realized then that he'd found someone to whom he could relate the tale. He wiped his eyes with the hem of his tunic and declared that his throat was burning from the salt tears he'd shed, glancing meaningfully at the cabinet where he knows I keep a bottle or two of wine. For medicinal purposes. It's plonk; our chef refuses to use it in his cookery. I poured a cup for Horio, whose tastes are less discerning.

Warming to his task...now, that's a rather apt expression, yes. I'm quite clever with words, I must admit...however, warming to his task, Horio spent the next fifteen minutes describing the death of Vitalis, details splendidly embellished.

It seems that the charioteer was murdered in a high class brothel in the Sixth district, a northern area of the city just past the Field of Mars. Horio's wife's cousin has lodgings on the same street as the brothel and he heard all the hullabaloo, what with the whores shrieking and imploring the gods and the Urban Cohort men shouting and stomping about officiously.

They say that Vitalis and several of his friends were

dining in the brothel, a respectable house that caters to the gentry. It was a private gathering to mark their forthcoming departure from the city to participate in the games in the south. Vitalis, so it is said, was making a speech when half a dozen armed thugs broke into the room and cut him down where he stood. Along with three or four of his colleagues. The killers, obviously relishing the event, laughed with fiendish glee as they hacked the bodies into small pieces and threw them out into the street, shouting, "Death to the Blue faction!"

Several of the house's girls were violated by the thugs, who also attempted to set fire to the building, but were prevented by the arrival of the police.

Only one of the killers was apprehended, but when questioned under torture he refused to name his accomplices. His last words before he died in agony on the rack, according to Horio's wife's cousin, were, "Freedom for Dalmatia!"

I informed Horio, as he was leaving, that my mistress, Ennia, is less than pleased with the quality of his asparagus and that we shall be looking for a new greengrocer should things not improve.

IX

"Very well, Macro, tell me about your visit to Ostia," Caesar said. "I suppose the city fathers sang you the old refrain about the condition of the docks."

"They did, Caesar. They insisted that I inspect them. There's only two serviceable docks remaining—and only flat-bottomed barges can use them. Unemployment among the wharf workers has adversely affected Ostia's commerce. As a result, there's an increase in crime. That was the main reason for my visit, of course."

Tiberius grunted. "Oh, very well, Macro. Give me your report when it's ready. But spare me the business about dredging the river mouth, will you? I'm quite aware that's the chief problem. But unlike most of my damned advisors,

I'm also aware that dredging is costly and I've already got too many commitments on the treasury. And if we can't afford dredging, then it's pointless to rebuild the docks, isn't it?"

"Of course, Caesar," Macro agreed. "But my report will recommend that we beef up the police in Ostia...at least fifty more men. And I suggest that the grain issue should be increased, because of the unemployment. With your approval, I'll prepare a report for the Prefect of the Grain Supply."

"Yes, yes. Very well, do that. Just don't harp at me about the dredging, is all I ask."

Macro inclined his head slightly, acknowledging the emperor's wishes. He knew by Caesar's ruminative manner that another matter was about to be mentioned.

"Now then, this business about Vitalis Hesper's murder. When was it? Yesterday? Day before? No matter. You're aware of it, no doubt?"

"Yes, Caesar, the charioteer. I received a report from my sub-prefect in the Sixth district. He believes that two men did the killing." Macro paused, then added, "There were five murders in the city that night, Caesar. About average."

"I'm not interested in the other four, Macro. But this one does concern me."

"Because he was an athlete, Caesar? Yes, I can understand that. Murder a senator, a poet, a general...well, that's life, isn't it? But murder a popular athlete and the entire world crumbles."

"Exactly," Tiberius growled. "It's the accursed times we live in. Last night there was a huge mob outside the palace, demanding that I find their hero's killer. "Avenge Vitalis!"—"Justice for the people!" they shouted. Repeatedly. Then the filthy scum threw rotten vegetables and eggs at the gates. It took a maniple of Praetorians to disperse them!"

"Two hundred guards to deal with riff-raff? Twenty of my men could have done that, Caesar," Macro snorted.

"Maybe so, but it took the guards half the damn night to restore order. With quite a few broken heads, I dare say. But the fact remains, the City is screaming for action. I've even had a senatorial delegation!" Tiberius snapped in exasperation. "I wonder just how many senators privately invest in racing stables while publicly deploring the rise of commercialism."

"Caesar, leave it with me. We'll make a good show of pursuing the matter. Let the populace see that we're serious. I'm sure the public clamor will fade in a week or so. In the meantime I'll assign a couple of sub-prefects full time to…"

Tiberius stopped him. "No, Macro." The prefect looked at him, puzzled.

"You, Macro. *You* will personally take charge. Anything less won't satisfy the rabble."

"Very well, Caesar." Macro hesitated. "But I can't guarantee that I'll find our man. You're aware that the majority of such murders go unsolved."

Tiberius smiled knowingly. "Ah, Macro, but you *will* find the killer, won't you? Or killers. You mentioned that two men may be involved. And, if it'll help you, I'm not fussy over who you find. Just produce him, or them, but don't take too long."

"It shall be done, Caesar."

"Another thing, this matter of old Aviola committing suicide. A most unlikely event, if you ask me. And the Vitalis fellow had been a guest in Aviola's home the night before the old man killed himself. Wonder if there's anything there, eh?"

Tiberius stood, their discussion over. Macro saluted and prepared to leave.

"Before you go, Macro, how *was* the charioteer killed? Nobody's bothered to tell me yet."

"Market place rumor says that he and several friends were hacked into a hundred pieces and flung to the street dogs," Macro grinned. "In fact, he was found in a whore's bed with his head removed."

"I'll be damned," said Caesar.

"And the weapon was left tidily beside him. It was a Praetorian officer's sword."

X

I informed Horio the grocer that his wife's cousin's version of the death of Vitalis Hesper is a pile of *merda*. Apparently, my recent remark about the asparagus wasn't wasted on him, as he called at the house mid-morning the next day with a basket of figs and six large cabbages, beseeching me to tell the lady Ennia that they were an unworthy gift in recognition of her most valued patronage and that he trusted that he would always have the inestimable privilege of being her most humble servant. And so on and so forth. Smarmy bastard, Horio.

I was able to present him the true facts of the killing because Macro told me about it last night. He and his wife dined alone and shortly afterward she retired. Macro sent for me to discuss a few household matters. Amongst other things, he's interested in having a mural painted on one of the *triclinium* walls, a banquet scene. He saw one in Ostia and was quite taken with it. I shall interview a few artists and get sketches and quotations for my master's consideration.

In a chatty frame of mind, he poured wine for both of us, inviting me to sit. He discoursed idly on trivial matters and complained about the endless demands placed upon him as Prefect of the Watch. Would you believe that one of the noble houses demanded that the *vigiles* rescue their pet cat from a tree? In Macro's view, that sea captain who imported the first cats from Egypt into Rome should have been publicly flogged and the cats sacrificed to an appropriate god—not that it's likely any of the deities would consider themselves honored by the act.

I ventured to ask about the Vitalis Hesper murder. When I repeated the tale I'd heard from Horio, he shook his head in disgust and told me the facts. By then we were well into our sixth or seventh cup of a wine. A vintage from Capua that Macro favors because, as he says, he's amused by its presumption although he believes that the grapes in the last vintage were probably picked too high on a southern slope and may have been bruised before pressing.

"I'll tell you something else, Anthus," said Macro, leaning toward me confidentially, "the emperor has ordered me to take personal charge of the investigation. Me, personally."

"You, sir? Why would Caesar want that?" I asked.

"Because Vitalis was an idol of the masses, and all Rome cries out for retribution," he sighed, then gave a rich belch. "In any event, Caesar says to produce the killer and be quick about it."

I assured him that if anyone could do the job, it was him.

"I'm not as optimistic as you, Anthus. I doubt that I'll ever find the murderer from what I know of the matter. That in itself isn't what bothers me. Caesar told me in so many words just to produce the guilty party, no matter who. Almost anybody will do. The populace will be happy and the matter soon forgotten by all."

"Well," I said, "that makes it simple."

"There's at least a hundred bandits I could nail for the job and not a soul would weep at their execution. And whoever we end up with will be executed in a spectacular style in the arena. Give the crowd some blood and entertainment and let them see that justice has been served. But," said Macro, "I'm not happy about such an easy way out. I want to deliver the real killer to Caesar."

I know what he was saying: the emperor will be contented when I present him with a criminal but the emperor will be impressed highly if I bring him the actual murderer. Another forward step in the progression of Sutorius Macro, *praefectus vigilum* of Rome.

"May one ask how you will proceed in the matter?" I ventured.

"Yes, one may." Macro grinned. "I reckon that first off I'll send for what's-her-name, the woman who runs the brothel where Vitalis got the chop. Yes, her and her girls. They should know what went on that night—probably sing like house-birds."

"Well," I suggested hesitatingly, "they might be frightened and apprehensive, sir. Either withhold information or distort it—you know, tell you what they think you want to hear."

Macro regarded me with patronizing patience. "Nothing that a bit of good old-fashioned judicial torture won't cure, Anthus. That's why we interrogate under torture, if necessary. That way, we know we'll get the truth, right? Yes, come to think of it, it might be a good idea to torture one or two of the whores on general principle. To encourage the others. Good idea."

Now, with all due respect to Macro, in my view he's an intelligent man and reasonably perceptive. But he's held high rank all of his life and sometimes loses sight of the basics. Such as your average person, be he patrician, plebian or slave, will babble like a brook under torture and agree to anything that's put to him, the truth be damned. But I wasn't about to give Macro a dissertation on the subject, however. Instead, I put on the look of a simple-minded slave trying to fathom his master's learned discourse.

Macro sloshed more wine into our cups. "Nothing but plonk, this. Grapes plucked too early in the season and too low on the northern slope," he sighed in resignation.

"And, damn your alien hide, don't sit there looking like a simple-minded slave trying to fathom my learned discourse. I know you, Quintipor. Something's on your mind, so out with it."

Quintipor. When he calls me that, he's feeling benevolent and I'm permitted liberties normally held in check. It's customary for a master to name a slave after himself, with the suffix *por*, a short form of *puer*. Thus, Lucius may call his slave Lucipor—Lucius' boy—and Flavius's slave will be Flavipor. These names are usually given to very young slaves and Macro probably felt I was too old for re-naming when I was purchased. But when he calls me Quintipor, it means "Relax, Anthus; forget you're a slave for a while."

I reflected a moment, then decided to stick my neck out. "I think, sir, that you'll learn much more through a less intimidating approach."

"Do you now? Less intimidating, eh? Well then, exactly what do you suggest? That I invite the whores to dinner and chat casually about the murder over a dish of honey-glazed partridge?"

I smiled dutifully. "Of course not, sir. But instead of questioning the women in an official atmosphere, why not interview them under relaxed conditions in their own house? We all know what women are like, sir—clucking like hens most of the time, whether they have anything to say or not. Now, the way I see it, if they could be led into talking about the night of the killing in a conversational manner, they'd probably squeak out a lot more information than they would half-frightened to death by a formal inquiry."

Macro looked dubious. "You may have a point, but surely you don't expect me to socialize in a brothel with a bunch of prostitutes? And how do you think they'd react? I can just hear madame what's-her-name, 'Oh, goody, girls! Guess who's dropped by for a pleasant chat? The Prefect of the Watch! Such a nice man and a real barrel of laughs. Quick, Lucinda, run out to the bakery and get some pastries. And you, Nerva, warm the wine.' Come now, Quintipor, you'll have to do better than that."

"Oh, I agree that a person of quality such as yourself can't fraternize with the whores, of course not," I assured him. "But when Caesar directed you to take personal charge of the investigation, that doesn't preclude your being assisted by others, does it?"

"No, I suppose not," he allowed. "You're suggesting I have someone else chat up the girls in the whorehouse, then? That's all very well, but *who*? I can't see my men clumping about in their hobnails charming the ladies. Never. It would have to be someone plausible—preferably well-spoken, articulate, yet restrained; courteous, sympathetic and understanding. An intelligent person capable of directing the conversation without it being obvious. Someone who can gain the confidence of others. Yes, all of that."

I nodded in agreement.

"But," he said, "I still have a problem, don't I?"

"Sir?" I said.

"Just where am I to find this paragon of investigatorial excellence? Tell me that, eh?"

I squirmed self-consciously, gazing modestly at the floor. "Well, *dominus*, there's always me."

• • •

I've pressed my luck with Macro, I thought. Following my modest proposal that he need look no further than myself for an agent to chat up the prostitutes, he stared at me. He's less than enthused, I said to myself. I was about to utter something in mitigation of my brashness when he chuckled.

I waited. Now what? I asked myself.

His chortling turned into laughter. After a few seconds it subsided and he refilled our cups. "Well, damn me, Quintipor, if I didn't think for a minute there that you were serious about visiting the whores." Another chuckle.

Which way do I fall? Back out right now with a few merry chuckles of my own? Or go for it while he's still in good humor? Let's go for it.

"Sir?"

"Yes, m'boy?"

"I *was* serious."

Eyebrows raised, again he stared hard. "But, but...you're a slave, man! Even were I to allow it, you don't honestly think that madame whats-her-name, Jucunda, would gush out her secrets to you, do you now?"

"Sir, what if she didn't know I was a slave?"

He snorted. "Ah, well now, not a slave, is it? May one ask just how you'd pass yourself off? *Praetor* of the treasury, maybe? Governor of Syria?" But I could see that beneath his derision he was giving it some thought.

"I'm reasonably well educated, sir, and articulate, as you've often said yourself. Why couldn't I be taken for a freedman? Or born citizen, for that matter? And you and your lady," I flattered him, "have always taken care to dress your servants well, allowing me to purchase a fine tunic from my savings. I'm sure that I could pass as a citizen."

"Well, hmm, I won't dispute that. But your physical appearance might cause suspicion. Still, you could be taken for a Ligurian or some such fair-skinned tribe, should the matter arise."

"I could use my former master's name," I suggested, sensing that he was warming to the idea. "Julius Viator Anthus."

"Ump," he grunted, but not in disapproval. "So, Anthus, if you're not to play the role of *praetor* or governor, just how would you represent yourself to the ladies of easy virtue?"

"What better," I said, "than what I am? Scribe and accountant. I could represent myself as an unemployed scribe seeking casual work. It gives me a valid reason to approach her."

I thought it imprudent to mention another aptitude that I could probably put to advantage, should I gain employment in the brothel. Like any experienced household slave, I'm well-grounded in the art of blending unobtrusively into the background—listening. This way I've learned much of the affairs of state through overhearing Macro's wealthy and influential friends when they're well into the wine after a good dinner. Why couldn't such experience be helpful to me in the house of Jucunda?

"After that," I smiled, "I'll just rely on my natural charm and gracious manners. Should it fail, *dominus*, nothing has really been lost."

Macro paced about for a minute, humphing to himself. Then he said, "Very well. We'll give it a try. And don't smile winningly at me, damn your alien hide! You've won your case. So then, that's that. When will you embark on this business?"

"Why not tomorrow, sir? Time is of the essence." I savored that last phrase. One of my finer contributions to linguistic expression. But then, I always did have a way with words. Macro had earlier declared that the affair had to be resolved "pretty damn quick," but "time is of the essence" has a certain genteel, classical, direct substance.

Macro downed the remainder of his wine and yawned noisily, stretching. With his arms straining above his head and standing tiptoe, he seemed a giant. He's quite tall, over five foot nine. Me, I'm about average height, five foot four.

"Good night then, Anthus. I don't think there's anything further to discuss concerning your venture to the whorehouse." He turned toward the door. "See me before you leave in the morning."

I cleared my throat in the discreet manner which usually signifies "haven't you forgotten something?"

"Uh, sir. There's the little matter of, um, expenses."

"Expenses?" said Macro. "Anthus, do you intend to hire a litter to transport you in style to the brothel? Or what?"

"Of course not, sir. But when I make my visit, it might be judicious for me to treat Madame Jucunda and perhaps some of her girls to whatever refreshment seems appropriate. And should I make progress in the matter, I believe it would be money well spent to ease their memories with a *denarius* here, a few *sesterces* there. And I'll need a little cash for buying a meal or two for myself."

"A *denarius* here and a few *sesterces* there! Damn and blast, Anthus! I've already told you that I can ease their memories, as you put it, with a spot of judicial torture."

I knew this for the ritual grumbling that it was. I've mentioned before that Macro isn't really a mean man, but where he'll spend ten thousand *denarii* without second thought, he'll cry like a baby over a few *sesterces*. It probably salves his conscience, helping him convince himself that he's a prudent man.

"Now, now, sir," I soothed, "I'm quite sure that I can be of more help to you in this regard than the rack or hot irons."

"Expenses," he grumbled. "Oh, very well, Anthus, damn your alien hide. How much do you think you'll need?"

"I was giving thought to a hundred *denarii* sir," said I, awaiting the explosion.

"A hundred *denarii*! A *hundred*! I swear by the cupbearer of Zeus that you believe I'm made of money! Do you think I'm King Midas? Or King, King…blast it! What's that other man's name?"

"Croesus, sir," I said.

"Yes, Croesus. Whatever. Two hundred curses on your head, Anthus. A hundred *denarii*! Oh, damnation, very well. A hundred. I'll give it to you in the morning. And now, have I your permission to retire, having let you talk me into who knows what asinine scheme? Never mind driving me toward bankruptcy!"

My master seems to forget that I'm his accountant, amongst other things. Of course I know that he isn't as wealthy as the fabled Midas or Croesus. But his and the lady Ennia's combined family fortunes exceed thirty million *sesterces*, including his handsome remuneration as *praefectus vigilum* of Rome.

It's not unlikely, either, that should the investigation proceed well, I'll be asking for more substantial expenses than a hundred *denarii*.

Petronia's back to calling me "your majesty" again. I don't know what it was I did, or didn't do, that set her off this time. She'll be more amenable, I'm sure, by the time I've finished looking into Macro's murder mystery. I suppose "murder mystery" is as good a way as any to describe the situation.

• • •

In the morning Macro renewed his ritual display of reluctance at adopting my suggestion, calling aloud upon Minerva, goddess of wisdom, asking why she'd deserted him in permitting him to agree to such a hare-brained idea. He's a bit of an actor in that regard and, like most of his social class, enamored with the sound of his own voice.

I allowed his solo performance for a minute or two.

Then, when he paused for breath, I joined the theatrics with a desolate sigh and downcast eyes.

"And, pray tell, just what is *that* supposed to mean?" he said.

"A pity, sir, such a pity. I truly believed that I could be of service to you," I replied, raising my eyes despondently to his. "But you know best, sir. As always. As you say, if Caesar isn't too particular over who's charged with the charioteer's murder...well, there it is. Why waste time and effort, and a few coins? Yes, perhaps better to torture a couple of prostitutes and have done with the matter quickly."

"Ump," Macro grunted.

"And you have countless thugs to choose from. All no doubt deserving of a fine public execution."

"Ump."

"It's all one to the emperor whether you reveal the actual killer or take the simple route and merely draw a name as in a lottery." I sighed loudly again for good measure. Macro pouted and pulled his lower lip between thumb and forefinger.

I continued my pantomime. "You see, sir, I thought that Caesar would be well pleased, should you demonstrate that the easy way, the path of least effort, is not the way of such as *yourself*. For lesser men, men of little stature, yes. But *not* for Sutorius Macro, a prefect of Rome."

We'd been talking in Greek, the language which signifies good breeding in today's Romans as it has for centuries. In a fit of cultural self-deprecation in the past, Romans conceded that their Hellenistic vassals were a polished lot and began imitating their elegant manners and social graces, including their speech. So most of the patrician and equestrian classes are bilingual. It's a sneering insult to say that someone "has little or no Greek."

When Macro and I are alone, we use Greek. Actually, my proficiency is greater than his but I play that down, stumbling now and then when we talk. It strokes his ego and costs me nothing to let him correct me, playing the role of instructive master.

Confident that he'd permit me to visit the brothel once our histrionic performance had ended, I was anxious to get it over with. I thought the best ploy would be to feign deferential abandonment of the scheme. The odds were that he'd groan in grudging assent and tell me to get on with it.

I switched from Greek to Latin and with eyes cast down in self-castigation, sadly intoned an old saying. I turned away, as though to leave.

"*Now* what are you babbling about?" Macro demanded. "The cobbler should not judge above the sandal? What's a damn cobbler to do with this, eh?"

I raised my hands, palms uppermost, in self-abasement. "Apelles, sir. The Greek artist of a few centuries back. A cobbler once criticized a sandal in one of his paintings. Apelles accepted that as just criticism by an artisan. But the cobbler had the temerity to then find fault with the manner in which the subject's legs were painted. That was when the artist put down the cobbler by telling him that he was qualified to judge the sandal but nothing more."

"I thank you, Anthus," Macro cried with mockingly exaggerated respect. "We simple prefects of Rome are so occupied with civic affairs that we tend to lose sight of the world of art and history. The rich tapestry of life often eludes us, hence we are ever in debt to our household staff who keep us informed of such matters. *But*, may I ask again what a cobbler has to do with our discussion?"

"Sir, I compare myself to the cobbler. He dared to venture beyond his limited knowledge and I also have done so. I should never have offered myself as your agent in tracing the murderer of Vitalis Hesper. The cobbler should stick to his last. And I should stick to my accounts."

I bowed and turned to depart. Before I'd gone two steps, Macro groaned and sighed grudgingly, "Soon it will be night—let's attend to business." A common expression, apt enough—but your average man on the street would probably put it "Let's get the show on the road."

I left the house an hour later. My head held all the information gleaned thus far by the City police concerning the death of Vitalis. My purse, tucked in the fold of my best tunic, held one hundred *denarii*. Expense money.

XI

The woman stared in concentration at the inlaid ivory chess board, then moved one of her pieces and took a red figurine from the board.

"Say farewell to your general, Ponto," she said.

The knight lifted his hands in mock despair. "Farewell, general. And with his loss, Procula, I surrender to your tactical genius."

She began to place the pieces in a cloth lined box.

"*Ludus latrinculorum*," she said. "The brigand's game. I wonder why it's called that?"

"I don't know and doubt if anyone else does," he replied. "It's an ancient game. They say it was brought from the east by the Greek Alexander. Who knows?"

He paused. "I apologize for not playing a better game, Procula. I don't seem to be in the mood lately. Forgive me for being such poor company."

She finished arranging the colored figurines in the box and, arising, extended a hand toward him. "Let's take a walk in the garden before we retire."

They strolled in silence beneath the starry autumn sky and when they reached the end of the garden, turned to walk back toward the house. After a few steps, she stopped and sat on a small stone bench. "Let's sit a few minutes," she said, "I want to talk with you where the servants can't overhear us."

"Talk? About what, Procula?"

"I'm concerned about you, husband. We've been married long enough for me to know when you're ill at ease. Ever since you returned from Rome four days ago you've been troubled. It shows in your every movement, every word. You pretend otherwise, but I know better."

He looked into her face and took her hand. "Yes. I'm in low spirits. But it will pass soon and I don't want to inflict my mood upon you."

"What happened in Rome? Tell me."

The knight glanced away briefly, then returned his eyes to hers.

"I killed a man."

Without a moment's hesitation she responded. "If you killed a man, there was a reason. Tell me the entire story. And I presume that it was related to his sending for you."

"Yes. He asked me to carry out an assassination in the interest of public morals and the welfare of the state."

He related to her all that had happened from the time that the centurion Priscus had departed from him after they had entered the Viminal Gate until he had left through the same gate three days later.

She listened in silence until he had finished.

"You have killed men in battle and you have also

decreed the death sentence for others in your role as military judge," she stated bluntly.

"Yes."

"And did you ever suffer low spirits on such occasions?"

He pondered the matter. "No. Sometimes I felt regret. But I never had a bad conscience. I was working within the rules of warfare and military justice."

"But the one you killed in Rome—you were the executioner and not the judge. It was a personal experience without the objectivity of your previous dealings in death."

"You state it well, Procula. Yes, it affected me as an individual rather than me as a soldier or official. I considered that I acted as an agent in the best interest of the state, but another part of my mind tells me that I slew a helpless, unarmed man."

He had been holding her hand while he talked but now he released it and pressed the palms of both hands to his face. Voice muffled, he continued, "Procula, we've just been playing the brigand's game, and that's how I feel now. I'm no better than a brigand myself."

She again took his hand firmly in her own. "Now listen to me, Ponto. Our families have served Rome for many years and we know the meaning of loyalty to the state and its moral code. We know also that in recent years there has been a laxity in public behavior that would disgust the founders of Rome. With few exceptions, the patricians are cringing sycophants who avoid responsibility and our own knightly class is far more concerned with making money than with public service and setting an example to the citizens..."

"Procula, I..."

"Please. Hear me out. Now then, you say that you washed the man's blood from your hands—and that you've been washing your hands compulsively ever since. I suggest it's your guilt that you're trying to wash away. But don't you see that there should be no guilt? You behaved honorably, doing what you did. Husband, you've had other men's blood on you in the past, not to mention your own, as witnessed by the battle scars you bear. The blood of the man you killed in Rome is of no more importance than that of those you slew in battle. In fact, it should be of far less concern to you. Your slain enemies were probably decent men, loyal to their own cause. But the one you killed a few days ago was no more than an arrogant lout from the provinces who abused his position as a popular folk hero by undermining Roman virtues."

Finished, she observed her husband while he gave thought to her words.

"I'm glad that I've told you about it," he said. "Your response has taken some weight off my heart."

She nodded and waited for him to continue.

"Something that's gnawed at my mind is that he suggested I'd be rewarded in some manner for having been his agent. Now I wonder if I'm guilty of allowing myself to be bribed. I tell myself that what I did, I did for the state and not for personal gain. Yet the doubt lingers."

"I know you better than you know yourself," she asserted. "You have never placed your own interests above those of Rome. Your record is unblemished and you've been twice honored for your service. You and I have more than adequate personal wealth and you have no need to accept bribes. Even if you had financial need, I know you'd never demean yourself by accepting them."

He smiled for the first time in days. "Your faith in me is a precious thing, Procula. May I never give you cause to lose it."

"I never shall, Ponto. You are a man of exceptional ability and I'm confident that Rome shall find a worthy position for you in the future.

Rising from the bench, she said, "And now, let's go inside. The evening grows chilly."

He chuckled as they walked toward the house. "So, my

love, you believe there may yet be a place in the history books for me?"

They had arrived at the door but before they entered, she put her hands on his shoulders and looked into his face earnestly. "I'll tell you this, husband, a thousand years from now, two thousand years, your name will still be known when those of emperors and kings are long forgotten."

XII

It took me an hour or more to walk to the district where Jucunda's house is located. It's only about two miles from Macro's residence but progress through Rome's streets is never swift, what with beggars, hawkers, litters, slave and client retinues and religious processions.

And the noise! I've mentioned that the upper classes love the sound of their own voices. But perhaps it's unfair to imply that only the privileged chatter endlessly. Everyone in Rome talks incessantly, barring a few reserved, taciturn people like myself. They prattle on at a mile a minute, raising their voices to be heard because they all talk at the same time. Resident aliens catch the disease quickly, too. Walk a hundred feet along any city street and you'll be assaulted by a dozen languages at full volume simultaneously. The Gauls are the worst...their arms wave as their mouths flap. The joke has it that if you tie a Gaul's hands behind his back, he's rendered speechless.

Rome is more than seven hundred and fifty years old and I suspect that its streets haven't been improved since the time of Romulus, the City's founder. They say there's more than fifty miles of streets in Rome now. Some of the larger ones have an orderly pattern, but most are a welter of narrow lanes snaking in every direction and zig-zagging up and down the Seven Hills. Very few are paved, so in the wet season the populace wades ankle deep in muck, enriched by slops and garbage chucked into the street by householders.

I'd like to visit Pompeii. I'm told the streets there are paved and run straight in a grid pattern. It's a small city south of Rome, a former Greek colony, not far from Neapolis. Its proper name is Colonia Veneria Cornelia Pompeianorum. There's a mountain called Vesuvius nearby and I recall from my student days that a Greek geographer, Strabo, claimed that it was once an active volcano. But there's nothing in recorded history that indicates the god Vulcan ever inhabited Vesuvius, so Pompeii is safe enough. Strabo—his name means 'squinty eyed'—was probably trying to invite attention to himself, as scholars do. It keeps their patrons happy.

The divine Julius decreed that landlords must keep the streets in front of their houses clean and if they didn't, the magistrates could have the cleaning done and charge the cost to them. This edict has been more honored in the breach than the observance and filth continues to pile up. Rome's engineers can build huge aqueducts and complicated engines of war, but its administrators can't keep onion peelings off the streets. They'll spend hours in the baths being steamed, scrubbed, scraped and perfumed, then step into the street and dance daintily to keep from soiling their sandals with stinking chicken guts or a dead dog.

That expression I just used…more honored in the breach…I rather like that. I do have a way with words, if I say so myself. I must start writing down my more clever and picturesque utterances. Who knows what future scholars and writers might be beholden to such an anthology of linguistic elegance?

I found Jucunda's house just as Macro had directed me, about two hundred feet from the corner of the Flaminian Way. The first thing I noticed when I turned into the narrow street was the gloom, even though the day was bright enough. Four and five storied buildings lined either side, most with overhanging balconies that almost touched over the middle of the street. It was like being in a tunnel.

I readily identified the brothel by its bright red door with a bronze satyr's head knocker and the faded painting of Cupido, god of love, above the doorway. Next to the brothel was a *thermopolium*—a rich, spicy smell of cooking emanating from its open door. A small potter's shop stood across the street.

As I stood looking at the house of Jucunda, about to knock on its door, a man lounging in the doorway of the potter's shop called out in a cheerful voice, "You're a little early, friend, if you wish to call on the ladies."

He gave me a gap-toothed grin as I turned to him. "The house doesn't entertain until the start of the ninth hour at this time of year."

The ninth hour—mid-afternoon. I would have thought that such establishments began business in the early evening. Not that I have much experience in such matters. Much experience? I have none whatsoever.

I returned his grin. "You guess my intentions, but the nature of my call is business rather than pleasure."

He was a tall, angular man, bald, with merry eyes. He wore a shop-keeper's apron and when he stepped toward me, I saw that he limped.

"Business, is it, friend? All I can say is that you'd better be cautious with Madame Jucunda. She can size up a situation faster than it takes to cook asparagus."

"You know the lady, then?" I said.

"Been neighbors a dozen years now. She's a tough old bird, make no mistake, but I like her. Been a good neighbor to me more than once. Gives me her pottery business, too. She runs an orderly house but being what it is, sometimes visitors get unruly after revels with the grape...a few cups and plates get broken, have to be replaced."

He looked at me suspiciously. "You aren't in the pottery business, are you?"

"No," I reassured him, "I'm a scribe and accountant. I'm 'between positions' you might call it. Looking for employment, even part-time. That's why I'm here. Perhaps I can assist her with her taxes. The magistrate's tax regulations get more complicated each year."

"Friend, you don't have to tell me," he said mournfully. Then, more cheerfully, "You'd better come in with me and share a cup while you're waiting."

"Thank you, but I want to call on the madame right away."

"Can't," he replied. "You missed her by a few minutes. She's away with a couple of her girls, probably shopping at the market. She operates a small dining room for her visitors as well as the other side of the business."

"In that case, I'll take you up on your offer," I said, following him into his shop. Seated at a table in the rear of the premises and surrounded with the cluttered tools and products of his craft, I accepted a cup of wine.

"I'm Bato Niger," said my host, seating himself across from me. "I drink to your success with the ladies."

Raising my cup, I inclined my head to him.

"What I mean is, to your success in satisfying Madame Jucunda," he explained.

Eyebrows raised delicately, I smiled questioningly.

"You know what I mean," he sighed. "Bottoms up." We drank.

"And I, sir, am..." I came close to saying Anthus, slave and steward of Sutorius Macro but checked myself in time. "Anthus. Julius Viator Anthus, who thanks you for your hospitality."

Bato refilled our cups and I cautioned myself to go slowly and nurse this one for a while. It wasn't yet noon and I had no wish to present myself across the street in a state of knee-walking *inebriatum*.

If I had to wait for the madame's return, this seemed as pleasant a way as any to do it. Besides, Bato might be able to assist me in my inquiries into the matter of the athlete's murder, living as close as he does to the scene of the crime.

"Assist me with my inquiries." Yes, another apt phrase, quietly expressive, discreet. Perhaps I shall pass it along to Macro as something he may wish to incorporate into his official reports. "The brick-maker Figulus assisted the Urban Cohorts with their inquiries into the theft of two goats." No. Upon reflection, I believe Macro would prefer to stick with a more graphic but honest narrative. "After being flogged and racked, the brick-maker Figulus confessed that he and his brother stole two goats."

Anyway, Bato and I passed the time bewailing the taste, dress and moral fiber of modern youth and deploring the shoddy products of so many of today's so-called craftsmen. He told me that he'd been discharged from the army after serving ten years.

"I was a private soldier in the Second Augusta. Mule driver," he said. "Had a catapult carriage team, six mules."

"Your limp, Bato, I couldn't help notice it. Is that why you were discharged?"

"Yup. Got that in Spain."

I nodded respectfully. "A battle wound, was it?"

"Well," he said mischievously, "that's how I tell it to

those who might buy a drink for an old veteran, but I'll be honest with you. Got kicked by a mule. Busted my leg. Actually the beast kicked me in the ass but I clipped my leg against a wagon wheel when I was in mid-air."

"So then you were sent home?"

"Not right away. The physician bound my leg with ashes from a boar's jaw. He apologized for not being able to treat it with virgin's spittle, but under the circumstances there wasn't much he could do about that. Anyway, the boar's jaw did the trick, more or less. I reckon they've gone as far as they can go with modern medicine. The old leg aches in damp weather but I'm not complaining. Seen men die in camp from less. After Spain, we were transferred to lower Germany and that's where I got my discharge from the flying horse."

He noted my perplexed look. "That's what we called our outfit," he explained. "Our emblem was Pegasus and Capricorn."

"Are you married?" I asked.

"No. My wife died a few years ago and I live here alone. Got a couple of rooms above the shop."

"Well, Bato, it must be nearly noon. I'd be pleased to buy you lunch. I see there's a hot food and drink shop across the street."

Beaming, he said, "Apio's *thermopolium*. I accept your kind offer, Anthus. It'll be a change from my usual bread and cheese that I was about to offer you."

He locked his shop door and we went across to Apio's, a modest establishment, but then it wasn't exactly located in the heart of the forum. Two large windows and the open door provided natural light at that time of day, but on the walls were several candle sconces and oil lanterns on small shelves for night lighting.

Along one wall ran a waist-high stone counter. A half dozen round openings in the counter top held metal pots, heated from below by oil lamps. A similar counter ran parallel to it about four feet away; also fitted with a half dozen metal inserts containing a steaming assortment of food. Between the counters was a table, laden with plates, bowls, cups and containers of chopped and grated vegetables, spices, hard boiled eggs and freshly baked bread.

At the far end of the shop was a *lararium*...a large wall niche decorated in red and gold. This was the family shrine, dedicated to ancestors and the *lares*, the household's protective gods.

A black-haired waitress, about fifteen, stood between the two counters, greeting Bato as we entered. He and the girl chatted briefly after he'd introduced me as his old friend, Anthus the scribe.

On the wall behind the food counters was a slate with the day's menu chalked on it. It's a small shop, more utilitarian than designed for gracious dining. The renowned gourmet, Marcus Gavius Apicius, might well have disdained Apio's *thermopolium*, but Anthus, the scribe, was pleased with it.

We both had thick, barley soup laced with slivers of mutton, then Bato enjoyed three large spiced pork liver sausages with peas and a celery and white wine sauce, and I had chicken dumplings with ginger gravy. The small pitcher of wine we shared brought the bill to three *sesterces*. Macro will weep like a child if I tell him I've squandered his money on a poor potter with a game leg.

Several people came and went while we ate, some calling out to Bato, others coming over to our corner table. Each time he introduced me as his friend, the scribe. Warming to my role, I obligingly put on what I hoped would pass for a scholarly countenance. I realize now that my relatively sheltered life within Macro's household had shielded me from the pecking order and the conventions of Rome's working classes. I sensed that Bato and his friends were deferring to me, not in an obsequious manner, but it was there all the same.

I'm sure that they considered me a *rara avis*. Someone who can read and write with fluency—and who's bilingual, as well—is a rare bird indeed, in their circle.

The fact is, Romans prize literacy and, although there's no public schooling, most people receive at least a rudimentary education. But the social status of teachers is low, many of them being slaves—as was my old Greek *magister*, by the way—so the quality of education is poor.

As we returned to the potter's shop, a slender black girl with closely cropped hair and fine features came out of the brothel. Bato called to her, "Has your mistress returned, Alis?" She replied in halting Latin that Jucunda was still away, then she set off down the narrow street, carrying a large straw basket.

"Alis is Egyptian," Bato said. "A slave. Jucunda has five or six slave prostitutes. The rest are freedwomen. Jucunda was a slave herself. German. Came here when she was a child. She treats her girls well, slave and freed. Oh, she berates them sometimes, threatening the whipping of their lives. Truth is, she doesn't own a whip. Doesn't need one. Her girls adore her."

"You seem to know a lot about her," I said.

He hesitated. "Yes. I do. My wife was once one of her girls. A slave. When I told Jucunda that I wanted to marry Sassia and asked if I could buy her freedom, she laughed and said, 'You haven't got enough money.' I agreed but said I'd somehow borrow it. She stared at me and quoted that old saying, 'Lovers are out of their senses.' I said yes, they probably are—but even so, I want Sassia. Then she took a cup from the shelf, a pretty cerulean cup with shoulder handles. She intentionally dropped it onto the floor and broke it."

Bato's voice was hushed and his eyes soft with reminiscence. "Then she said, 'Damn. That was my last cerulean cup. I want another; in fact, I want fifty of them. Can you make cups as good as that one?' Yes, I told her. 'Very well, potter,' she said, 'Bring me fifty cups and Sassia is yours.' She kept her word. Sassia and I were very happy for six years...and when Sassia died, Jucunda loaned me the money for her tomb."

He looked toward the brothel. "Yes, Anthus, I know a lot about her," he said.

We'd been standing in front of his shop as he told his story. "Wait here," he said. "I'll get a couple of stools and we can sit and wait for Jucunda's return."

We settled with our backs to the building. "I sit out here most evenings when the weather's good," he said. "Not too exciting for a young fellow like you, but I enjoy watching the people come and go. What with Apio's eatery and the brothel, there's usually something going on."

He inclined his head toward the intersection of the narrow street and the larger Flaminian Way. "I often go down to the corner in the evening. Old friend of mine sells hot chestnuts there when he's up to it. He's a discharged soldier, too. Lost an arm and an eye in the Rhineland. He was in the Twentieth Valeria. Yep, old Ignatius and I often wile away the time lying to each other about our legion days."

Bato sat up and leaned toward me animatedly. "Hey, I said that there wasn't much excitement around here...but did you know that it was in Jucunda's that Vitalis Hesper was murdered?"

I did my best to suppress any overt display of interest. "Who? Hesper...Hesper...um, yes, I seem to remember hearing something about that..."

"C'mon now, Anthus—the charioteer! Everybody's heard of him!" Bato cried, amazed at my ignorance.

"Ah...yes, of course. Vitalis Hesper. Of the Red Stable."

"Blue," Bato said. "He was of the Blue faction."

"Blue...now I recall. Yes. And he was actually murdered in that very house. Well!" I hesitated briefly. "It's coming back now. They say his killers cut him into pieces and threw them out into the street. Horrible!"

He snorted. "That's pure goat dung. I was here the whole time and it didn't happen like that at all. What happened was the killer cut off his head."

I shook my head wonderingly. "And you were sitting here at the very time?"

"Well, not *all* the time, exactly. I was down the street for a while chatting with Ignatius. It was mentioning him a minute ago that reminded me of the murder, see?"

"How so?" I queried.

"When I was sitting here earlier that night I saw a man enter the brothel. About an hour before sunset. 'Well,' says I to myself, 'you're not the usual run of client for that place, are you?' It was his appearance and the way he walked. He was wearing a *paenula*, a good quality one, and had the hood pulled well over his face. Seemed a bit odd. It wasn't raining and the weather was cool but pleasant enough."

"Perhaps he was embarrassed about going into the house, trying to hide his face?" I suggested.

"By all the gods, friend, you must lead a sheltered life," he laughed. "Nobody's embarrassed about going into a brothel. Well, maybe some of the more pious citizens or public figures, but then they wouldn't be visiting one, would they?"

"But it seems that the cloaked man didn't want to be recognized, or at least, have his face remembered," I said. "Did you see him when he left the place?"

Squirming happily at the chance to tell his tale, Bato continued. "Sure did. Like I say, it was mentioning old Ignatius that brought it to mind. That night after I'd sat here awhile I walked to the corner to visit with him. Suddenly Ignatius interrupted whatever we were jawing about and called out 'Buy some chestnuts from an old soldier, sir?' I turned to see who he'd spoken to, and by Pollux, it was the same cloaked man I'd seen entering Jucunda's earlier."

He waited for some expression of awe at this revelation and I obliged.

"Isis, Osiris and Horus!" I gasped. "The same man?"

"The very same," he nodded eagerly. "And he still had his face hidden in his hood. Well now, he stopped and stared at Ignatius. 'Old soldier, are you? Your name, rank, legion, line and cohort!' Well, me and Ignatius can smell 'officer' at five hundred feet and we both knew that this was one, the way he stood, the way he snapped the question. And it weren't no question, either—it was a bloody order, is what it was."

Shaking his head wonderingly at the recollection, he went on. "Standing at attention, Ignatius rattled off 'Ignatius Carbo, sir! Duplicarius, *hastati*, fourth cohort, Legion Twenty Valeria. Sir!' Damn me, if I wasn't standing at attention myself! The cloaked man said, 'The Twentieth, eh? Your commander was Pomponius Culleo, then; and your emblem was the bull.' Poor old Ignatius looked puzzled, then replied, 'No, sir, my commander was Flavius Artemus and our emblem was the boar.' At that, the officer said 'Yes, *emeritus*, you're right.' Then he handed a gold coin to Ignatius and strode off without another word."

He paused, awaiting my reaction. "A gold piece," I breathed reverently. "Probably more than your friend would make in a week of selling chestnuts. But tell me, you said he called Ignatius '*emeritus*.' I'm not sure of the meaning of that."

"It's an old soldier who's served with distinction and been honorably discharged. Not a term used lightly, so when the officer called Ignatius that, it was a compliment. And it showed that the cloaked man knew the army. When he gave Ignatius the wrong emblem and name of his commander, he was putting him to the test."

"Which your friend passed, yes," I nodded.

Glancing about cautiously, Bato leaned toward me confidentially. "That was the night of the murder. About the same time, and I think..." He stopped, once more looking around apprehensively.

"Yes?" I encouraged him.

"I think the officer was the killer."

Masking excitement at this gratuitous bit of information, I said, "Well, yes, he was in the house at the time, it would seem...but what about Madame Jucunda and her girls? They must have seen him. What did they report to the police? Or do you know?"

"Between you and me, friend, the story they told the police was pure twaddle. I haven't heard Jucunda's version from her own mouth, I admit. We've had a few chats since then, but she steers clear of any talk about that night."

Puzzled, I said, "Then how do you know what the police were told?"

"By putting two and two together," he replied. "About an hour after the officer had given the coin to Ignatius, one of the whores ran out of the house screaming murder and hollering for the police. The neighbors took up the cry, and in a few minutes a small detachment of the Urban Cohorts pounded down the street and charged into the brothel. I was about to go inside but stayed here to see what would happen. I was thinking that after all the fuss died down, I'd go over to ask Jucunda if I could help her."

Making mental note of all this to inscribe later for Macro, I urged Bato on. "Then what?"

"A man was posted at the door of the house and he refused to let anyone leave. There was a bit of shouting and complaining and one young roisterer—taken with drink, I'd say he was—got rapped smartly on the head with a cudgel when he tried to leave. Anyway, after a while the police left the house and the man in charge saw me sitting here and came over. I stood up and said, 'Greetings, centurion.' He weren't no centurion, that's for sure, but most of those people like being bumped up a few ranks when addressed by us ignorant civilians."

He interrupted his story and looked toward the street corner. "There's your lady. That's Jucunda."

A middle-aged woman, handsome, of average height, came along the street accompanied by two younger women. All three carried baskets laden with their market purchases. As they drew close, the older woman smiled across at Bato, then they entered the house.

"I'll take you over in a few minutes, if you want," the potter said. "Introduce you to the madame."

I told him that would be appreciated but first I wanted to hear the rest of his tale.

"The detachment commander asked me if I'd been sitting here long, and when I said that I had, he asked if I'd seen two cloaked men, one tall and one short, run out of the house. I told him, quite honestly, that I hadn't but then added, not so honestly, that I'd gone for a couple of minutes into the yard at the rear to relieve myself and maybe the men had left when I was away. That way, the police couldn't say that the girls had lied. That's obviously what Jucunda told them, isn't it? That two men in cloaks had done in the charioteer and run out the front door."

"Seems so," I agreed. "But you saw no such men, so I wonder why she lied. But then, I suppose you told the police about the cloaked officer?"

"Hell, no," Bato said cheerfully. "They didn't ask about him, did they? And I wasn't going to inform on a senior officer and get involved in the gods know what."

"Senior officer?" I said. "How do you know?"

"Apart from his upper class accent and the fact that he oozed power of command, I knew when he handed the coin to Ignatius."

I looked bewildered.

"Yes, friend. On his little finger—I saw it plain as day—he wore an equestrian's *annulus aureus*.

"The gold ring of a knight!" I cried. Now I was truly astonished.

"Enough of my chatter," Bato cheerily said. "Let's meet Madame Jucunda. You'd best give her your sales talk before the house opens for business."

As we crossed the road, Bato touched my arm. "A few minutes ago you referred to the goddess Isis and her family, an exclamation you made."

"I did? I don't recall, but if you say so."

"Yes. Well, I thought I'd mention that it might be better if you didn't swear by Isis when you talk with Jucunda. What with the cult being outlawed and all. Well, it can be a touchy matter, if you know what I mean."

I took his meaning at once. The worship of the Egyptian goddess has been condemned by the authorities for more than a hundred years, as a threat to Roman morality. Recently, Tiberius has renewed suppression of the cult, yet in spite of this it flourishes behind closed doors while its members pay lip service to the state religion.

The potter was telling me—and it showed that he trusted me even on such brief acquaintance—that Jucunda was a follower of Isis and that I shouldn't take the name of the goddess lightly if I wished to be on madame's good side.

Jucunda greeted Bato with the ease of old friendship and nodded courteously to me.

"Anthus is a scribe and accountant," he told her happily. She observed me inquiringly as he continued. "Speaks Greek, too, very accomplished gent, my friend is. But he wishes to have a private chat with you, so I'll be getting back to my shop. Drop in and see me for a minute when you're through here, Anthus."

Bato left us and Jucunda turned to me abruptly. "Be seated and tell me what you want to discuss. But before you start, I wish to know who you are, other than a new friend of Bato's. You're Roman born, your accent says so. Are you freedman or slave?"

I recalled the potter saying that Jucunda could size up things quicker than it takes to cook asparagus. A popular saying, that. It was, so I'm told, one of the late Augustus Caesar's frequent figures of speech.

"Most observant," I said, "I was indeed born in Rome. But you presume that I'm either slave or freedman. Might I not be born freeman?"

"You might be, but I doubt it. Nor have you answered my question. I'm not interested in Socratic dialogue, scribe. Well?"

Socratic dialogue? I'd best deal carefully with this lady, I thought. "Freedman, ma'am," I lied. "May I ask how you knew I'm not freeborn?" I smiled, as though in admiration of her perspicacity.

"Your accent and manner of speaking…too good for a person of your station. You've received a better education than most. And you're a scribe. A born freeman with a good education normally comes from a family influential enough to settle their sons in better positions than that of scribe. You're a good cut above the average Roman—that can only mean that you've acquired excellent schooling yet you're restricted in your aspirations. And that spells 'slave.' I suspect that you were educated as a child while in the service of a wealthy, if not noble, household and have been employed in such houses ever since."

This was a new experience for me. My life so far had been spent largely in association with slaves, ex-slaves, tradesmen and people of little consequence. Apart from occasional chats with Macro, my immediate social life is circumscribed and I'm rarely exposed to witty dialogue or intellectual observations by my peers. Madame Jucunda both intimidated and stimulated me with her self-confidence and perception.

"I'm what you describe, ma'am," I said, inclining my head respectfully. "You impress me with your power of deduction."

Her demeanor up to now had been stiff, on the formal side, but now she relaxed in her chair and smiled, not warmly, but still, a smile.

"And now, Anthus the scribe, why are you here?"

I told her that I sought employment and hoped that I might be of some use to her, perhaps part-time. She thought about it briefly, then shook her head.

"No, I can't afford the luxury of an accountant. I've been able to deal satisfactorily with the tax farmers. And I've told them more than once that the prostitutes of Rome must be the chief support of the treasury, the head fees they charge us."

Her sudden tone of resentment prompted me to commiserate. "Ah, ma'am, how very true," I said dolefully, hoping I wasn't overdoing it. "It's as they say, the rich grow richer and the poor grow poorer. Honest proprietors such as yourself and our friend Bato the potter are squeezed dry while the privileged classes squander fortunes on feasting and finery."

I must confess that my sympathy wasn't all that sincere. It's true that a few of the aristocrats scatter money with gay abandon, but it's the artisans and tradesmen who generally profit by it. And by the same token, the wealthy classes pay heavy taxes. Tiberius Caesar doesn't show favor to the upper classes, not when it comes to coin of the realm, he doesn't.

As I've mentioned before, I hear quite a bit about what goes on in the corridors of power. Now, there's another neat turn of phrase, just off the top of my head. 'Corridors of power.' Yes, I like it.

But I digress—as for Jucunda, my sympathetic manner appeared to soften her even more. Now she proceeded on a recital of the endless vexations which face a professional woman of her ilk: being a mother to her girls, teaching them, nursing them, counseling them; looking after the accounts; maintaining the premises and its inventory; overseeing the kitchen and dining room operation; ensuring that the clientele are satisfied; dealing with occasional rowdies and employing discretion with the wealthier and more fastidious clients; and of course, maintaining a good rapport with the *vigiles, cohortes* and municipal officers, especially the magistrates who approve her brothel license.

Yes, I thought, tremendous responsibility for a woman. I wondered how she'd become the owner of a brothel. I guessed her to be about forty—plumpish, but not fat. She had reddish gold hair, as befits her occupation. She's handsome rather than beautiful, with a wide mouth, and straight nose. But her dominant feature was her blue eyes, wide set and accented with black eyeliner. Petronia had told me that eyeliner was made from powdered antimony blackened with nut-gall. She wore three or four rings on each hand and a pair of pendant ear-rings of light blue stone set in gold. A matching blue and gold necklace harmonized with the blue trim at the neck and bottom of her white gown. The overall effect was of conservative good taste.

She finished her litany of tribulations and I nodded in condolence. "I said before, ma'am, that I admired your ability to assess my background. I'm even more impressed with your ability to cope with so much diversity in the running of such an establishment as yours." I also reflected to myself that her task to a large degree paralleled my own stewardship of the Macro household—with a few minor variations.

"You're a courteous young man, Anthus," she said, "but you don't have to call me ma'am. I expect that from my grocer and butcher in view of the considerable trade I give them, but you may call me Jucunda."

"Thank you, Jucunda," I replied, then added with shameless flattery, "A delightful name for a delightful lady." She smiled. Her name does mean pleasing, agreeable, delightful, sought after and the like. It's also the name of a renowned Roman family.

"My birth name is Elsa," she said. "I came to Rome

when I was a small girl. My father was a minor official in a small German village. My parents, along with dozens of other families, were taken as slaves in reprisal for an attack by local insurgents on a squad of Roman soldiers on patrol. We were lucky, really. Every tenth member of the village was executed."

"An unhappy beginning," I said.

She shrugged indifferently. "Yes. But I don't believe in looking backward. What's done is done. For that matter, I'm not sure that life in a German village would have been too happy. I've heard the stories of rapacious land-owners who make their own law, brigands, inter-tribal warfare. No, at least here in Rome there's a semblance of law and order. I'm a practical person, Anthus. Make the best of your niche in life and never stop working to improve it. If life as a slave can be more secure and comfortable than uncertainty and misery as a freeman, then to hell with freedom."

"But you're free now and it's better than being a slave, surely?"

"Yes, because I've worked hard and done fairly well. And now I'm a slaveholder myself. But my slave prostitutes are well treated and I give them their freedom when they reach the age of thirty." She paused. "Sometimes before that."

"How did you acquire the name Jucunda?" I asked.

"My master was Aulus Jucundus Cornutus, of a noble family. His brother was a senator and now his nephew is. He was a widower and I was his mistress. When I was twenty-four, he died and freed me in his will, leaving me a generous bequest. That enabled me to establish this house. Although my patron is long since dead, I honor him by retaining his name."

She fell silent for a moment, probably thinking of her former master. "Well now," she continued, "I really don't need your services, not on a continuing basis. But to help you out, I'll hire you to look over my bookkeeping system and see if it needs improvement. That's to include both brothel and dining room. I'll pay you two *denarii* a day and your mid-day meal for five days. If after the five days you need more time, you'll have to do some fancy talking to convince me. What do you say to that?"

What did I say to that? I was very pleased with myself, as I'd made a favorable impression upon the madame and had learned valuable information from the potter. And although it may seem a small matter, this was a milestone in my life. For the first time in my thirty years, I was to be paid wages for my work.

"Madame Jucunda," I said, "that is most satisfactory. Thank you. I'll return tomorrow at the start of the second hour to start work." She nodded agreement.

"And now, if your house rules permit the hired help to purchase wine on the premises, may I have the pleasure of offering you a cup of your finest vintage in appreciation of your assistance to me?"

A few minutes later we were toasting one another with Falernian. Nothing but the best for my employer and me. Macro would sob his heart out, were I to tell him.

XIII

Pierced by her mother's withering glare, Livilla sank weakly onto a couch in Antonia's sewing room. Her air of bored indifference had changed to one of terror at her mother's words. Heart thudding, she gasped, "What did you say?"

"You heard me well enough," Antonia snapped, "but you've spent your life hearing without listening, so I'll say it again. It has been reported to the emperor that you murdered your husband with the assistance of the commander of the Praetorian Guard. Need I add that Tiberius is less than pleased with the news that you were instrumental in his son's death?"

Striving to control her panic, Livilla said with an edge

of indignation, "Who dares to make such an accusation?"

"Who indeed? One no longer able to testify in the matter. The charioteer Vitalis Hesper. Your late lover, I'm told."

"You accept the word of an athlete, a Greek nobody, that I would do such a thing!" Livilla said with venom. "How dare…"

"Hold your tongue!" her mother hissed. "You're in no position to play the injured party, so curb your arrogance at once or you'll regret it! I'll remind you that other members of this family have been exiled for life for much less serious crimes than you are accused of."

The younger woman's bravado crumbled and she slumped, staring bleakly at the floor.

"Daughter, your accuser is dead. Murdered. A coincidence? Or is it connected to his accusation, I wonder? He informed someone that you told him you and Sejanus had poisoned your husband. And, by further coincidence, the person he told was Senator Valerius Aviola, poor old Aviola who took his life the very next day."

"But…"

"I ordered you to remain silent!" Antonia, still standing, glared into her daughter's teary eyes.

Antonia continued, "Earlier that same day Aviola had been summoned by another of your lovers, Sejanus. How much coincidence are we expected to accept?"

Antonia walked to the window and looked out, her back to Livilla. Then she turned to face her daughter.

"Very well, then, your defense is undoubtedly that the accusation is only hearsay, an utterance made by a drunken athlete of humble origin to a doddering oldster. Both are dead, a strange coincidence, as I've already said. But the fact remains that a third party overheard the charioteer and on his testimony a judicial inquiry could be convened."

She walked toward Livilla, eyes fixed on her face.

"So, daughter, you're in deep trouble. You have only

one thing in your favor. Tiberius Caesar, a man you display contempt for, has a strong sense of family loyalty in spite of the dour exterior he presents in public. Without stronger evidence, Tiberius does not wish to investigate the subject further. But he will certainly do so should additional information come to light." Antonia paused. "You're fortunate that Tiberius is not only your father-in-law, but your uncle also."

Expressionless, Livilla nodded in acknowledgment and opened her mouth to speak. Antonia raised her hand.

"I'm not finished! There will be no formal investigation, for the present, by wish of Caesar. But I'll say this. As my daughter, you shame me. You've brought dishonor to the Claudian and Antonian families from which you are descended. You have conducted yourself in a manner which disgraces the imperial household. The meanest slaves in this house display more nobility and dignity than you do."

She pointed her finger at the door.

"Now go. But not far, daughter. You are restricted to the confines of the imperial palace by decree of Caesar."

XIV

I well remember the first time I walked this road, Serapio Priscus reflected, as he strolled along the Flaminian Way in the late afternoon sun. I was seventeen years old, a newly trained recruit in Legion Twenty Valeria. Thirty-two years ago—can it really have been that long?

Of *course* it was that long ago! Don't start making fatuous, rhetorical remarks, Priscus chided himself. You're not some mincing aesthete; you're an honorably retired chief centurion of Rome, so behave accordingly.

His cohort, Priscus recalled, had just completed a six week training period on the Field of Mars, close by the Tiber in the City's north-west. They had marched north to rejoin their legion which was camped outside the old town of Luca, by the Arno river. There, they received their orders to march east, to relieve a garrison in Illyricum.

He had been armed with two spears, a two-foot thrusting sword, body armor and a wood and iron shield. He carried also three days rations and a forty pound pack weighted with saw, ax, pick, bill-hook, iron frying pan and assorted other pieces.

Priscus had done well, promoted to centurion at age thirty-one. Nine years later, he became *primus pilus* of Legion Ten Fretensis, then stationed in Syria. As the legion's chief centurion he had commanded the senior century of battle-tested veterans, the legion's shock troops. More than that, he had been staff officer to his *legate*, his advice often sought over that of younger, more senior officers with less experience.

And now he was retired. His discharge certificate, imprinted on a thin brass sheet, had been presented to him two days ago.

Tiberius Claudius Caesar Augustus Nero, imperator, pontifex maximus, holder of the tribunician power, consul, grants honorable release from military service to Chief Centurion Titus Serapio Priscus, son of Verecundus of the Quirine tribe, who has completed thirty-two years and twenty-nine days service in four legions and six auxiliary cohorts stationed in Syria, Illyricum, Vindelicia, Pannonia and Germany, namely the Legions Twenty Valeria, Ten Fretensis, Fifteen Apollinarus and Twenty-One Rapax. Twice he was awarded the silver spearhead, six times the detachment banner and also the Gold Crown and the Rampart Storming Crown. Because of his exemplary service and excellent conduct he is exempted from the payment of taxes for ten years. This certificate of discharge is done on October 10, year 778 since the founding of the city.

Now he was settled into a comfortable apartment in the Ninth urban district, an easy walk to the heart of the city. His savings and tax free pension left him in agreeable circumstances and in no hurry to plot out the future.

Marriage? Perhaps. At his age it would be pleasant to have a decent, sensible woman to share his home. If she was a good cook, all the better, but that wasn't important. Thirty-two years of army camps had left him undemanding in that respect. Rich food and excellent wine had no priority, not that he didn't appreciate them. Priscus subscribed to the old proverb, "more people die partying than in war."

Another consideration was that he would be expected to acquire household servants, should he exercise his privilege of entering the knightly class. That would resolve the matter of whether or not a future wife could cook.

Reflecting idly on such matters, he walked with care, picking his way through the patches of slime and muck, which glistened from the rainfall earlier that day. Priscus was looking for the brothel recommended by an old friend, the house of Jucunda. It discouraged the riff-raff, so he was told, and treated its visitors with respect, and Priscus was a healthy man with a normal desire for occasional female company.

He arrived at the narrow street to which his friend had directed him. It ran off to the left of the main road and he followed it a few hundred feet. Yes, there was the brothel, proclaiming itself by the Cupid above the door. He rapped and a young red-haired woman opened the door, bowed her head with a sunny smile and stood aside for him to enter.

The sun had set when Priscus left the house a few hours later. It wasn't yet dark but would be by the time he'd walked home. There was no curfew but prudent citizens stayed indoors at night or traveled in groups for fear of the brigands who flourished in spite of the large police force. He had little apprehension, being a professional man-at-arms, and one who carried a knife under his tunic. But he also knew better than to tempt trouble, so set out at a good pace.

The cool night air made him wish he'd worn his cloak;

autumn would soon yield to winter. At the corner of the street a hot chestnut vendor was dousing his small brazier, about to close business and trundle away his two-wheeled pushcart. A few hot chestnuts will warm me on my way home, Priscus thought.

"Any chestnuts left?" he asked. The vendor turned to him and Priscus saw that he had lost an arm and an eye.

Ignatius Carbo stiffened. Sensing 'officer' for the second time that week, he looked respectfully at the sturdy, grizzled man, illuminated in the dusk by the flickering tapers secured to the sides of the pushcart.

"Ah, sir, I do have a few left, yes, sir. I'll heat them a little for you, sir." Carbo blew life into the dying coals with a small leather bellows which he managed with his one hand. The surface of the brazier rippled with renewed flame, lighting up the old vendor's seamy, scarred face. Priscus knew him at once.

"Ignatius Carbo! Duplicarius Carbo, Legion Twenty Valeria. Do you remember me, old comrade?" Priscus cried.

Looking closely at him, Carbo said, "Ah, sir, my one eye isn't as sharp as it once was, no, sir. But I was sure that I knew you for an officer. Let me see now. Where was it?"

"We served together in the Twentieth Valeria, many years ago. The last place was in Germany."

Still uncertain, the old man made an appropriate reply. "Yes, indeed, sir, now I recall. I served under you in the sixth cohort, or was it the fifth? Of course, sir."

"No, old friend, it was I who served under *you*. You were a *duplicarius* when I was a recruit. You taught me well, Carbo. We were in Illyricum, then in Germany. I was there when you lost your eye and arm."

Peering intently at Priscus, Carbo had a glimmer of recognition. Still unsure, he said, "It was long ago. In winter. There was a young soldier in my squad who saved me from a German ax-man. I'd taken an arrow in my eye.

His name, I think, was Priscus."

"Yes, Serapio Priscus. Twenty-seven years ago. I am Priscus, comrade. Yes, I slew the ax-man, but not before he'd ruined your left arm," Priscus said quietly.

The old man stared a moment at Priscus, as though bewildered. Then he wept silently, wiping at his good eye with a ragged sleeve. "I'm sorry, sir," he snuffled.

"Sorry, *emeritus*? Let's be happy instead! By Jupiter, we'll celebrate our reunion, that we will!" Priscus said heartily. "After all, Carbo, I owe you a drink or two. After you were invalided home, I was promoted in your place. Here, let me help with your pushcart. I'll see you home, then we'll find a late night tavern."

A few hours later the two old soldiers relaxed contentedly, having re-fought several battles over many cups of wine in a gloomy tavern close by Carbo's shabby lodgings. Carbo had listened with fascination to the story of Priscus' rise to the rank of chief centurion and of his service in various provinces, shaking his head in honest admiration and steadfastly refusing to call Priscus anything but 'sir.'

"You called me '*emeritus*' earlier, sir," Carbo said after a brief lull in their conversation while they reflected on the knavery they'd both witnessed amongst members of the quartermaster staff.

"I did indeed."

"Not many days ago another man called me that. Nobody has for twenty-five years or more, then twice in a week it happens. First, another officer, then you, sir."

"Who was the other man?" asked Priscus.

"I don't know. I've been thinking about him ever since, but although he seemed familiar somehow, I can't place him." Carbo related the story of the hooded man who had queried him, then left abruptly after giving him a twenty-five *denarii* gold piece.

"And he was of the equestrian order, sir. I didn't notice it myself, my eye being a bit cloudy these days, but my friend Bato, the man I told you about, swears that he wore a knight's gold ring. He certainly had the polish and manner of a born aristocrat."

"From what you say, he must have been an officer and probably a senior one," Priscus agreed. "Well, who knows, perhaps he'll return some day and you'll learn more, eh?"

Priscus summoned the landlord to bring more wine and a plate of cold pork and barley sausage. As they munched, he said, "Talking of the old days, guess who I spent a happy evening with not many days ago?"

He told Carbo of his visit to the knight's villa and their return to the city the following day.

"Yes, I remember him when he was a tribune, sir. Yes, I do. We had some fine officers back then but none better than him, no, sir." Carbo sighed in happy reminiscence.

"And imagine him recalling my name after so many years," Priscus said. "I felt honored."

"Yes, sir. Just as you remembered me," Carbo responded. "Both you and him are good officers. Rome will be fortunate if those that follow are half so good."

Priscus grinned. "Thank you, Ignatius. But we're becoming far too serious and it's getting late. I have a good walk before me and more wine inside me than I'm accustomed to."

Carbo arose and drained his cup. "My quarters are modest, as you've already seen, sir, but it would please me to have you stay with me tonight. I have a spare couch and you're welcome."

They walked to the door and Priscus put his hand on the other's shoulder. "In view of the hour, I accept, my friend."

It rained lightly as they walked along the muddy street to Carbo's apartment building. "I appreciate your kindness, Ignatius," Priscus said. "You and I have marched enough in the rain in days past, eh? We don't need it now."

Carbo didn't answer, but appeared deep in thought.

Suddenly he stopped and stayed Priscus with his hand. "Our talk tonight of the old days—it's coming back to me now. The cloaked man who gave me the gold coin!"

"Yes?" Priscus prompted him when he hesitated.

"Now I know who he is, sir. His voice, manner, everything about him. He's the man you escorted to the city. Our old tribune in the Twentieth!"

XV

"Three *sesterces*! Anthus! You have the nerve to stand there and tell me, without flinching, that you spent three *sesterces* for some wretched potter's lunch?"

Glowering, Macro shook his head in utter despair at my prodigality with his money. I waited.

"Tell me, Anthus, why don't you do things in proper style? Invite the entire population of Rome to three days of games in the *circus* at my expense!"

It was early evening and I was giving him my report on the day's events.

"Now, now, sir," I soothed, "you know I wouldn't spend such a sum unless I thought it would show good return. The potter was quite informative, and he eased my approach to Madame Jucunda."

Macro humphed grudgingly but paid attention as I told him of the mysterious hooded man and of my employment for the next few days in the brothel. He waved me to be seated.

"Ump. Well, I admit that you seem to have made progress. Didn't subscribe to your hare-brained scheme at the start, and still don't, damn me," he grumbled. "However, now you're into it, we may as well see it through."

"Thank you, sir. My only wish is to serve you well. I'm honored by the trust you have in me," I said in my most unctuous manner.

"And stop being unctuous, damn your alien hide," he growled. "I get enough of that from my junior officers. Now, holler for that new boy, Rufio, or whatever his name is, to fetch us wine."

"Rufinus, sir," I said. Macro makes a great display of forgetting his servants' names, but like many of his ways, it's purely an act.

The young slave brought in a flagon and two cups. I must tell the boy—he's only seven—not to make such exaggerated bows. I know he's trying hard to please, but a simple inclination of the head suffices for informal occasions.

We discussed the matter for twenty minutes. I didn't tell him that Jucunda had lied when she reported the charioteer being slain by two fictitious men. No need to get him fussed unnecessarily. And, after his anguish over the three *sesterces* I'd paid for lunch, I refrained from telling him that I'd spent double that on wine for Madame and myself.

"How much is she paying you for your survey of her accounts?"

"A *denarius* daily, sir." Well, a half truth, at least. "And my lunch."

He sighed in mock relief. "Well, that's good news, at

least. Now you won't need to fritter away good money in eating establishments, eh? And your salary will help offset the lavish expense account you talked me into, damn me for a soft-hearted fool."

Being a slave, my earnings are the property of my master. Even so, I was still a *denarius* daily to the good.

"Very well, Quintipor, see me again tomorrow night. But remember—Caesar isn't going to wait forever while you're merrymaking with potters and prostitutes."

I bowed and made to depart. "And tell that lad, Rufus, to hustle in more wine."

"Rufinus. Yes, sir."

• • •

Not in the best of moods, I arrived at Jucunda's the next morning, having trudged two miles through a steady drizzle. My *paenula* kept me fairly dry but it was soaked by the time I arrived and my sandals squelched as I walked along. As for the next fool who says, "Ah, yes, but the rain is good for the farmers," a pox upon him—or may the god Faunus transmute him into a frog, to dwell his remaining days in a swamp.

A chirpy girl with a mass of red curls opened the door and conducted me to Jucunda's private quarters, where that lady eyed my damp condition. "Emmachia, take the cloak to the kitchen to dry." She glanced at my feet. "And the sandals."

I removed the cloak and sandals and passed them to the redhead. "Bring a pot of heated wine and two cups," Jucunda told her. Emmachia left, twittering happily.

"She seems in good spirits," I observed.

"Em is getting married in a few weeks. We'll miss her. She's marrying a stone mason, a decent young man, or I wouldn't have let him purchase her freedom."

Bato came to mind and how he had bought his wife's

freedom for a few dozen ceramic cups.

"Observing that I'll be studying your accounts, may I ask what price you set on a girl such as her?"

"Oh, well, it depends, of course," she hedged. "You know how it is…"

"No, I don't, really," I said, "but I'd like to know, as it may assist me in understanding how your business operates."

"Um, well, Em's been here eight years. I bought her from her father, a drunken ne'er-do-well. She was fifteen then. She's had a far better life here than she'd ever have known with him, the son of a bitch."

Emmachia returned with the wine and said that she'd bring my sandals when they had dried.

"Here, this'll warm you," Jucunda said, passing me a cup and gesturing me to sit at her table. "Then you can start on my accounts. I'm not paying you for social chit-chat, scribe."

"My thanks, ma'am," said I, "but you were about to tell me the price of the sprightly Emmachia."

I knew that she wasn't at ease with my question. She replied, "For a girl with her appearance, good nature, age and health—oh, I could get two thousand *denarii*."

I sipped the hot wine. Ah, this is the stuff that killed auntie, I thought appreciatively. Not the excellent Falernian we'd had yesterday, courtesy of Macro, but not plonk, either.

"Two thousand," I mused. "Now where would a young mason get that amount? Surely that's three or four year's wages for him." I was thinking again of Bato and his experience with Madame.

"Anthus, if you must know, the mason will be doing a few jobs for me in the house, renewing some of the hearths, that kind of thing."

You're compassionate under your business-like veneer, aren't you, Madame? I thought. You probably bought

Emmachia for about five hundred *denarii* and you've made it back twenty or thirty times, but you're good-hearted enough to give your girls their freedom for a token payment of goods or services.

"And," I winked knowingly, "by freeing her *inter amicos*, you avoid paying tax to the state." I had presumed that Jucunda would grant Emmachia her freedom "between friends"—a common method which only required the slaveholder to gather a few friends together to witness the document of manumission.

She stared humorlessly. "Yes, so I do. And now, speaking of taxes, I'll take you to the office so you can start earning your wages."

For the next hour I sorted through Jucunda's recent business records which she filed neatly on a couple of shelves. Others from previous years were in a wooden chest. Some were inscribed on paper and others on waxed tablets, the latter used when receipts were required from municipal officers. Her accounts went back to year 755, apparently the date she started her business. She'd told me that she was twenty-four when her master died and she'd operated her house for twenty-three years, which made her forty-seven, give or take a bit either way.

The house could accommodate fifteen prostitutes but, according to her records, at present there were only eleven. There was a separate account for each woman who'd ever worked for her, seventy-one of them, including present staff. Each account was prefaced with a short narrative on the woman concerned and they were assembled in chronological sequence of the prostitutes becoming members of the house.

I examined every sixth or seventh record, which I considered an adequate audit to learn Jucunda's method and assess its consistency over the years. Looking at one for the year 761, the subject's name caught my eye, Sassia...I remember Bato saying that was his wife's name.

I read her brief history, learning that she had been a born slave, purchased by Jucunda for twelve hundred *denarii* in 761 and freed seven years later, when she was twenty-five. Bato had told me that he and Sassia had been married six years, so she was about thirty-one when she died.

Other than the memories of her husband and friends, I mused, her only impact on the world are these half dozen lines in a brothel's ledger. Those who remember her will soon be gone, too, and the brothel accounts flung onto a garbage heap. Who then will know that Sassia passed this way?

I forced myself to stop musing on such things and got on with the brothel accounts. I wanted to do a good job for Jucunda, not so much a noble work ethic as wanting to soften up the old girl if I was to learn anything pertinent about the night the hero of the Blue Stable got more than he'd bargained for in a prostitute's bed.

The morning was half gone when Emmachia returned my dried sandals and said that my cloak was drying nicely, too. "Such a handsome cloak it is, sir," she said, "Like a rich man's, even a knight's."

"I'm afraid that I'm neither," I smiled. "But you're quite right. It was a wealthy man's *paenula*. He gave it to me when I was working for him." That was the truth, but I didn't bother to explain that the rich man was Macro and he'd wearied of it, giving it to me in a moment of expansiveness.

In an off-hand way I said, "I suppose that in a respectable house such as this, you have a few visitors from the wealthy class—even senatorials and equestrians."

Emmachia appeared willing to chat. "Oh, a few, sir. Mostly the younger ones celebrating or having a night out." She giggled. "But sometimes their fathers, too."

"Like father, like son," I smiled.

Again the giggle.

"You mentioned my cloak, Em. Have you seen another like it recently, or what?"

"Yes, just last week. I opened the door to a man, early evening it was, and I knew right away that he was quality. His posture, the way he spoke, and he was wearing a cloak like yours. I remember especially because he had the hood over his head, even though it wasn't raining or cold."

"A new visitor, was he?" I asked, trying not to appear too interested. Luckily for me, though, she was the talkative type.

"Actually, he wanted to see Madame. I took him to her room, the one that you were in earlier. Maybe he was a magistrate or somebody like that, here on business. I didn't notice him after that. I was probably working in the kitchen."

Her eyes widened and she put a hand to her mouth. "Yes, I *was* in the kitchen. You see, Madame went there and told me to look after Dorcas. She's quite young and wasn't feeling well. She was in Madame's room and looked terrible. She'd been crying. Anyway, Madame told me to put her to bed in one of the top floor rooms that aren't being used. I wondered why not in her own room, but found out later." She paused, looking at me dramatically.

"Yes?" I prompted.

"Well, sir, that's where the athlete was murdered."

"What athlete?" I said. Not too fatuously, I hoped.

"Why, Vitalis Hesper! Surely you know about him!"

Bato the potter and I had gone over this same ground yesterday, but I doubted that he and the guileless Emmachia would compare notes later.

"Hmm, Vitalis…" I reflected cogitatively, then snapped my fingers in sudden recollection. "Of course! The charioteer! You mean that he was murdered in this *very* house? Here?"

"Oh yes, sir. Right in Dorcas' room, next floor up. They cut off his head. The sword was still there when the

Urban Cohort men arrived."

"They? How many assassins were there?"

"Two. Madame and Dorcas, they saw two men in cloaks running down the stairs and out the front door. Madame was just coming out of her room to check things in the dining room. Some athletes were having a banquet that night. And Dorcas was coming from the kitchen with wine and fruit to take up to her room. They both saw two men running away."

Emmachia paused, looking toward the door apprehensively. "I really should get back to my duties, sir."

"A minute or two more, Em. If Madame comes looking for you, I'll tell her that you were helping me."

The anxious set of her face turned to a smile when I said, "I hear that you're to be married soon."

"Yes," she beamed, "and I'm being freed! That's why I work in the kitchen and sometimes answer the door," she explained.

"I see," said I, not really seeing at all.

"When it was agreed that I was to be freed to marry Lucullus," she explained, "Madame said that I wasn't to work upstairs any more, but I could help the cook and act as door porter. She says a married woman shouldn't work as a prostitute, nor one about to be married."

"Well, now," I reached into my tunic and withdrew two *denarii*, "this isn't much, Emmachia, but please accept it as a wedding gift. May good fortune always attend your home." Wouldn't Macro be ecstatic?

Her eyes moistened. "This is my very first wedding gift. Thank you. With this I'll purchase my *flammeum*." She spoke of the traditional flaming orange veil that covers the head and upper face of a bride. I was pleased that my present would be so visible.

"Before you leave, Em, you mentioned a man in a *paenula*, who wished to see Madame Jucunda that night. Had he departed before the other two men fled the house?"

She frowned. "Well, sir, I guess he must have. Like I said, I was in the kitchen helping Clodia, our cook. We heard shrieking and then Madame burst in and told Clodia to run out and fetch the Urban Cohort. Most worked up, Madame was. That's when she told me to take care of Dorcas."

"Most curious," I said, not wanting to press the girl too openly. "And then the police came?"

"In two or three minutes. The neighbors had taken up the cry and there must have been a patrol on the large street at the end of our road because they came quickly. I was still with Dorcas in Madame's room when they got here."

"And the cloaked man had left before that," I mused. "I suppose that quite some time had passed from when you first let him in the door until the two men were seen running off?"

Emmachia pondered this. "It was still daylight when the man arrived, but the sun was low. I'd say he came near the end of the eleventh daylight hour. And the sun had gone down when the police arrived, although it wasn't dark yet. Probably well into the first hour of the night."

I recalled Bato saying that about an hour had passed from when he first saw the man entering the house until he gave the gold coin to the chestnut vendor. That indicated that he'd left the house about an hour before the police were summoned.

"I wonder how the two men got into the house...the ones that were seen running away later? Well, somebody obviously tended the door while you were in the kitchen."

"Sir, that's the strange part of it...nobody let them in. None of the girls. The only ones who saw the men were Madame and Dorcas. We don't know how they got in. The door is always locked, day and night, and has to be opened from the inside."

"Emmachia! Blast you, girl, I've been searching everywhere for you!" Jucunda stood in the doorway, arms akimbo.

"Oh, Madame..." Emmachia replied.

I leapt up. "I apologize, ma'am, for taking up Emmachia's time. She was good enough to bring my dried sandals to me and I asked her to assist me for a few minutes. She was a great help."

"Ah, a great help, was she indeed?" Jucunda said. "Pray tell me in what fashion?"

"I asked her to ensure that these tablets were in the correct chronological sequence," I answered uneasily.

Jucunda stepped forward, picked up a tablet and handed it to the girl. "Very well, what name and date is on this?"

Tearfully, Emmachia stammered, "I don't know, Madame."

Taking the tablet back, Jucunda turned to me. "The girl is illiterate."

I felt a fool. And felt poorly over having gotten poor Em into trouble. "It was wrong of me to lie, ma'am, but I didn't want the girl to be chastised because of me. It's my fault, not hers. I chatted to Em a moment when she brought the sandals and said that I'd heard of her forthcoming marriage. She was so happy, telling me about it, that we talked longer than we should have. My fault alone, ma'am."

Through her tears, Em said, "And Madame, he gave me two *denarii* for a wedding gift. My first gift!"

Looking at both of us in silence a moment, Jucunda motioned the girl to leave us. "All right, Em, go back to the kitchen. Clodia's got her hands full with a banquet tonight."

Alone with Jucunda, I awaited her rebuke. Instead, she shook her head in wonderment. "Somehow, I find it difficult to be annoyed, Anthus. I'm paying you two *denarii* a day and you've already given away your first day's wages to a girl you only met a couple of hours ago."

I shrugged. "The cursed hunger for gold, as the poet says, isn't one of my foibles, ma'am. It pleased me to give the girl a wedding gift."

"So now we're quoting Vergil, are we?" she said evenly. "Well, quote away all you wish, but preferably on your own time. My accounts await you, scribe," then added dryly, "now that Emmachia has put them in order for you. I'll send a girl to tell you when your meal is ready."

I felt sorry over having compromised good-natured Em, but my discomfiture was offset by satisfaction at having the girl corroborate and expand upon Bato's tale of the mysterious hooded man.

The charioteer hadn't been killed by two men. Indeed, there never were two such men in the house. The murderer was the knight, who else? But why? And why did Jucunda wait an hour before calling the police? Why had she lied about seeing two men running away? How long had Vitalis been dead when his body was found?

Why had Dorcas been upset? She and Jucunda were the only ones to see the "two men." So Dorcas, like Jucunda, had lied. And Vitalis had been murdered in her bed.

My speculation was interrupted by some girls chattering in the hall. I returned to the accounts. I didn't wish to be dismissed on my first day.

• • •

When I returned to the brothel the second day, I examined the records which showed each girl's earnings, withdrawals and the balance owed her.

Of Jucunda's eleven girls, three were freeborn, two were freedwomen, and six were slaves. The five free girls were given a percentage of the money they earned for the house, averaging six *denarii* weekly, about the wages of an unskilled laborer. And better than the two hundred and twenty-five a year paid to legionary soldiers.

The slave prostitutes received one *sestertius* per day, about ninety *denarii* a year. The slaves were provided their clothing by Jucunda; the others had to buy their own. All, regardless of status, received free accommodation and meals.

In contrast to most slaves in the city, Jucunda's girls were well off. Apart from their small allowance from the madame, they received around thirty *denarii* a year in gratuities from clients. Although Jucunda had the right to keep slave gratuities for herself, she permitted them to retain their money.

I found no fault with Jucunda's accounts. I suspected she'd been well educated while domiciled in the house of her late master, Jucundus Cornutus, witness her remark about "Socratic dialogue" and her recognition of a line of verse by Vergilius Maro, and her orderly accounts kept in a well-formed, literate hand.

Then my attention was seized by an entry in Dorcas' account. On October eighth, Jucunda had credited her with one hundred *denarii*. A hundred silver coins or four gold ones!

The girl had only been with Jucunda a little more than six months, during which time she'd acquired forty-six *denarii*, three *sesterces*, with a balance of seventeen *denarii* at the end of September.

Had good-hearted madame advanced Dorcas more than a year's allowance? Not likely. Or had a client with more money than sense been loose in the house on October the eighth? No, the day before; Jucunda always posted her accounts first thing each morning. Dorcas had acquired her large sum during business hours the night before, on October seventh. Probably four gold coins; it's unlikely anyone would carry around such a large number of silver ones.

Somebody else had been given an *aureus* that night. The chestnut vendor, and by a man who'd just left the brothel.

Anthus, said I to myself, it's time to have a good chat with Dorcas and old Carbo. Between them I might learn a few things, including the name of the generous man in the hood. I won't know 'til I've tried. As the poet says, "Fortune goes to the bold." That's Vergil again. No, I'm wrong. It was the African playwright, Terentius Afer, who wrote it. Terence should know, having started life as a slave, like myself, and ending up one of the darlings of high society. His sentiment is good, but I'd have expressed it "nothing ventured, nothing gained." But then, I do have a way with words.

I had my mid-day meal with some of the girls in the kitchen. Jucunda had taken three of them to the market for provisions. This chore was rotated amongst the girls and they enjoyed it. It gave them a few hours away from the house, mingling in the hubbub of the streets and enjoying a meal in a *thermopolium*, to which Jucunda treated them.

Clodia's thick, spiced pea and lentil soup, served with bread and cheese, was as tasty as any I'd had in Macro's kitchen. I won't mention that to Petronia, cooks being rather testy over their peers' accomplishments. Ever since Petronia was elevated from scullery maid to assistant cook, you'd think she was president of the chef's guild. But our chef is pleased with her. He's a freedman, a Gaul, which means two things: he talks with his hands and slathers sauce on everything. His accent is worse than Petronia's. If you heard the two of them conversing, you'd despair over the future purity of our beautiful Latin language.

Dorcas was one of the girls I dined with. A quiet little thing but friendly in her reserved fashion. She has a Greek name but looks Spanish. After lunch I asked her to come to the office on the pretext of wanting her to confirm some details in her account. After querying a couple of unimportant things, I said, "The one hundred *denarii* you received last week, Dorcas, an amount that large should have a notation of the donor."

Her eyes widened but she said nothing.

"It's for your own good," I explained, "it protects you

from being accused of stealing. The account shows that visitor so-and-so gave a gratuity of a certain sum to the girl so-and-so on a certain date. Nothing is hidden. Had the girl stolen the money, she wouldn't be foolish enough to give it to madame to credit to her account. Do you see?"

She nodded mutely, eyes downcast.

"So then, Dorcas," I said, placing the account before me as though to write on it, "what was your benefactor's name?"

"Sir, I don't know," she whispered unhappily.

"Oh. Well then, let's just give a brief description—color of hair, eyes, that sort of thing. Better than nothing, eh?"

She nodded in misery while I waited. Then she said, "I couldn't see his face, sir. His hood covered it and the light in madame's room was dim."

Yes, Emmachia had told me that she'd taken the cloaked man to Jucunda's room. So, Dorcas had been sent for. And the charioteer was in Dorcas' room upstairs, no doubt waiting for her to return to him.

Emmachia had told me also that the visitor had worn a "rich man's cloak," just like mine.

"His hood was up, I see. He wore his cloak, then." I affected a light tone. "It must have been a quality cloak if he was wealthy enough to leave such a large gratuity, eh?"

"He...he was a gentleman by his accent and the way he talked, sir." She began to weep quietly. "But madame told me I was to never talk about it, not ever. And now I'll be in trouble."

I stood and put my hand on her shoulder. "No, you won't, Dorcas, I promise. I won't tell your mistress we spoke."

She looked up, forcing a smile, her cheeks wet. I grinned back at her. "When he gave you the hundred *denarii*, it must have filled both your hands, eh, Dorcas?"

"Oh no, sir. It was four gold coins," she replied, less

troubled now and wiping away her tears.

Then I pressed my luck too far. "Dorcas, I understand that you're the only one of the girls who, with your mistress, saw the two men who killed the charioteer."

She ran wailing from the room.

When Jucunda returned late afternoon, I was engrossed in my work. I assured her that her accounts were in good order. "Yes, ma'am, I swear by the goddess that your books are as well kept as any I've seen."

"How unusual to find one of your vocation invoking a goddess," she replied. "It's my understanding that scribes and accountants dedicate themselves to Mercury. Isn't he the patron of businessmen as well as being messenger of the gods? Or does Anthus, in a show of sympathy for his less privileged sisters, subscribe to the worship of Juno or Ceres, the great deities of marriage and fecundity? Perhaps Diana the huntress or the hearth-watcher, Vesta?"

She left before I could reply.

I hadn't handled that too well. I'd hoped to leave the impression with Jucunda that if I wasn't actually a follower of Isis, I was ready to learn something of her religion. I got that idea when Bato hinted to me that madame was a member of the suppressed sect. By professing to share her religious bent, I might ingratiate myself with her.

More astringent minds than mine might question the ethics of using religion to enhance my position but such things never prick my conscience. The end justifies the means, say I. And there've been several others who followed the same code. Consider the divine Julius and the divine Augustus. As far as that goes, consider the gods themselves. They've played many a rotten trick upon one another, never mind how they toy around with we mortals.

I was about to leave for the day when Jucunda came in. "I was abrupt with you earlier, Anthus," she said.

"Oh, no, ma'am," I protested. I'd decided to address her as madame whilst in her employ, despite her indication of less formality a few days ago.

"Oh yes," she said. "But I suggest to you that there is a goddess who welcomes equally the worship of men and women in all stations of life."

Putting on my humble mask, I nodded in comprehension. "Yes, ma'am, but her cult is in disfavor and one such as myself must be cautious in seeking to learn more of, of…"

"Isis," she said.

"Are you a follower?" I asked in a low voice.

She raised her eyebrows. "As you said, her cult is outlawed. I must be about my business. Until tomorrow, farewell."

Jucunda has told me that she's a member of the Isis cult, without having said so, which may be helpful in my future dealings with her.

I left the brothel, hoping that the chestnut seller would be at his corner and, sure enough, there he was. As I drew near, he called out, "Buy some chestnuts from an old soldier?"

"How much, old soldier?" I asked.

"Ten for a *sestertius*, governor. But for you, sir, being a fine gentleman like I can tell, twelve for the same price."

"You're a shameless, flattering rogue, Ignatius Carbo," I replied cheerfully. "But I'll have some of your chestnuts."

He peered closely at me. "You know my name, sir? But I don't think I know you, do I?"

"I'm a friend of your friend, Bato Niger. He's told me many commendable things about Ignatius Carbo of the Twentieth Legion."

The old man beamed. "Ah, well now, Bato's a good man, that he is. Did his time in the army, too."

"Bato told me that just a week ago a senior officer stopped to have a word with you. Someone you'd served with in the old days, was he?"

"That was strange indeed, sir. When he talked to me,

I thought I knew him but just couldn't place him. My eye isn't too good and it's been some time since I left the army. But he seemed familiar. And then, just a few nights ago it was, I'll be damned if another retired officer didn't greet me as an old comrade. A centurion, a *chief* centurion! Well, sir, we went to a late night tavern and talked about the old days. He told me about meeting one of our old officers recently, one that was in Germany with us."

He pointed to his face. "That's where I lost my eye and arm, sir. That's why I remember him now, even though I didn't recognize him when he stopped to talk. Gave me a gold piece, too, he did. Yes, sir, he was one of the men that helped the surgeon when I lost my arm. A tribune he was then."

"He must be a knight to have held that rank," I said. "What is his name?"

Carbo told me the name—Pontius Pilatus—although he used the familiar vocative case of the knight's *nomen*, Pilate. However, it meant nothing to me.

Two small boys ran up to the cart, one holding out a coin, the other presenting a straw basket. Carbo apparently deemed the urchins to be "fine gentlemen" like myself, for he put twelve chestnuts in their basket. The boys scampered off, and I tackled Carbo again.

"Did the centurion say where he'd met the tribune?" I asked, hoping Carbo wouldn't wonder at my curiosity. But the old man obviously enjoyed yarning with whoever would listen. He related with relish how the centurion, one Priscus, had served his final months in the army with the Praetorian Guard, and that one of his last duties had been to deliver a message to the former tribune at his country estate, then escort him back to the city.

"A chief centurion, that's rather high-priced for a simple messenger," I mused. "Whoever dispatched him must have possessed *auctoritas*. Did Priscus mention who he was?"

"No. Don't think he knew. Anyway, he said he parted company with the tribune once they'd reach the city gate, the Viminal. Then Priscus went back to the Praetorian camp outside the wall. Oh, yes, before he did, he watched our old tribune for a minute or so, and apparently saw him turn his horse left into the Vicus Patricius."

And two days later Vitalis Hesper, the Blue hero, was murdered, I told myself. On the same evening that the knight visited the brothel and gave Carbo a gold coin.

I said goodbye to Carbo and handed him a *denarius*. "Ah yes, sir, your chestnuts," he grinned. "I almost forgot, what with us chatting away. Fifteen for a fine gentleman like yourself, sir. And three *sesterces* change."

I told him to keep the coins and buy a drink for himself and the potter. I took four or five chestnuts and munched them on my way home.

It had been a good day, I thought, going over what I'd learned. And I knew the name of the charioteer's killer. He'll be easy to locate. Macro will be pleased with me.

I wondered what would follow after I'd told Macro that a Roman knight had murdered Vitalis Hesper. It really wasn't too difficult to visualize. Macro would interrogate those people whose collective testimony would be adequate to incriminate the killer. Priscus would testify that he had accompanied Pilate to Rome and Carbo would say that he spoke to him on the street corner close to the time of the murder. Bato would say that the man who spoke to Carbo had entered the brothel about an hour earlier.

Jucunda and Dorcas would tell why they were given money and by whom, and Bato would expose their lie about two men seen fleeing the house.

Knowing Macro, the interrogation will be swift and efficient. I hope it doesn't necessitate judicial torture. The thought of Jucunda and Bato being tortured—well, it needn't come to that—not if they cooperate.

Shortly after, the knight's head will be presented on a

platter to Caesar by Macro. Figuratively speaking. Undoubtedly the knight will be invited to open his veins or take poison, befitting his position.

Macro *did* say that Caesar wished an early solution. It's only been three days since I started. I'm sure that I'm doing the right thing. But I hope they don't torture Bato. Or the madame and her girls.

Still, it's none of my business, is it? What are these people to me, really? I set out to locate a killer, not win admirers. I'm trying to prove to my master how clever I am. I'm trying to earn my freedom. Why shouldn't I?

Petronia asked if I liked my supper. She was all smiles and attention tonight. I told her yes, but I don't remember what she served me. She said I was behaving in a remote, distracted manner. She didn't say that exactly, she hasn't the vocabulary, but that's what she meant.

Young Rufinus has just told me that Macro is ready to see me.

Forgive me, Bato and Jucunda…but Anthus has to look after himself.

XVI

Pilate and his wife sat in their garden, enjoying the sunny October afternoon, one of autumn's few remaining balmy days.

"I don't think I mentioned the chestnut seller," he said, "the other day when I told you of my visit to the city."

"No," Procula said, "you didn't."

"After I'd left the brothel, at the foot of the street an old chestnut vendor called to me, selling his wares. He referred to himself as an 'old soldier.' He'd lost an arm and an eye. I shouldn't have stopped, but I did. I remembered a skirmish long ago in a German forest when I commanded a cohort in the Twentieth. One of my men lost an arm and an eye. I helped hold him down while the surgeon took off his arm. I remember it snowing heavily. There was no time to return him to camp for treatment. His arm had been half-severed by a battle ax. A dead German soldier was lying a few feet away—no more than a boy—ax still in his hand. There was blood…"

She watched but said nothing as he massaged his hands gently, as though washing them.

"That soldier never cried out or whimpered while the surgeon worked on him. It took four of us to restrain him. He gurgled in agony, but nothing more. When his stump had been bound and his eye dressed and he'd been given a drink, he croaked his thanks to the surgeon. Then he looked at me with his remaining eye and whispered, 'Sorry to be such trouble, sir.' Then he fainted. I left him to his companions, as I had other things to see to. I never saw him again. He was sent back in a wagon train the next day. I knew his name, but forgot it over the years…but I never forgot that day. Soldiers have cursed and raged at me in the agony of their wounds, but that poor man apologized for having disturbed the routine by sacrificing an arm and an eye to Rome."

"The street vendor, was he the same man?" she asked.

"Yes, Procula. I was sure it was him. To be certain I questioned him about his service and he gave the correct answers. When he gave his name I recognized it. Ignatius Carbo."

"Did he recognize you?"

"I'm certain that he didn't. My face was hooded and it was dusk. He gave no sign of recognition. He sensed that I was an officer, but that's hardly a rarity. Another man was nearby. I'd guess an old soldier also, the way he stood at attention when I talked with Carbo. I gave Carbo an *aureus*. I was sorry to see the wretched state he'd come to. Then I walked away."

After a brief pause, she said, "I'm sorry for such men. They deserve better from the state, after their service. But,

Ponto, I'm glad that he didn't recognize you."

"Yes," he agreed. "Otherwise, I would have had to kill the poor fellow."

XVII

"What word from the brothel, Anthus?" Macro cheerily greeted me, waving me to a seat.

"Gratifying news, sir," I replied unhappily, "I wish to…"

"Good! Good!" he interrupted. "Fine! So you're winning the whores' confidence, eh?"

"Yes, sir. And I wish to report that…"

"Glad to hear it, m'boy. But you'll be pleased to learn that you have more time than we thought. Yes, take the pressure off a little."

"Sir?" What's all this, I wondered.

"Caesar. Sent for me today. Wants me to go to Capreae. I'm leaving tomorrow morning and will be away seven or eight days."

How nice for you, I thought to myself. Capreae, an island in the Bay of Neapolis, is said to be quite beautiful. I've heard that Caesar has twelve villas there.

"May one ask the nature of your trip, sir?"

"The emperor's taken it into his head that he wants to go there for an extended stay. I'm to inspect the island with a view to security."

"And the matter of the charioteer's murder, sir?" I asked.

"You're to stick with it, Quintipor. Both Caesar and myself wish to see what you come up with."

"Then I'm to continue my investigation in your absence?"

"Yes, no change there. Well, a small change," Macro said. "But first, tell that lad Rufus to fetch a jug of the grape. The Falernian."

After instructing Rufinus, I returned to Macro to learn what the "small change" would entail.

"I told Caesar that I've planted a reliable man in the brothel and that he's made out quite well with the whores…"

"I beg your pardon, sir?" I said, straight-faced.

"Damn your alien hide, you know full well what I mean! I've told Caesar that the way it's going, we'll probably find our men in a week or less."

Men. He still accepts the story of two men seen running away, I realized.

"You mentioned a small change in my investigation."

"Yes, but it won't affect what you're doing. Caesar's being nagged by the athletes guild and its senatorial friends to find the killers, so two days from now he'll announce their capture. They'll be kept in custody until the Plebian Games next month, when they'll be publicly executed in the arena."

"Not to be hanged and flung onto the Stairs of Mourning?" I asked. That was the usual fate of criminals, be they men, women or children, before their bodies were thrown into the Tiber.

"Nothing so conventional," Macro replied. "These lads will provide a spectacle for the mob. Crucifixion with burning pitch, perhaps. Or a wild beast show."

"And who are these criminals, sir?"

"Haven't decided yet, Quintipor. I've given a list of worthy candidates to my legate. He'll select a couple and pick 'em up tomorrow and deliver their confessions to Caesar. The matter will be announced to the senate the next day."

Macro held up his wine cup. "Just where did you acquire this deplorable stuff?"

"Crispus the wine merchant, sir. He's supplied the house for years," I answered. "Lady Ennia directed me to deal with him. He caters to many of the noble houses."

"Good for him. But tell him from me that this particular vintage is eminently unquaffable, and that its insouciance borders on petulance. Damn me, Quintipor, am I not a reasonable man? I don't quibble over a cheeky or presumptuous wine, but by Zeus, I will *not* tolerate one that sulks! Yes, you just tell Master Cestius that!"

"Crispus, sir. I'll most certainly have a word with him."

"Ump."

"Now, about my investigation, sir..."

"And you can also tell this Crassus fellow that I suspect the grapes were bruised and probably plucked too early in the morning."

I waited to see if my master had further words for the ears of Crispus, the wine merchant. When none were forthcoming, I ventured back to the topic of murder.

"It's my understanding, then, that although two men will be found guilty of the charioteer's killing, you wish me to continue my attempt to locate the true murderer and that I may do so during your absence."

"Exactly. Now Caesar, you understand, won't really

care whether you find the killers or not under the circumstances."

"In that case, why do you wish me to stay with the job, sir?"

Macro dropped his blustering style and became serious. "Anthus, I've given thought to what you said a few days ago, when you suggested that there were other ways than the rack and the whip to investigate crime. To be honest, I didn't think much of your idea and I suppose I was more or less humoring you when I approved your suggestion. But I've given it second thought and I'm interested in seeing what you produce. Also, you commented on taking the easy route, which anyone can take and which I suppose most people do. But I have no wish to be lumped in with most people. As a prefect of Rome, I have a responsibility to follow my conscience in what's best for the state."

He refilled our cups in silence.

"In short, Anthus, after our talk, I knew that an honest effort should be made to find the Vitalis Hesper killers. More than just seizing a couple of handy thugs to satisfy Caesar's wish for a speedy conclusion."

Reading my thoughts, he continued.

"I admit that the easy way is now being taken, but it's Caesar's wish. Remember, Anthus, that Tiberius Caesar is ruler of the entire world, other than a handful of barbarian tribes which are beneath the dignity of Rome. Neither you, nor I, nor the Council of Conscript Fathers are in a position to question his motives."

"Let my will stand as a reason," I said, quoting someone from the past—it may have been the divine Julius, but I'm not sure. More bluntly, one might say, Don't argue; just do as I say.

"Exactly, Anthus," Macro nodded. "Caesar has no need to justify his action to anyone. And in this instance, his reason is plain. He wants to prevent social unrest. The populace gets excited over the small issues, because they don't understand or bother to consider the larger ones. They're happy as long as they have grain and festivals. But the charioteer's death gives them something juicy to chew on and injects excitement into their lives for a few days. Let 'em chew on it too long, and the hotheads will take over with their mindless vandalism...public statues toppled and so on, even fires."

Fire, I thought. The horror of all city dwellers. With buildings jammed close together on narrow streets, an unchecked fire can level a block of buildings in an hour. Macro's duties as Prefect of the City Watch include the organization of the city fire fighters. His jurisdiction is extensive, to the point where he has authority to fine and flog shop-keepers and householders who fail to observe such fire regulations as keeping a specified supply of water available on each floor of their buildings.

"So the emperor will declare that the two murderers have been caught and will soon be on public display in the arena," he said. "The mob will be happy and there'll be two less scum in the city."

I knew that Macro was right, of course. The likes of us, more especially the likes of me, don't offer unsolicited advice to Caesar or query his actions. Did I mention earlier that messengers never collapse, gasping at my feet, bearing urgent summons from senate or palace? So, if Caesar wishes to have two murderers to slake the public thirst, then he shall have them.

"But," continued Macro, "I still want the real killers found. When I return from the south, I hope to find your investigation completed so I can present a neat package to Caesar. Let him see what clever fellows we are, eh?"

I liked the *we* bit. "A week should be adequate, sir," I said.

"One other thing that Caesar mentioned," he added. "He seems to think that the killing may have something to do with Aviola's death. Not sure I follow that myself, but you might think about it."

"Aviola, sir?" I remember hearing the name somewhere recently. Where was it?

"Senator Valerius Aviola. Nice old gentleman. Not too bright, but did his duty to the state. I told you about him committing suicide, before you sallied forth to the whorehouse."

"Ah, yes..." I lied. "There was some mention. Could you refresh my memory, sir?" Macro hadn't said a word about Aviola earlier, not one word.

"Vitalis Hesper had been at a dinner party in Aviola's house the night before the senator took his own life. Can't figure out why Aviola would kill himself...popular enough old boy, in good health seemingly, tons of money. Then a week later the charioteer had his head removed. The emperor wonders if there's a relationship between the two events. Seems unlikely to me, but ponder on it so we can tell Caesar the thing wasn't overlooked."

Macro continued in a lighter vein. "Now, I've told my wife that you're busy with important work for me and won't resume your full-time duties in the house until I'm back from Capreae. I've told her that you're overseeing the copying of revised administrative orders for the *vigiles*, and that Caesar himself is awaiting the completion of the task."

"Sir," I agreed, my mind not fully on what he was saying. Aviola. *Why* does that name stir my memory?

I was jolted into full attention by Macro's next remark. "I'd better give you another hundred *denarii*, Quintipor. If you run short while I'm away I don't want you asking my wife for money; she'd only wonder what was going on, and this business is between you and me."

Surprised at this unexpected event I assured him of my prudent stewardship of his money.

"Perhaps a sausage or two for your potter friend," he winked, "but, damn your alien hide, I don't want you throwing any wild parties, eh?"

In a flash it came where I'd heard of Aviola. "Wild parties." When Macro jokingly said that, I immediately thought of Marcus Soter, the caterer's man whom I'd met recently. He'd told me that he was on his way to assist the gentry in getting well-oiled at a party in the house of Senator Valerius Aviola. The date fitted. That was the party that had been attended by Vitalis.

After I'd taken my leave of Macro and wished him a successful trip, I went straight to bed. It had been a busy day. Tomorrow would be even more so.

And now I had several days reprieve, hopefully enough time to determine how I could reveal the killer's identity without creating trouble for my friends in the small alley off the Flaminian Way.

XVIII

At first light I was up to see Macro off to Capreae with his escort of ten men. The horses' breath plumed in the crisp October morning air and Macro and his party were muffled to their chins in long woolen riding coats. Young Rufinus and one of the dining room attendants served cups of hot, unwatered wine and Petronia's cinnamon sweet cakes to the mounted men. Then they trotted off, followed by a slower moving baggage wagon with its own mounted escort. Brigands still existed along the inter-city roads.

Back in the warmth of the kitchen, Petronia gave me breakfast and asked why I was away from the house so much lately. I told her the story about the secretarial project in the master's civic office and that I'd be busy with it for a week or so yet.

"You see other woman, I hit her on head," she declared tenderly, holding up an iron frying pan. I assured her that I wouldn't "see other woman" and promised to bring her a gift in a few days.

When I arrived at Jucunda's house, most of the girls were still eating breakfast, half asleep. Madame was already at work in her office and I told her that I wished a couple of days off, using the excuse that I'd learned of possible employment with a city merchant and also with a wealthy house in the suburbs. This she accepted readily enough and wished me well. I declined her offer to pay me for my two days work thus far, assuring her I'd return to finish the job.

Then I set out to call upon Marcus Soter. A half-hour walk brought me to the *insula* where he and his family lived in a three-room apartment on the fifth floor, the top floor. The cramped hallways and stairwell of the dismal apartment building, with their smudged, greasy walls, reeked of stale cooked cabbage, onion and rancid oil.

The drab, dispirited woman who answered my knock listened in silence while I gave my name and asked if I might see Marcus Soter. Unspeaking, she motioned me to enter, and left me standing by the entrance as she disappeared into an adjoining room. Two small children, boys, I figured—to me all children look the same until they're about six years old—played on the bare floor with some colored wooden blocks. One ignored me while the other stared at me fixedly. I'm not used to small children, there not being any in the Macro household, other than little Rufinus, our new slave.

With the child gazing at me, I thought that some benevolent gesture on my part was called for. Smiling, I said hello in the condescending syrupy tone we employ when addressing less intelligent forms of life.

The child responded at once. Scrambling to its feet, it ran to me and kicked me hard on the shin, then rejoined its sibling on the floor, giving me no further notice. The small bare foot hadn't hurt but I was given pause over its owner's conviviality. The Greek philosopher was probably thinking of children when he defined the human being as a two-legged animal without feathers.

Muffled conversation came from behind the woolen drape covering the door of the room the woman had entered. I realized that I'd probably caught Marcus still in bed. Although most Romans arise at dawn, there are late-sleepers, those whose employment keeps them up after the seventh night hour that marks the start of a new day. Marcus would be one of those, his job with the caterer requiring him on duty at parties until the sun was closer to rising than setting. If I'd disturbed his rest, I'd find out shortly.

While waiting, still standing by the entrance, I looked around the room, which was about ten feet square. I'd never been in a working class *insula* before, or in any kind of apartment building for that matter. I guess I'm a good example of those slaves of wealthy houses who are naive about living conditions of the lower classes in free society. There are exceptions, of course, but from what I've observed recently, I'd say that the slaves of the great houses are much better off than most freemen.

I noticed that the room contained only two stools, three-legged affairs that had seen better times. There was a *cathedra* type chair with a sloping straight back and a worn, red cushion covering the seat. The only other furniture was a small wooden table about fifteen inches square, supported by one central leg that was secured to a square wooden base not much smaller than the table top. On the table were an unlit ceramic oil lamp and a small plaster bust of the Praetorian Prefect. That didn't surprise me. Sejanus shows up everywhere these days. I've already expressed my views on the subject.

A copper brazier smoked half-heartedly in one corner,

its scant warmth heating the air for a few feet at best. The shutterless window was only half-covered with a leather curtain, allowing some illumination along with a cool draft. The dismal chill of the room made me wonder what it would be like in the winter months just ahead.

Two wood and leather buckets of water stood against the wall close to the window as required by the fire regulations.

Running the length of the wall opposite the entrance was a wide masonry ledge, covered with a thin mattress and a couple of crumpled blankets. It was probably the children's bed at night, and a sitting bench by day.

Through an open doorway I could see into the kitchen, where another brazier glowed weakly, its thin smoke drifting lazily into the outer room. A four-legged table held a large stone jug and assorted bowls.

The woman returned, still unsmiling but her demeanor toward me had improved. "Marc will be out right away," she said. "I thought maybe you were a fire inspector or a tax man, at first, but Marc says you're a friend of his. Here, be seated." She honored me by indicating the chair.

"Thank you, uh..."

"Antistia," she introduced herself. She glanced at the children. "Did Paulina kick you?"

"Oh, no," I lied. "We've been getting along famously."

She glanced at me doubtfully, then raised her voice to the child. "This man is a personal friend of the emperor's and if you kick him he'll have you sold as a water carrier."

Water carriers are considered scum, the lowest order in the slave hierarchy, but Paulina, unimpressed, studiously picked her nose.

Sleepy and rumpled, Marcus appeared, greeting me in a friendly way and my conscience was eased when I learned that he hadn't been working the night before but worshipping at "the temple of Liber," the god of planting and growth, more especially that of the grape. The Greeks called him Bacchus.

"I hope Paulina didn't kick you," he said.

"What? Little Paulina?" I said in disbelief.

"She likes kicking people lately." He turned to the child. "This man is the Prefect of Egypt and, if you kick him, he'll have you flogged."

When I reminded Marc of our meeting on the street recently and that he'd mentioned part-time work that might interest me, he suggested we repair to a tavern where we could discuss the matter.

Soon we were seated in a small, noisy public house not far from Marc's dwelling, a pitcher of wine before us, courtesy of my master, Macro. I took it from the landlord's greeting that Marc had spent the previous evening in the place. We observed the preliminary ritual of cursing the weather, sighing over the shabby workmanship of present day artisans, and shaking our heads over the manners, taste in clothing and general lack of virtue in modern youth. Then we got down to business.

"All right, Marc," I opened, "tell me about this part-time work."

Not one to mince words, he said, "I'm an informer."

So, my friend is a *delator*, a paid informer who passes personal information about people to someone who, in turn, imparts it for a fee to high ranking officials. I mentioned before that the patrician and equestrian classes walk on eggs these days, never knowing when they'll be accused, falsely or otherwise, of breach of conduct. They say that Sejanus alone has dozens of such informers, as do the imperial family.

"I've heard of such," I said, "but know nothing about it."

He told me about it. He didn't reveal the name of his employer nor did he know what was done with his information after he'd reported it. Nor did he care. He was well paid for easy work and that's all that mattered.

Marc asked me to respect his confidences, not that he was doing anything illegal—still, it was wise to keep the matter private. I assured him of my discretion.

With access to wealthy houses through his job, Marc was in an ideal position to overhear the chatter of the privileged classes. His instructions were simple: to note any comment or action that appeared to reflect discredit or insult to the state and its officers, or question the authority of the established order. Is it any wonder that the highborn walk in trepidation, knowing that every time they sneeze it could be interpreted by a tailor's assistant as an insult to the emperor?

I refilled his cup. "Are you paid the same amount each time you have something to report?"

"It varies...the more important the information, the more I'm given." He drained half his cup with one swallow. "My last job, I got four hundred *sesterces*. That's pretty good, but usually I get one, two hundred, about once a month. The gentry are careful what they say these days, so things are a little slow."

We'd been talking close to an hour, mostly him talking and me listening. I poured the remains of the pitcher into his cup and signaled the landlord to bring another.

Taking a gamble, I asked, "The four hundred *sesterces*, was that the time you were working in the senator's house, the night Vitalis Hesper was a guest?"

He looked at me questioningly. "Hey, how'd you know that?"

"When we met last week, you told me you were on your way to work at the senator's house. Later, after Vitalis was killed, I overheard Macro telling someone that Vitalis had been a guest of Senator Valerius Aviola the week before." Having been a slave himself in a large house, Marcus could accept my statement readily enough.

"Yeah. Well, that's why I mentioned this informer work to you, Anthus. You're in a position to get information that certain people would be happy to pay for. And look, if you're leery of getting in too deep, we could make some kind of deal. You give your information to me and I pass it to the man I work for, then we share the proceeds."

"Tempting, Marc. I'll think about it. Here, pass your cup."

"Good stuff, this," he said, again knocking back half his cup in one swig.

"There's certain merit to its provocative aftertaste," I agreed. "And I'm rather amused by its cheeky bouquet; yes, a flirtatious little wine." Macro would have been proud of me. Marc wasn't impressed, however. "Lay off, Anthus," he sighed, "I hear enough pretentious crap from the highborn bastards."

"So, Vitalis Hesper was there that night," I prompted.

"Yeah. The exalted athlete was getting potted and opened his big mouth when he should have kept it closed. And I just happened to be standing close by."

I remembered the wall *graffito* about the charioteer. "They say he was quite a ladies' man. Doing a little bragging that night, was he?"

Marc reached for the wine pitcher and slopped some into his cup, dribbling a little on the table. "Bragging is right, too true, mate." His exaggerated, solemn nod was jarred by a belch. "Bragged about the wrong lady, though, the stupid bastard. Sure did. Told the old senator that he'd enjoyed the delights of the emperor's niece, then he had a few things to say about Sejanus. How stupid can you get, huh? Guess you don't have to be too bright to drive a bloody chariot."

"How did the senator react?"

"Poor old guy nearly had a fit, told the charioteer to shut up, then tried to ignore him." Marc fell silent a moment. "Real nice old man, the senator. Very polite, even to us servants. Nice man. Gave us all a ten *sesterces* gratuity, too. Most of the noble houses don't give you a thing. But he did. I was sorry when I heard that he died a few days ago. Nice old man."

I didn't tell him that the report he'd made of the senator's dinner party possibly had led to the nice old man's death. I wasn't sure about that, but the pieces were beginning to fit together.

That the knight had murdered Vitalis, I was sure. The question was why. I now knew that Marcus had informed on Vitalis, and, unwittingly, on the senator at the same time. The senator had committed suicide the day after his party. Why? The charioteer had been murdered by the knight a week later. Another why? Knights don't go about murdering people. It might be in their nature to arrange such a thing, but surely they'd have the deed executed by an agent, paid or otherwise. There's a thought. Was the knight someone's agent? If so, his principal would have been someone in high authority.

Marc said that the person he reports to isn't anyone important. In fact, he's a former slave. Who employs him, then? Marc was well paid for his disclosure about Vitalis and the senator. Therefore, Marc's employer knew that he had valuable news to pass to his own superior. Information that concerned the emperor's niece, Livilla. And Sejanus, the Praetorian Prefect.

My thoughts were broken by Marc knocking over his cup. I moved smartly to avoid the spilled wine dribbling onto my tunic, calling for the landlord to bring a cloth, which he did cheerily, such incidents being commonplace. Marcus was drunk. After his imbibing the night before and having had no breakfast, an hour and a half of steady drinking had left its mark. I had the start of a mild glow myself and I'd only had one to his three, I'm sure.

"You all right, Marc?" I asked. Not one of my more brilliant utterances, but what does one say under the circumstances?

"Yeah. Sorry 'bout that," he mumbled. "Hey, lemme

get us another jug of juice."

"I have to leave, Marc. Want me to walk you home?" It wasn't yet noon but I had things to do before nightfall.

"Home? Not goin' home yet. Stay here awhile...don't have to work today. No parties in fancy houses tonight for old Marc."

I stood up. "Marc, where is the senator's house?"

"What senator? Lots of senators, eh?"

"Valerius Aviola, where you saw Vitalis."

"Oh, sure. Lessee. On the Ardeatinan Way. Yeah, just inside the Tullian wall. Nice man, the old senator."

On my way out, I discreetly asked the landlord if one of his tavern boys would make sure Marc got home safely. He took the three *sesterces* I held out and assured me deferentially that he'd see to it. I suppose its my well-bred accent that does it.

XIX

Sejanus smiled placatingly. "Caesar, I'm surprised to find you concerned over a small matter like this."

"The Praetorian Guard is *not* intended to do police work!" Tiberius said. "The Valerius Aviola business was clearly something that should have been referred to the Urban Cohorts, if indeed it required action at all. Which I doubt, from what you've told me."

"I realize that the senator's apprehension was more a subject for the police, but I considered his fears to be groundless, the fancies of advancing age, perhaps. To satisfy him I detailed a detachment of the Guard to be stationed around his house. I was sure that in a few days he'd have forgotten his fear of assassins, and the men could be quietly removed."

Tiberius snorted. "I knew Aviola and he was not in his dotage! He was only nine or ten years older than me. Am I beginning to meander mentally also?"

"Never, Caesar."

"Yes. Well, I'm most concerned about this. I'll accept that you acted in good faith. But I can't understand why Aviola went to you instead of to Macro who's better organized than you to track down any thugs that may have been harassing Aviola—if in fact there were any, which I doubt. No, there was some other reason why he talked to you, of that I'm sure." I'm very sure, Tiberius thought, looking at the Praetorian Prefect. And your lies are an insult to my intelligence.

"With no disrespect to my colleague, the senator intimated that he'd feel more secure with a guard of my men rather than one from the Urban Cohorts."

"Indeed?" Tiberius said with exaggerated surprise. "Most strange, that. I should have thought that Aviola had a healthy respect for the city police."

"I don't understand, Caesar."

"No? Well, last month the senator donated half a million *denarii* to their welfare fund. The most generous contribution probably ever made; most certainly the largest during my time in office. And you can be sure that every member of the police knew about it. They made Aviola an honorary legate, did you know that?"

"No, Caesar. Nor of his donation."

"Amazing, Sejanus! I would have thought your informers might have reported it. Well, don't feel bad about not knowing. Aviola was generous with his wealth but never sought public recognition. Not everybody's like you and me, Sejanus, ensuring that our deeds are well publicized. No, don't protest! You know it's the truth. You and I are kneaded from the same flour."

Sejanus smiled silkily. "Caesar jests, surely. The populace knows of our actions because you are First Citizen and I am one of your executive agents…"

"Caesar does *not* jest!" Tiberius interrupted. "Caesar is too mystified over the matter of Aviola's suicide which happened on the very day that you say he asked for protection. And one other thing. The athlete who was murdered shortly after, he'd been a guest in Aviola's house the day prior to the senator committing suicide."

"The two deaths can't be connected, Caesar," Sejanus protested. "Pure coincidence, surely. The charioteer probably had many enemies, being a colorful public figure."

"Perhaps. Perhaps not," Tiberius said. "I hope to find out."

Sejanus shrugged sceptically. "It's doubtful that the killers will be found now. A week has passed and there were no witnesses."

"But all Rome demands that the killers be found." Tiberius paused, looking at Sejanus knowingly. "The police will find them soon, I expect. Macro has several choice suspects to choose from."

The prefect's expression cloaked his alarm as Tiberius continued. "As for Aviola, we'll learn more upon his son's return to Rome. He'll assume his father's seat in the senate."

"What do you mean, Caesar?"

"What I mean, Sejanus, is that Aviola left a letter for his son. One written a few hours before his death. It seems probable that it may explain his taking his own life, doesn't it?"

"But how do you know of such a letter?" Sejanus asked.

"Claudius," said Tiberius.

"Claudius?"

"Yes, Claudius. I know you consider him a fool. And like many others, some day you'll find that you're wrong. But my misunderstood nephew is often useful to me. He has an open nature and gets along well with people, given half a chance. I sent him as the imperial family representative to offer our condolences to the house of Aviola. It's expected, you know, even if the succeeding *paterfamilias* isn't present, as in this instance. After Claudius had finished with the formalities, he had a chat with the steward who told him that he held a letter to be given to the eldest son when he returns from Egypt."

"But, Caesar, I've told you that the senator was full of imagined fears when he asked me for protection. His letter might be similarly deranged."

"Well, we'll just have to wait and see, won't we?" Tiberius said. "I'm particularly interested in learning what Aviola wrote because I'm informed that the charioteer had told Aviola something concerning the death of my son. Yes, his letter may prove a most interesting document."

Sejanus inclined his head respectfully. "I must go now, Caesar. I have a meeting this morning with the Urban Prefect."

"It will not be summer forever, Sejanus," Tiberius muttered after the prefect had gone. "The day of reckoning always comes—and I'm already planning yours."

His thoughts turned to Sutorius Macro, who had departed that morning for Capreae. Yes, a good man, Macro, he reflected.

• • •

By late morning Macro's party of horsemen were thirty miles south of Rome on the Appian Way, the "queen of roads" built more than three hundred years before to link Rome with the cities of the south. The weak sun had dissipated the morning mist and the riders had removed their cloaks. Approaching a long uphill grade, Macro signaled the column to rein in from the trot to a walking pace.

Beside Macro, at the head of the group, his aide took off

his helmet, wiping the perspiration from his forehead.

"Warmer than when we set out, eh, Milo?" Macro said.

"Indeed, sir," the junior officer replied. "Your steward offering us a hot cup before we departed was much appreciated. Most thoughtful of you, sir. And the sweet cakes, like the ones my father's cook makes. From a recipe by Apicius, I believe. Delicious."

Macro grunted in acknowledgment. The hot wine and cakes had been Anthus' idea.

"A fine steward you have, sir. Seems most capable and very courteous. Handsome fellow, too. Is he Ligurian, perhaps?"

"He's a Briton, but Roman born." Macro glanced mischievously at his aide, who was competent enough but inclined to be pompous and rank-conscious. "Grandson of a king, is Anthus."

"Really, sir! Yes, yes, he does possess a certain air of gentility. How very interesting. Has he been with you long, Prefect?"

"Twelve, thirteen years. I bought him when I needed an *amanuensis*. I was looking for a secretary and an accountant and found both of them in Anthus. His previous master had him well educated. Speaks better Greek than I do, but doesn't let on. Oh, he's a cunning bastard is Anthus, but I'm onto him. We play a game, he and I. I'm the big, bluff master shouting and fussing and he's the patient long-suffering servant guiding me discreetly where he's decided I'm to go."

The younger man put on his helmet. "It sounds like a good relationship."

"It's an excellent relationship, Milo. I'd trust him with my life, damn his alien hide."

And it's none of your business, Macro thought to himself, but it won't be much longer before I grant freedom to Anthus. Maybe a gift for the approaching Saturnalia. He's thirty years old, been a slave all his life, always been loyal and conscientious. He's earned his freedom. I'll ask him to stay on as my steward. Wonder when he'll get around to asking permission to marry the kitchen girl. Maybe I'll do the bully act and tell him he can't have her unless he stays on as household steward.

They had reached the crest of the incline now and the horses were breathing easy. Macro's aide read the prefect's thoughts. "The canter, sir?" Macro nodded.

They eased their horses into a trot for half a minute, giving the men behind them time to replace their helmets, which most had removed during the uphill walk. A moment later the troop broke into the most graceful and flowing of all equine gaits, the canter.

XX

After leaving Marcus Soter in the tavern, I had a quick mid-day meal in a *thermopolium* where the prices were higher and the food not as good as in Apio's next door to the brothel. I suppose the downtown location gives the owners the right to skin the customer. Going by the chatter in the kitchen, which I could overhear, the place is run by Greeks. There are old jokes about what happens when two members of the same race meet, and they go that when two Greeks meet they immediately open an eating house. They also say that when two Britons meet they sit around doing nothing because they haven't been introduced. I don't really follow that one, but the only Britons I ever knew were my mother and, of course, the great-hearted King

Tincommius who sold us into slavery.

The house of Valerius was fairly close to where Marcus had described. Thinking on the matter as I walked there, I'd decided to present myself honestly as the slave-steward of Macro's household.

Behind an eight foot stone wall was a paved courtyard about fifty feet square, beyond which was the senator's house, a two-story building of simple design, sparing in external ornamentation. A double gate of bronze scrollwork in the wall was unlocked. It would be secured at nightfall and, being a noble house, a night watchman would no doubt be on duty. Closing the gate behind me, I approached the front door of the house, on each side of which stood a huge stone tub of late blooming flowers much like those in the *peristyle* of Macro's house.

My arrival had been observed from within, for the door opened as I was about to knock. A young man in a servant's tunic, perhaps a dozen years younger than me, spoke before I could announce my business. "This house is in mourning for its late master, Senator Valerius Aviola of happy memory." Unless your business is urgent, don't bother us, he was telling me.

"All honor and respect to the spirit of the departed Valerius Aviola," I said, inclining my head. "My name is Anthus, steward to the household of Quintus Sutorius Macro, *praefectus vigilum*. I come to see the steward of this household on behalf of my master who is absent from the city at present."

He studied me briefly and I passed inspection as he bade me enter. "Wait here, please. I will inform him."

For the second time that day I found myself waiting inside the entrance of a strange dwelling while the subject of my visit was being informed of my arrival, but the mean quarters of the Marcus Soter family were in marked contrast to the tasteful opulence of this house. While admiring its tiled mosaic floors, fluted columns, magnificent wall decorations and expensive furnishings, I wondered if a small patrician child would appear and deliver me a welcoming kick on the shin.

"Please come with me." The servant had returned and beckoned me to follow him. The entrance hallway opened into the *atrium*, the principal hall of the house, a spacious rectangular room. Its walls were richly decorated with gold paint simulating curtains which were embellished with the heads of cupids, fauns and satyrs. On either side of the *atrium* were three or four smaller rooms; these, I figured, would be used as guest rooms or for whatever purpose the owner wished. At the far end of the *atrium* was the *lararium*—a large niche fronted by a waist-high stone altar—the shrine of the household gods, containing several portrait busts of family ancestors.

Then we passed into the *tablinium*, the living room, about one third as large as the *atrium*. On one wall I saw an immense mosaic of the sea-god Neptune and his wife Amphitrite, done in rich red, blue, gold and silver. Set into the opposite wall was a *nymphaeum*, a deeply recessed niche about four feet wide and six high. A fountain emptied into a large circular pool in front of the niche. In the center of the pool stood a two foot high bronze *putto*, a small boy bearing a dolphin on his right shoulder. A life-size tragic mask adorned each side of the niche and the entire structure was covered with intricate blue and white mosaic tile patterns. This place, I knew, was dedicated to the muses and the demi-goddess nymphs who inhabit the seas, rivers, forests and mountains.

At one side of the living room a wide archway led into the dining room. As we passed it I glanced inside and noted the bright murals and stucco relief decorations. A large number of *triclinium* couches were arrayed in orderly patterns. On one of these Vitalis Hesper had reclined recently, drinking too much wine and discoursing too freely within the hearing of Marcus Soter, the caterer's man.

We entered the *peristyle*, a large courtyard within the confines of the house but open to the sky, surrounded by a two story high portico on all four sides. I estimated that the tiled roof of the portico was supported by thirty or forty fluted pillars. The grassed garden area had flagstone walkways and was graced by several statues, stone benches, fountains and water basins.

I paused, admiring a large marble statue which stood on a square pedestal at the far end of the *peristyle*. It was larger than life, the figure of a naked man, right arm at his side and the left hand gripping an upright spear, its butt resting on the ground at his feet. I'd never seen such a lifelike piece, from the facial expression to the ridged veins in the hands and arms. Its beauty impressed me.

My escort sensed my appreciation and waited patiently beside me. "The Spear Bearer," he said. "The Greek sculptor Polycleitus's athlete. The original is five hundred years old, done in bronze. This copy is only about eighty years old and it's not considered to be a good one."

"Thank you," I said. "You're well informed."

"Such things interest me. Our late master of happy memory, knowing of my inclination, taught me all that he could and then paid scholars and artists to educate me further."

"And do you pursue any of the arts yourself?" I said.

He hesitated. "I write poetry. I was freed by my master's will and it's my wish to write poetry the remainder of my days, if I can find a patron."

"I wish you well. May I know your name?"

"I was born Titus Calpurnius but was sold into slavery in my native Sicily as a child, so became merely Titus. Now, as a freedman, I'm Aurelius Valerius Calpurnius. But should I ever become a recognized poet, I'll use my birth name. I'm sure the Valerian family wouldn't wish to be identified with a scribbler of bucolic verses."

As I listened to this young man and watched him, I had

a premonition such as most people, I'm sure, experience at least once in a lifetime, that he would achieve his goal.

"Titus Calpurnius Siculus," I said, "your poems will be read by scholars for millennia to come."

"Calpurnius of Sicily..." he mused. "Yes, I thank you for your kind words. But Tiro is awaiting you." He led me through a door under a side portico, then along a passageway that skirted a large kitchen and what were probably several storerooms and offices. Titus ushered me into a small room at the end of the passageway. A tall man arose from the table at which he'd been seated.

"I welcome you, Anthus, steward of the house of Sutorius Macro." His voice was deep and vibrant like that of a tragic actor. "I am Aurelius Valerius Tiro, steward of the house of Valerius."

We made a contrast, Tiro and me. I, with my pale skin, yellow hair and blue eyes; and he, a foot taller than me, with dark brown eyes, crinkly, close-cropped hair and skin the color of a ripe olive, the silky sheen of his black flesh accentuated by his pale blue tunic.

Tiro's use of the *tria nomina* was, I think, engendered by double pride of a sort. Only the free and the freed may use the three names: the given name, the clan name and the name of the family. Tiro was proud to be a freedman and was proud to bear the clan name of Valerius, that of his late master. He had adopted his master's given name of Aurelius and kept his own given name of Tiro as his *cognomen*, which would perhaps someday become the family name of his descendants.

It seems to me that Roman names are overly structured, but like many Roman concepts, there are always variations on the theme. The upper classes are the worst offenders, if indeed, such a thing is an offense, which I don't think it really is. They tend to take on indicative names, with the nobility setting the style. Defeat a tribe of Germans in battle and you add "Germanicus" to your list of names.

Clobber some fractious Slavs on the frontier and you glorify in "Pannonicus." Then again, there are those families which traditionally use two names only—for example, the republican heroes, Marcus Antonius and Gaius Marius. Well, you get the idea.

That expression I just used, "variations on the theme." Rather nice, that. And right off the top of my head, too. I must include it in my proposed lexicon of sententiously evocative phrases.

Tiro dismissed Titus with a few gentle words. "A fine young man," he said after Titus had left. "He's our scribe and was well thought of by the master."

"We talked briefly as he brought me to you," I said. "He told me that he writes poetry."

"I'm literate, but not too well educated and unable to judge the merits of poetry. But our master considered Titus gifted. In fact, he indicated to me recently that he had been planning to give Titus his freedom soon and offer to become his patron."

"Will Titus leave the house to seek his way, now that he's a freedman?"

"He's agreed to remain as scribe and as my assistant until the eldest son returns from Egypt. I've been asked to stay on as steward, which I've decided to do, even though the senator left me money in his will, more money than I shall ever need. The son is somewhat less amiable than his father, but none the less honorable or mindful of his responsibilities as a patrician. I shall inform him of his father's thoughts concerning Titus and perhaps he will carry them out in respect to his father's memory."

A middle-aged woman entered the small office, carrying a tray holding a single wine cup, a jug of wine and a plate of cakes. She placed it on the table and left wordlessly.

"I offer you refreshment," Tiro said. "I will not join you because I'm denying myself wine and rich food for one year in memory of my master."

I poured a trickle of wine into the cup and broke a small piece from one of the cakes. "I acknowledge your courtesy by taking one sip of wine and one bite of cake." I drank the dollop of wine and ate the cake morsel. "The rest I deny myself in respect for your state of mourning."

His expressive eyes showed that he was favorably impressed by this.

"Anthus, you say that you're here on behalf of your master, Sutorius Macro. Why does the prefect send his steward to see me, I wonder? I presume that it's an unofficial visit. Otherwise the prefect would have despatched one of his officers in all his plumed finery to attend to the matter, surely." There was bitterness in his speech.

I started to speak but he cut in. "If there's hardness in my tone, I apologize. It's not you who causes it. But, you see, this house in recent weeks has been attended by officers, and their men. They came one afternoon and departed the next morning. And during their brief stay my master took his own life."

"Yes, Tiro. I come here informally, but on a matter of concern not only to Macro but also to you and the house of Valerius." He said nothing but I knew that I had his full attention.

"I wish to know the circumstances of your master's death and also to learn what you may know of the charioteer, Vitalis Hesper." Tiro's eyebrows raised but he waited silently for me to continue.

"The prefect has been ordered by Caesar personally to look into the murder of Vitalis Hesper. Now, why Caesar is so interested, we can only guess at; but I suggest that in part, at least, it's because the senator took his own life for no obvious reason...yet shortly afterward Vitalis was murdered. I'll tell you in confidence that both Caesar and Macro believe that the two deaths may be related." This wasn't exactly true, but close enough to the mark.

"The two events were related," Tiro said. "But before

we talk further, tell me why it is that you have been chosen to come to me. A slave acting as emissary for a prefect is rather unusual, you'll admit."

"A slave," I said. "Like you were until recently. Tell me, did your late master trust you?"

"Completely. As I did him."

"Tiro, it's the same with me and my master. And he's entrusted me with the task of finding out all I can about the deaths of the senator and the athlete. He believes that an informal approach will result in freer discussion than if you were to be interviewed by an officer of the Urban Cohorts."

"Surely you know that I've already been interviewed by such. By two of them, in fact."

"Yes, but they only queried you on the death of the senator. Macro has made me privy to the records and I know that the only result of their talk with you was confirmation that it was a case of suicide, reason not known."

Tiro nodded in affirmation.

"Any simple-minded stable boy could have reached the same conclusion, Tiro," I said. "The question isn't how the senator died, but why. Did the police pursue that at all?"

"No."

"That's why I'm here now. Using your own words, 'a slave acting as emissary.' The police aren't really trained to investigate crime of this nature. In fact they see no crime attached to the matter at all. An old man committed suicide, that's all. Nothing whatever to do with the killing of Vitalis. But after the few things I've learned the last day or so, I suggest that there's a common factor in the two deaths."

Tiro's black face was impassive. I couldn't tell whether I'd convinced him or not on the validity of my task. After the encouraging progress I'd made so far, I desperately needed his cooperation.

The fragments of information given by Bato the potter, the prostitutes Dorcas and Emmachia, Ignatius the chestnut vendor and Marcus the informer—they all fitted together, but I needed more facts. Actually, I'd already accomplished what I'd set out to do. I knew the name and social position of the man who killed Vitalis. That's all Caesar asked for, isn't it?

Yesterday I was on the verge of telling Macro who the killer is, but his bumptious lord and master routine stifled me momentarily. And when he said that I had a few more days to study the matter, I admit that a wave of relief passed over me. Wave of relief. Yes, another excellent description; I'll add it to my thesaurus of clever speech. I really must get to work on it soon. Who knows, perhaps in the not too distant future, similar to Titus the budding poet, I shall be seeking a wealthy patron to support and encourage me in my literary undertaking. I'd have to dedicate the finished work with the usual flowery exaggeration about his devotion to the arts, greatness of spirit and unflagging zeal in the cause of so on and so forth. Well, I wouldn't object to that as long as he or she—there's lots of wealthy ladies around—kept the *sesterces* flowing freely as I wield my stylus for the benefit of future scholars.

But I've wandered from the subject. I must learn to control such flights of fancy.

Tiro had been staring at me with concentration while I spoke and I knew that he was giving full thought to my words. I continued.

"When I said that my investigation is of concern to this house, I meant that should we be able to prove that the deaths of the charioteer and your master were connected, it follows that the reason for the senator's suicide will be…"

"You weren't listening, perhaps," he interrupted. "I stated before that the deaths *were* related."

Now it was my turn to stare in silence.

"Very well, Anthus," he said, "I'll tell you what I know."

He began with the night of the senator's dinner party for three dozen guests, the usual mixed gathering of legislators, artists, soldiers and athletes. The guests were assigned to the *triclinium* couches according to rank and status as guests of honor. The senator's custom was that when the dinner and entertainment were over, the guests would change positions in order to socialize with others than those who had been their neighbors at dinner. By chance, the charioteer had ended the evening reclining next to his host.

Tiro had been in attendance from the arrival of the first guests to the departure of the last, six hours later, overseeing the household staff and the temporary catering assistants. Most of the time he'd been standing close to his master's couch, his usual location on such occasions. Some time past midnight, during the seventh night hour, he'd gone to the kitchen to pay the entertainers, a troupe of Egyptian jugglers and dancers who were, by the senator's orders, partaking of refreshment before they departed. Upon his return to the dining room he'd observed a startled expression on Aviola's normally affable features. Vitalis was talking to the senator who, uncharacteristically, spoke sharply to his guest and then turned away from him. A wine server, one of the caterer's men, was standing close by.

When the guests began to leave later, Tiro was occupied with his duties but he saw Aviola and Vitalis conversing alone in subdued voices. The next morning Valerius Aviola arose early, although he normally stayed abed a few extra hours after one of his parties. His vestment servant helped him put on his *toga*. As is well known, it's impossible to drape oneself without help in an eighteen foot length of fine woolen fabric, seven feet wide.

The senator told Tiro that he was proceeding to the imperial palace to request an audience with Caesar. He wished to be accompanied by his scribe and three other servants, two to precede him, to ease his passage through the crowded streets, and two to follow. The silver-haired old man was well-known and respected by the populace and his figure, in its white *toga*, would by itself have moved the people to make way for him ungrudgingly.

For that matter, as I learned later, Aviola was an honorary legate of the Urban Cohorts and could readily have been provided with a small escort to attend him whenever he chose. He wasn't the kind of man who took advantage of such privilege, however.

Tiro told how the senator and his servants were about to leave the house when a tribune of the Praetorian Guard arrived with a detachment of men. After a brief exchange with the officer, the senator told Tiro that he had been summoned by the Praetorian Prefect on an urgent matter. His visit to the imperial palace would have to be deferred.

A couple of hours later Aviola returned, escorted by two centurions and a squad of guardsmen who were posted outside the doors and windows of the house. The senator told Tiro to advise the household staff that they were unable to leave the house but that they shouldn't become concerned because it was only a temporary restriction. He said that he would be busy in his office for several hours and didn't wish to be disturbed.

Then he did what Tiro said was an unusual thing. He said that he wished to have chicken in hot thyme sauce for his supper. The senator rarely decreed what he wished to eat, relying upon his chef to plan the menu without interference. Tiro knew that this was one of his master's favorite dishes. He didn't know until later that Aviola had chosen his final meal.

Hours later, when the senator had finished his lonely supper, he sent for Tiro and invited him to sit and share a jug of wine. The two men talked of small matters for the better part of an hour and no reference was made to the soldiers posted outside the house. Aviola didn't mention it and Tiro refrained also, assuming his master wished to avoid the subject.

According to Tiro, Aviola then said that he was going to relax in his bath before retiring and that he didn't wish his bath attendant's services. He said goodnight to Tiro, then took the steward's large, black hands in his own small, pale ones, holding them tightly. "I enjoyed your company tonight, old friend," he said. "Thank you for your years of loyal service."

Shortly after midnight Tiro was awakened by a trembling, near incoherent male slave, the young man responsible for night patrolling both inside and outside of the house as a precaution against fire and thieves. Barred by the guards from going outside, he had followed his routine faithfully inside, making silent rounds of the building. When the lamplight still glimmered from under the door to his master's suite of rooms long after the old man was usually asleep, he ventured to open the door quietly to see if his master had taken ill or fallen down. He wasn't in his bed nor anywhere in the room, but lamplight shone from the adjoining bath chamber. The night watchman called out softly, then louder. When there was no response, he went to the bath chamber door and looked in.

It was Tiro and Titus, eyes burning with tears, who drained the bloody water, washed their master's body and carefully carried him to his bed. They remained with the body until daybreak, when Tiro opened the front entrance and told the sentry there that the officer in charge was required at once.

By mid-morning the guards had left the house and within minutes of their departure two servants exited, each bearing a sealed letter: one addressed to the *pontifex* of the sacred temple of Minerva, an old friend of the senator; the other to Lucinius Gallus, *juris consultis*, learned man of law.

Tiro then related how two days later the body of Valerius Aviola was taken to the rostrum of the Forum where, befitting his rank, a public funeral was conducted. The priest of Minerva made sacrifice in the presence of several masked men dressed in purple-trimmed *togae*. The masks were lifelike representations of the dead man's ancestors. Tiberius Caesar was present, as was his nephew Claudius. Three hundred senators attended and double that many of the knightly order. There were two honor guards, a century each from the Praetorian Guard and the Urban Cohorts. All four city prefects paid their final respects: the Urban Prefect, the Prefect of the Grain Supply, the Prefect of the City Watch, Quintus Sutorius Macro; and the Praetorian Prefect, Lucius Aelius Sejanus, who was in the foremost rank of mourners and seen to brush away tears during the eulogy.

Tiro had been talking for twenty minutes. When he finished, he asked "Well, Anthus, does that assist you in any way?"

"It does. Yes. And it's consistent with the things I've learned earlier. The conversation between the senator and Vitalis seems important. A pity that you didn't overhear it." Courtesy of Marcus Soter, I knew what that dialogue had entailed, but I didn't wish to let Tiro know that.

"Tell me more of the letters you mentioned...the two despatched with the servants and the one left for you personally by the senator. Also, you said that there's another being held by you for his son."

Tiro hesitated a moment, then stood up. "Wait here," he said, then left the room. He returned a minute later and, sitting again across the table from me, placed a scroll before me.

"When Titus and I carried the master's body to his bed, at its foot was a *capsa*. On its lid was a small piece of parchment with my name written on it. Nothing more, just 'Tiro.' The scroll box was unsealed, so I knew that I was intended to examine its contents. Inside were four letters, all sealed. One for the priest of Minerva, one for the family lawyer, one for the eldest son, and one, which rests before you now, for me. You may read it."

Aurelius Felix Valerius Aviola to his loyal and loved steward Tiro. I have this day written three other letters but this one is the most difficult. When you read this, my spirit shall be waiting in whatever place it is to which spirits are consigned prior to joining those of their ancestors, should they be judged worthy.

I shall not explain the reason for taking my own life other than to state that under the circumstances it is the only recourse I have to safeguard the interests of my family and my servants. In time the reason will possibly become known to you. I am compelled, however, to say this much for your own protection. My summons by the Praetorian Prefect earlier this day and the subsequent posting of soldiers around the house concerns a matter which was voiced by the athlete Vitalis Hesper during the dinner party last night. It is obvious that he was overheard by an informer who wasted no time in passing the information to Lucius Sejanus. It is my belief that Vitalis Hesper will be arrested shortly but will be killed before facing trial. It will most likely be proclaimed officially that he committed suicide.

I think it unlikely, but should you be questioned by any office whatsoever on the matter, deny any knowledge. If necessary, consult Lucinius Gallus, whom I have instructed in my letter to treat you as client-freedman of the Valerian clan and agent of my estate pending the return to Rome of my son Felix.

I leave three letters in your care. At first light tomorrow advise the officer of the soldiers outside the house of my death. The soldiers will be withdrawn soon after, I'm sure. When they have left, send the letters to the priest and to Lucinius Gallus, with whom my will is deposited. The letter to the priest requests that he advise the emperor of my death at once. Should he be barred from the imperial palace, he will advise the Urban Prefect, who, as senior prefect of Rome, will surely have access to Caesar. The letter to the juris consultis instructs him to execute my will with haste and to arrange my funeral rites.

> *The letter to Felix you must retain for him until he returns to the city. Advise him at once by letter of my death and tell him that you hold a letter for him which will set forth the circumstances of recent days. Also I ask that you write to my son in Spain and my daughter in Noricum, telling them that their brother Felix will communicate with them in due course.*
>
> *The terms of my will grant manumission to yourself and all of the household staff and also to fifty-three others in my outlying estates. I should like to have given freedom to many others who have served me well but you are aware that under the law I can only free one-fifth of my slaves. I have bequeathed you a sum of money which will suffice to let you spend the remainder of your days in comfort and I have also left varying amounts for the others.*
>
> *From one who has long admired and respected you and knows your true worth, farewell, Tiro, for the last time.*

Carefully I rolled the letter back onto its turnstick and placed it on the table.

"This letter could prove dangerous to you, Tiro," I said. "I wonder if perhaps you should destroy it."

"I've considered that," he said. "I prefer not to."

"At least keep it well hidden in a secure place."

He didn't answer but his look of forbearance expressed his opinion of such unnecessary advice.

"It certainly indicates that the two deaths were linked," I continued, "and the senator's prediction about the fate of Vitalis came true, more or less. I suggest that the Praetorian Prefect didn't wish to risk the public outcry that would have been raised if the athlete had been arrested—better to have him slain by a hired assassin."

Tiro nodded agreement at this, saying nothing.

"The priest was able to notify the emperor without interference, was he?"

"He didn't even try." Tiro's features flickered with the

hint of a smile at my bewildered glance. "The priest of Minerva is a sly old fox, Anthus. He knew that Caesar's visitors were being screened by Sejanus's orders, so he went to the house of the noble Claudius and informed him. Claudius at once went to his uncle. The Praetorians wouldn't dare hinder a member of the imperial family. In fact, later that day Claudius called here in the formal capacity of Caesar's representative to express the condolence of the imperial family. He appeared genuinely upset over my master's death. Claudius had been a guest here several times and was shown more respect and consideration here than he receives in most houses."

"Did he inquire about the reason for the senator's suicide?"

"In his guarded fashion, yes. More like wondering aloud why such a thing should occur."

"And your response to that?"

"I told him of the manner in which my master had been taken away and later brought back by the guards. I told him of the letter that I hold for the return of his son, and of the one which was left for me."

Again, the merest hint of a smile as Tiro said, "And, like you, Claudius cautioned me to safeguard the letters."

"You can charge both the noble Claudius and myself with insulting your intelligence, I agree," I said, "but it shows that we're both concerned about your welfare."

"Your concern is appreciated. Although I once believed that law prevailed in Rome, the events of recent weeks have proved me wrong. I know that the letter I hold for Felix probably contains damning information, most likely concerning the Praetorian Prefect. It worries me."

"Let arms yield to the gown," I sighed. "Cicero," I responded to Tiro's querying glance. "That's what we're supposed to believe—that the military must defer to the civil power. It's more fiction than fact. The regular army is under control, but the legions are all in the provinces. The Praetorians, instead of playing their intended role as personal guard to Caesar, have become a force unto themselves commanded by the second most powerful man in Rome. Second? No, he shares top place with the emperor and the more bored Tiberius becomes with his executive power, the more it's usurped by Sejanus."

"You seem to know a lot about the political scene," Tiro said.

"I'm the steward of a wealthy house headed by a prefect of Rome. Who better than yourself would know of the conversations I'm privy to in my position?"

The question I'd anticipated from Tiro earlier came now. "Anthus, if that is really your name, how do I know that you're the steward of Sutorius Macro?"

My answer was simple. "Come with me to his house. I'll introduce you to his wife, our *domina*, Ennia. As steward and freedman of the late senator you can justify your visit to her by offering thanks to her, in her husband's absence, for the honor paid to Valerius Aviola at his funeral by the Urban Cohorts."

For the first time since we met, Tiro smiled openly. "No, Anthus," he chuckled softly, "I'll leave such courtesies for the senator's son to observe. But I do accept that you're who you say you are. And, I'd heard of you before."

At my quizzical look, he explained. "When the senator was made an honorary legate of the police recently, he invited Macro and several of his officers and other dignitaries to a reception here following the ceremony. Your master is a most bluff and hearty man, as you well know. The gathering was in the *peristyle*, it being a pleasant day. I was present, overseeing the servants, and the prefect Macro approached me and said, 'So you're Aviola's steward, eh? Fine figure of a man you are and seem to know what you're doing.' Then he called out to my master who was standing close by. 'I'll trade you stewards, senator. I need an imposing fellow like this to lend some dignity to my household. You can have my worthless yellow haired, blue-eyed Briton, Antonius, or whatever he's called. He'll rob you blind and chase after the kitchen wenches, and those are his better points.' He also damned your 'alien hide' a couple of times, I recall."

I shrugged resignedly. "That's my master, all right."

"Does he really forget your name?"

"Just his clown act, Tiro," I reassured him. "Once he pretended to forget my name completely in front of some guests. Turned to them and said, 'I'll be forgetting the names of my damned hounds, next.' In fact, he doesn't own any dogs. Lady Ennia won't allow it. She wheezes and gets all puffy-eyed within a hundred yards of a dog. The physicians say that it's a phthisis caused by her mother being frightened by a dog a few months before my lady was born."

Tiro leaned forward, interested. "Ah, phthisis. My master's daughter likewise suffered from that but she was cured by a Greek physician. He gave her thinly sliced raw wolf's liver soaked in watered wine and made her inhale the smoke from dried cow dung."

"I'll remember that, Tiro," I said. We reflected a moment or two on the marvels of modern medicine. The conversation of the last few minutes seemed to have relaxed Tiro considerably.

"Anthus, you and the noble Claudius are correct, I know. The letter I hold for Felix would be of great concern to the people who caused his father's death if they knew of its existence. And they're surely clever enough to presume that such a letter may exist. It's well hidden but I wonder now just how safe it is in this house. Claudius even suggested that I let him take custody of it until Felix returns…but I declined his offer. A member of the imperial family, no matter how well-intentioned, is too close to the Praetorian Prefect for my peace of mind. But…"

"...the letter should be kept some place other than here," I finished for him. He nodded in agreement.

"Tiro, give it to me. What more secure place could there be than a strong-box in the house of the Prefect of the City Watch?"

"Do you swear by your gods that you will keep it safely and return it to me when Felix Valerius returns to Rome?"

This huge black man probably came from the far reaches of the upper Nile. And from his accent I knew he wasn't Roman born. Did he follow the religion of his native country? I gambled on it.

"I swear by Isis, Osiris and Horus and by the *lares* of the house of Sutorius under whose protection I place myself." There, that was a pretty good scope.

He stepped toward me and hugged me in his great arms. "You have sworn by the mother of gods. I place myself in your trust." He released me and stood back. "I will bring the letter."

The sun had gone down by the time I got home, and I was well soaked by the cold drizzle for the second time in the last few days. My spirit was undampened, however, as was the letter from Senator Valerius Aviola to his son. It was safe and dry in the folds of my cloak. And soon it would be safe and dry in my strongbox. But not until I'd opened and read it.

XXI

Sejanus waited with sullen impatience as his wet cloak was removed by an attendant and another gently rubbed a soft towel over his damp feet and sandals. He was then escorted by an usher to the emperor's office chamber.

"I will inform Caesar that you are here, Prefect," the usher said, inclining his head respectfully.

Alone, Sejanus wondered what pressing affair had caused the emperor to send for him on such a wretched night. Still, he was accustomed to Caesar's sudden impulses and snap decisions of late. He'd often been summoned to the palace with little notice—or none at all, like tonight. Yet, he mused, such petty inconvenience was a small price to pay for the progress he was making toward his goal. A few more years only, then...

His thoughts broken by the emperor's entrance, Sejanus bowed. Tiberius grunted an acknowledgment and sat down heavily at his desk, without inviting the prefect to sit. Waiting for Caesar to speak, Sejanus wondered if he was still ruffled over their recent conversation concerning the suicide of that old fool, Aviola.

Without preamble, Tiberius informed Sejanus that the imperial administration was being moved from Rome to Capreae in the immediate future. Astonished at the emperor's statement, Sejanus recovered quickly, his alert mind recognizing what such a move might mean for him.

"But why, Caesar?" Sejanus asked. "Why do you wish to move your court to Capreae?" His elation at the emperor's words was hidden by his concerned expression.

"Because," Tiberius said, "I'm weary of Rome. I'm weary of niggling patricians and complaining plebians, of priests and processions, of endless petitions and importunings. I'm weary of the plotting and scheming, the dodging and maneuvering. I'm weary of senatorial bombast, palace intrigue and the indiscretions of my family. *That* is why."

And I'm weary of you, Praetorian Prefect, Tiberius said to himself. From now on, I'll keep you at arm's length. I have given you far too much authority and now I must slowly cut you down to size.

Sejanus, too, had silent thoughts. The gods favor me, he cogitated. With Caesar in self-imposed exile more than a hundred miles from Rome, my position will be enhanced. But I mustn't appear pleased. I'll urge him to reconsider. Be careful, though...he's been in a strange mood lately. And he hasn't invited me to sit but leaves me standing before his desk like a school boy.

"Caesar, I well understand your patience being exhausted by unceasing complaints and demands from every direction. Do I not endure the same endless clamor, as one of your chief executives? But, Caesar, to govern Rome and its provinces, it's necessary to hold a wolf by the ears, which you have done commendably."

Sejanus smiled reassuringly. "And as for palace intrigue, you have nothing to fear, surely. Nor from the imperial family."

"I'll be sixty-seven years old in a few more weeks," Tiberius said. "After a lifetime of soldiering and politics, I think that I'm entitled to some peace and quiet. I intend to find it on Capreae."

Caesar has scant regard for the gods of the state religion, Sejanus mused. He's more inclined to believe the world is governed by predestined fate, hence his trust in astrology. More fool him. But I can be sure that he's consulted his court astrologer about this move. And I can be sure that the old charlatan will have told Caesar exactly what he wanted to hear.

"Caesar, are you certain this is an auspicious time for such a move? Have you consulted the soothsayers? And your astrologer?"

"Of course I have!" Tiberius snapped. "And the signs are favorable, most favorable."

Yes, thought the prefect, they are. Especially for me.

"The city will be a much poorer place without you, Caesar," Sejanus said, at once regretting the tired cliché.

"That's the kind of gibberish I'd expect from some fawning fool in the civil service, Sejanus, not from you. Now then, be seated. We have several matters to talk about, and the first one is Calpurnius Piso. Very well, I'm aware that he's getting on in years and has a fondness for wine. But he's been City Prefect thirteen years and I intend to keep him in the post."

"Whatever you wish, Caesar. But, as you say, Piso isn't the man he used to be and…"

"No, he isn't. However, Piso has rendered outstanding service to Rome for many years, as his fathers did before that. I'm not going to retire him, not yet. And for the past year his duties have been much lighter, since I placed the Urban Cohorts under Macro."

Ah, the ambitious Macro, Sejanus thought. Prefect of the City Watch with seven thousand *vigiles* and half that number again in the Urban Cohorts—a force of more than ten thousand fire fighters and policemen. They outnumber the Praetorian Guard and many are former legionaries. In effect, Macro has his own army. Macro, the shrewd, designing bastard, with his facade of genial bluster.

"You don't think Sutorius Macro is overly burdened, Caesar? I recall that when you first appointed him commander of the urban police it was a temporary arrangement."

"It was. But I'm satisfied with the way it's worked out and Macro assures me that he can handle both jobs. He has reliable deputies and he's a capable administrator. So he'll remain head of the *vigiles* and the *cohortes urbanae*, for the present."

"And what of me? Will I continue as your senior administrative officer, Caesar?"

"Yes. No change in your present duties. You will see to the routine operations but refer anything on the policy level to me. We'll work out a dispatch-box routine later. And the City Prefect and Prefect of the Watch will report to me directly also. The Prefect of the Grain Supply will continue to report to you."

"What staff will accompany you to Capreae?"

"I don't know, yet. Most certainly a number of secretarial and financial clerks, household staff and a detachment of guards. How many guardsmen will depend upon Macro's report when he returns in a few days."

"But Caesar, there are no barracks or military facilities on the island," Sejanus protested.

"No, by Jupiter, there aren't," said Tiberius. "We'll have to build them, eh? In the meantime, Sejanus, your

Praetorians will just have to camp under the stars like regular legions on campaign, won't they?"

XXII

Anxious as I was to read the senator's letter, I put it in the important papers box in my room, to be opened later. I changed into a fresh tunic and dry sandals and went to the kitchen, where Petronia greeted me happily.

"Is much special tonight eating like when you are small boy in Britannia," she beamed. I've told her repeatedly that I was born here in Rome and haven't been more than a few miles outside the city. But she has a fixed picture of me as a tiny barbarian romping in the fields and forests of Britannia, when not otherwise occupied worshipping rocks and trees.

With a proprietary flourish she set before me a dish of fried squash, boiled onion and what appeared to be a huge meatball the size of an apple.

"Is Briton." She pointed with pride at the meatball. "Egg."

"Egg?" I said.

"Egg," she confirmed. "Recipe bring back in person by Julius Caesar after he conquer wicked pagans in Britannia. Is from north where is savage barbarians."

"Ah, Caledonia," I replied. I remember from my geography lessons that the northernmost part of Britannia is called Caledonia, peopled by a wild race that specializes in sheep and cattle stealing, plundering and general marauding of the more peaceful tribes that dwell to the south.

"Eat now. We talk later," she decreed.

Tentatively I cut the steaming meatball in half. Inside was a hard-boiled egg. It was delicious. Petronia told me later that the egg was thickly coated with sausage meat, rolled in spiced bread crumbs and cooked in hot oil.

"You like?" she asked. "Just like when you are little boy eating Briton, no?"

"Yes, Petronia, my dove," I said. "I enjoyed my Caledonian egg. Just like when I was a small boy. Now, give me a kiss."

My days were fully occupied with the investigation of the Vitalis Hesper murder, but I still had my responsibilities as steward of the Sutorius Macro household. Each night I spent an hour or more resolving domestic problems and preparing a work schedule for the following day. So, after a brief dalliance with Petronia, I went to my office to hold court.

The head dining room servant dragged in young Rufinus, charging the terrified child with having broken a pottery bowl. I listened to the plaintiff, a crotchety faultfinder at the best of times, then dismissed him. Alone with the tearful boy, I cautioned him to be more careful in future, gave him a couple of candied apricots, patted his shoulder and sent him on his way.

Next was Zosimus, Macro's personal wardrobe servant. He's illiterate and asked me to read him a letter he'd received that day. The letter was from his freedman brother in Beneventium, a town southeast of the city. It had been written by a scribe, the brother being illiterate also. It advised that Zosimus' mother had died recently and the brother had seen to the funeral and asked if Zosimus was able to assist with the expense. Zosimus, a quiet, dignified man about twenty-five years old, wept silently and told me that he only had ten *denarii* in savings but he would send it all to his brother at once, if I could arrange it for him. I told him to keep his small hoard and that I would give him twenty *denarii* to send, a gift from his master and mistress. I knew that Macro would approve. He's often told me that he considers Zosimus a good man. As I've mentioned before, Macro will rant and carry on over a few *sesterces* but he's not mean about serious matters.

The last business of the evening was with Cerdo, our Gallic freedman chef. They say that the divine Julius brought back almost a million slaves from Gaul after his campaigns there seventy-five years ago. Cerdo's ancestors weren't among them; had they been, Cerdo would be speaking fluent Latin and thereby easing my administrative problems. Cerdo wasn't introduced to the delights of slavery until he was twelve years old and he's never quite caught the hang of the language even after twenty-five years.

Our relationship is delicate in that although I'm a slave and he's freed, I'm his senior in the household hierarchy. That's not an unusual situation, however. Even in the imperial household there are officials—former slaves and non-citizens—whose authority is such that the senatorials and equestrians fawn over them and curry favor openly.

Cerdo and I get along well enough. I treat him respectfully and always offer him a cup of wine at our meetings. He has an inclination toward the grape, like most good cooks.

It probably has something to do with the heat in the kitchen.

In his execrable Latin he described the wickedness of our fishmonger and the insulting quality of his eels and shellfish. As for the butcher, he'd promised weeks ago to deliver some sows' wombs—a favorite of the lady Ennia—yet none had appeared. And the greengrocer's delivery boy had been apprehended by Cerdo in a compromising situation in a storeroom with Sarra, our new scullery maid. Nor could Cerdo be expected to create his wonderful sauces from the poor quality eggs, olive oil, anchovies and assorted spices which cunningly rapacious merchants—"may the gods infect them with a foul disease!"—provide to the house, yet charge top price.

I let him describe the incredible miseries of being chef in a wealthy household, as he waved his arms and shed a few tears. At the third cup of wine he wound down and sighed in resignation at his hopeless plight. I assured him that I'd have a word with the various suppliers and have a talk with the girl Sarra. I'll certainly tell her to watch her step but I'll forget about the tradesmen. Complaining is a sacred ritual with Cerdo. Were he chef to the emperor, once a month he'd be sobbing on Caesar's shoulder, deploring the utter depravity of Rome's merchants.

Domestic duties finished, I went to my private chamber, secured the door and removed from the strong-box senator Aviola's letter to his eldest son. It was in a purple, cloth-covered cylindrical parchment container, appropriate to the senator's rank. The metal caps at either end were wax-sealed in two places, each seal bearing the imprint of a signet ring, a boar's head, undoubtedly the emblem of the clan Valerius. The seals were affixed on either side of the caps where the rims snugged onto the side of the cylinder.

I heated the tip of a fine pointed bronze needle in a candle flame, then cautiously inserted it under a seal, withdrawing and reinserting. I re-heated the needle several times and after about ten minutes the seal was loose enough to remove intact. I removed the second seal in the same way and put the two pieces of wax in a table drawer to await their reattachment. There were five sheets of papyrus inside the container. I unrolled them gently and laid them side by side on the table top, weighting the tops and bottoms to keep them flat.

I saw Tiro's trusting face and heard his voice. "Do you swear by the gods…"

Yes, Tiro. I swore. But I only said I'd keep the letter safe for you. I didn't say I wouldn't read it. Shaky reasoning and ethically debatable. But I find myself in a messy scenario in which ethics have been laid aside. "Fight fire with fire," as the old saying goes.

A man who knows he is about to die can be explicit and that's what the senator's letter was. I won't repeat it all—much was of an intimate, family nature and as I read it I was uneasily aware of trespassing on private ground.

The letter told how Aviola had decided that it was his duty to advise the emperor of the story told by the drunken charioteer concerning the death of Drusus, Tiberius Caesar's son. If Vitalis was indiscreet enough to tell such a thing to a Roman nobleman, how often had he repeated it in lesser social circles? And to some degree, *lese majeste* was involved in that it impugned Livilla, a member of the imperial family, and also accused the Praetorian Prefect of sedition and murder.

I read how the senator's intended report to Caesar was aborted by a summons from Sejanus and how the exchange between the two men had convinced Aviola of the prefect's moral corruption and his designs upon the principate of Rome. It told how Sejanus had given Aviola a choice in his manner of death: to be tried in the senate by his peers, most of whom were in dread of Sejanus and subject to his manipulation, or to commit suicide. The choice was obvious, not only for the preservation of his family honor but also for the protection of their social and financial status. Were he to be condemned in the senate as a criminal, Aviola's entire estate—money, land, slaves, chattels and investments—would be confiscated by the state, leaving nothing to his heirs. Were he to die by his own hand, his will would remain valid and family honor intact.

The details of his house arrest were set forth, including the names of the two officers who had escorted him to his house by orders of Sejanus. He noted that they had treated him with courtesy and seemed embarrassed over the role which had been imposed upon them.

The senator counseled his son to not act impulsively over the matter but to establish himself as a member of the *optimates*, the conservative faction of nobles from the older families whose influence was greater than that of the "new men" of lesser pedigree. Once established as a Conscript Father of Rome, he should inform the emperor of the events of the twenty-four hours which preceded Aviola's suicide.

The only part of the letter I'll quote is this:

When you take your senatorial oath you will swear by Jupiter, Earth, Sun and by all the gods and goddesses that whenever you perceive or hear anything being said or planned against Caesar you will lodge information about this and will be an enemy to whoever says or plans or does any such thing. Apart from your oath of allegiance, the honor of the clan Valerius demands your loyalty to Caesar who is the embodiment of the state. Your ancestors have served Rome for centuries. Your grandfather was a trusted companion of the young general Octavian, now the deified Augustus. I, in a more limited capacity, also served the state to the best of my ability, firstly as a young man of the republic and for the past fifty years as a soldier, magistrate, priest and senator of the empire. Rome is being led into the future by Tiberius Caesar and his task requires the loyal support of such men as yourself.

As he had in his letter to Tiro, the senator predicted the death of Vitalis Hesper by the machination of Sejanus. And he commended to his son a dozen or so men who are loyal to Caesar and who know Sejanus for what he is. One of those named was Macro.

I spent the next hour making a copy of the letter, then replaced it in its cylinder and reattached the seals. I put it in my important documents box and took the copy to my steward's office, securing it in the strongbox with my household accounts.

I was tired and not without cause. Up at daybreak to see Macro and his party off to Capreae, then my visits to Marcus Soter and Tiro, adjudicating the household staff problems and the business of opening and copying the senator's letter.

Too bad that Macro's away. Tonight I could have given him the senator's letter, incriminating Sejanus in the deaths of both Aviola and the charioteer. And I could have named the agent used by Sejanus to murder Vitalis in the whorehouse. Not a bad four day's work.

As I drifted into sleep I remembered that I still had something like one hundred and ninety *denarii* left of my expense money.

• • •

Impressed by my expeditious solution of the Vitalis Hesper murder, Caesar appointed me to the equestrian order, awarded me half a million *sesterces* from the imperial treasury and decreed three days of public games in my honor. Beaming with approval, Caesar watched as my former master, the prefect Macro, placed his hand in brotherly fashion upon my shoulder.

"It's well into the first hour," he said as I looked into his blue eyes. Strange, that. Macro has brown eyes.

"Time to arise, Anthus." Giton, our night watchman, shook my shoulder gently again. "Are you awake?"

"Ump," I responded.

With the exception of late night workers and high society rowdies, the inhabitants of Rome start their day at dawn to take advantage of the daylight hours. In our household, the night watchman's final duty before his watch ends is to awaken the servants at the start of the first hour.

Giton remained beside my bed, waiting assurance that I was awake. To satisfy him I again grunted without enthusiasm and shifted reluctantly into a sitting position on the edge of the bed. After he left, I stood up, yawned, scratched and began to prepare for the new day, the dream of a knighthood and a half a million *sesterces* fading.

After a breakfast of porridge and honey and a chunk of bread I went to my office to consider my day's program. I removed the copy of the senator's letter from my strongbox and read it once again. Last night, in the excitement of reading it for the first time, I'd been convinced that the senator's words were a direct indictment of the Praetorian Prefect, Sejanus, in the deaths of both Aviola and Vitalis.

And now, reflected in the cold light of day...there's a rather good phrase, "cold light of day." I must note it for my literary compendium. And now, looked at dispassionately the following morning, it still seemed a damning document.

My task has been completed now, leaving only a few tag ends to tidy up. And of course I'll have to return to the brothel and terminate my business with Jucunda. I owe her that, at least, after the consideration she's shown me. I'll tell her I've found employment and won't be able to complete the audit of her accounts. That won't upset her, I'm sure, as she only hired me out of kindness. And I'd like to visit Bato the potter again; maybe buy him lunch at the *thermopolium*. I've barely dipped into Macro's expense money, so why not?

In contrast to yesterday's bleak drizzle, the morning was sunny and scented with the mellow fragrance of autumn. Before I'd walked a hundred yards, I removed my cloak and carried it over my arm. As I drew closer to the heart of the city, the street noise increased. I've never been in any other large city but I'm certain none could be noisier than this one.

As I made my way through the crowded streets my ears were battered by the cries of sidewalk vendors, the shrill piping of school children reciting in unison at the top of their voices, the clank and rattle of metalsmiths, the chanting of priests, beggars whining and wailing, the discordant drone and jangle of street musicians, litter-bearers shouting for gangway, poultry squawking and passers-by gabbling in a dozen tongues.

It's been a long time since I was in the city after dark, but I recalled that the noise which begins at curfew is almost as bad as in the daylight hours. The divine Julius decreed that vehicles were not permitted to use the streets in daylight, traffic congestion being that bad even in his day. The regulation still exists, so the carts and wagons make their appearance after sunset—horses and mules hauling loads to the market places and construction sites with drivers shouting and cursing one another at the top of their lungs. It's said that only the wealthy obtain a good night's sleep in Rome, but only because they can afford to live in sheltered villas on the city outskirts. I wonder, does Caesar sleep well? His palace is only a stone's throw from the forum at the heart of the city. Of course, it's protected by thick walls and surrounding courtyards.

Now as I approached the forum, on my right was the Temple of Concord, originally constructed of wood about four hundred years ago to celebrate the end of a long battle between the patricians and plebians. If my old schoolmaster told what they were fighting over, I've long forgotten.

Anyway, the present temple is used as an art museum. The original building burned down—most places in Rome eventually do—and was rebuilt in stone about a hundred and fifty years ago. And on my left, the Curia, where the senate meets. An ugly building, to say the least. It's being renovated at present after the usual fire damage.

I entered the forum, the heart of Rome, or as some boast, the focal point of the entire world. Standing at the northwest end of the area, I stared at the huge pillars which line the central space, each topped by statues larger than life. Immense public buildings and temples surround the central promenade. The Greek city of Athens is reputed for its architecture but surely it's a poor second to the glory of Rome. The Greeks may be long on culture and art, but their engineers could learn a few things from ours—so I'm told.

During the past week I'd seen more of the city than I had in several years, visiting widely dispersed locales in pursuit of my investigation. Perhaps it was the contrast between the sedentary existence I led in the Macro household and the colorful sights and bustle of the streets, but I wanted to learn more of this huge city and its splendid sights.

Why not now, I thought? It would be several days before Macro returned from Capreae. I could call upon Jucunda tomorrow. Today I'd treat myself to a leisurely stroll wherever my fancy led me. And the weather was most pleasant. As the poet said, "Enjoy today, put little trust in tomorrow."

The broad pavement was crowded with people, mostly men, although a few working-class women and female slaves were to be seen. The highborn and wealthy women rarely appear on the streets and, if so, they're usually enclosed in a litter carried by servants.

I paused to watch a money-changer at work, one of several dozen transacting their business under the long portico of the Basilica Julia, the huge civil law courts on the southwest side of the forum. Fascinated by his colorful costume and sing-song eloquence—an Armenian, I thought—I was startled by a loud voice. It came from a tall, muscular man bearing a heavy staff; a servant whose task it was to clear a path for his master in the crowded streets.

Jumping aside, I bowed my head in respect as a senator passed by, followed closely by a dozen or more of his clients, the hangers-on who form the retinue of an influential man. I knew him to be a senator by the broad purple border of his tunic and his red shoes decorated with crescent-shaped silver buckles.

No sooner had he and his chattering retinue passed when again I was ordered to make way, this time for a priest of the cult of Bellona, goddess of war. He and his attendants appeared placid enough, but they're known as the "frenzied" cult because of their custom of slashing their arms with knives during religious rites.

I could have spent most of the day in the forum, admiring the buildings and statues, but I wanted to explore further afield, so settled for a brief sight-seeing. Perhaps, I thought, I could arrange to bring Petronia here sometime soon. I imagined her wide-eyed wonder at being surrounded by so much grandeur.

On the opposite side of the open forum space from the Basilica Julia was another grand edifice, the Basilica Aemilia; it had been rebuilt recently after being gutted by fire. Passing in front of it was the *Via Sacra*, one of Rome's oldest and most important roads. They say that for centuries religious processions and the army's triumphal parades have followed the Sacred Way, en route to the Temple of Jupiter Best and Greatest atop the Capitoline Hill.

But it was the south end of the forum I found most interesting, with its three temples dedicated to the divine Julius, Castor and Pollux, and the goddess Vesta. The temple of Julius Caesar was erected by Augustus, fifty years ago, I believe—and just think!—on the very spot where Julius Caesar was cremated and where Marcus Antonius delivered his funeral oration. A platform at the front of the temple is used as a *rostra* for public speakers.

I was much impressed by the temple of Castor and Pollux, "the guardians of Rome"—however, what I found most memorable of all was the temple of Vesta. Not because of its splendor or size, for it's quite small, really. Its pure simplicity appealed to me, a white rotunda with a domed roof. A wisp of smoke drifted from the hole at the roof's center; this was from the Sacred Fire, tended by the Vestal Virgins. The fire, which burns perpetually, is the symbol of Rome's existence and well-being. Vesta, goddess of hearth and family, is one of our most revered deities. The six virgins who serve her are of noble birth and chosen for the honor when they're between the ages of six and ten. The house of the Vestal Virgins is close by, almost adjoining the temple.

I then wandered over to the edge of the Sacred Way to admire a large equestrian statue. From there I could see the roof of the Temple of Jupiter Best and Greatest to the west and, to the south, the walls of the emperor's palace on the hill beyond the House of the Vestal Virgins. In a week or so Caesar will be reading my report, I thought. Well, Macro's report, but my work. Gazing at the palace walls I imagined myself approaching the palace gates and demanding an audience with the emperor.

"Who?" cries Caesar. "Anthus! Dammit, man...don't just stand there! Bring him to me at once! Mother, put on your best gown and see to some refreshment, quickly now! Ah, Anthus, my dear fellow, such a delightful surprise...please excuse the mess in here...I've been discussing aqueduct repairs with these gentlemen. You may leave us, senators...I'll try to fit you in some time tomorrow. Well now, Anthus, do be seated..."

Then, shouting and cheering dispelled my daydream.

A crowd had gathered near the *rostra* of the Temple of Julius Caesar and, curious, I joined it. The focus of attention was a *praeco*, a herald who was positioning himself for his daily proclamation of the latest news. These "town criers" were also paid by artisans and tradesmen to advertise their skills and wares. The citizens often grumbled that such commercial announcements outweighed the news items.

The crowd quietened as the herald indicated that he was about to make his announcements. He'd do this two or three times, then move to a new location. His vibrant voice carried easily to where I stood at the back of the gathering, about fifty feet from him.

"By order of the City Prefect, the citizens are advised that the murderers of the charioteer Albino Vitalis Hesper have been seized and taken into custody. They are Cyrus Publius Merula, freedman; and Glaukios, an escaped slave. They have confessed to their crimes and have been sentenced to public execution by crucifixion and burning. This will be done on the Ides of November on the ninth day of the Plebian Games. Let each man tell his neighbor that justice shall be done on behalf of the senate and people of Rome."

As the crowd roared its approval, the herald waited for the noise to subside before making announcements of lesser importance. The gathering began to break up, people drifting away in small groups, chattering animatedly about the capture of the killers.

I also sauntered away indifferently, close behind four or five men who were speculating loudly upon the type of execution that the two criminals would suffer. They mentioned the three common kinds of crucifix—the heavy posts being formed into the shape of an X, a Y or a T. I know that the T shape, the *crux immissa*, is the most common, where the criminal's wrists are roped or nailed to the ends of the crossbar at the top of the upright post and his ankles similarly secured to a small ledge which partly supports his weight. I overheard them say that in recent years a fourth type has been used, although it doesn't resemble a *crux* at all. It's a horizontal beam supported at each end by upright posts and the criminal is hung from it by one arm and one leg.

I've never seen a crucifixion but have been told that if the criminal is to be burnt as well, he or she is smeared with pitch or oil and a brush fire is then lit beneath the victim. Actually, there's very few crucifixions in Rome; it's more common in the eastern provinces, being a Syrian practice originally. Here, hanging and beheading are the usual methods. I've never seen one of those, either. Where did I learn all this? I suppose from listening to Macro and his friends.

So, then—as foretold by Macro, the killers of Vitalis Hesper have been apprehended. Two men selected from the police roster of local thugs. They both may well deserve execution for previous crimes, but it's ironic they're going to die for a murder they didn't commit. But only a few of us know that: Caesar, Macro, a few of Macro's staff officers...and yours truly, Anthus. I'm in high class company in that respect, aren't I? Oh, yes...there's a couple of others...Sejanus and his agent, the knight.

The executions will take place about four weeks from now. By then Tiberius Caesar will know the name of the true murderer and the name of the man he acted for. But you can bet on it that won't save the skins of the two thugs.

While musing on the matter, I meandered into the Vicus Tuscus, the narrow lane leading to the southwest out of the forum. Making slow progress because of the crowds, after about ten minutes I arrived at the northern end of the Circus Maximus.

One of the first things I'll do when I become a freedman—think positive, Anthus—is attend the races in the circus. I've only seen the races once—a few years ago when Macro took me with him on a business trip to a small town north of Rome. It was a small racecourse, but I thrilled to the spectacle of the horses and chariots and trick riders. A slave isn't privileged to attend the circus usually, but Macro used his influence to get me into the section reserved for freedmen.

The Circus Maximus is the largest racecourse in Rome—in the empire. Well, its name tells you that, doesn't it? Three-eighths of a mile long and more than six hundred feet wide, it seats a quarter of a million spectators. A quarter of a million! Races are held about two hundred and forty days of the year, with a dozen or more races per day.

Macro's a racing enthusiast and he's described the Circus to me in detail. He said the main feature is the *spina*, a raised platform that runs lengthwise down the middle of the course. It's decorated with the shrines and statues of various deities who favor the sports. Each race consists of seven laps around the *spina*.

The charioteers drive from one to six horses and there are specialty events where trick riders perform such stunts as picking up a piece of cloth from the ground at a full gallop. One I'd really like to see is the "standing race" in which the riders have two horses and ride them with one foot on each steed. A variation of this is when the rider jumps back and forth from one to the other. Some day I'll see for myself.

The charioteers belong to one of four factions which are known by their racing colors: the Red, White, Blue and Green Stables. In every city and town with a race-course there's a local following of each faction, with intense rivalry that goes back for centuries. Their ardent followers belong to clubs, wear distinctive costumes to the races and regularly brawl in the streets and molest ordinary citizens. In recent years the Blues and the Greens have become the most popular. The top charioteers do quite well for themselves. They tell me that the late Vitalis Hesper, in the last ten years, earned more than ten million *sesterces*! Pretty good for a Greek nobody whose father was probably no more than a goatherd.

There were no races today or I would have heard the roar of the spectators a mile away. I walked along the east side of the circus, down its length to the south end. The outside marble-covered walls have three levels of arcades, the ground level occupied by a variety of taverns and shops. Here I browsed along the stalls of nuts, fruit, pastries, cheese, cold meats and bread. The souvenir shops displayed miniature horses, charioteers, gladiators, chariots, cheap plaster busts of celebrated heroes, and pennants in the four faction colors.

On the spur of the moment I entered a shop which featured Blue Stable souvenirs. Several dozen small busts, purporting to be those of Vitalis Hesper, were on a counter top. I picked up one, thinking I'd perhaps buy it as a memento of my recent activity. Being a non-racing day, business was slow, and I was the only potential customer.

The middle-aged, greasy proprietor approached, eyeing my good quality cloak. I was wearing my best tunic and sandals, so presented a respectable appearance. I nodded to him curtly, saying "Good morning, my fine fellow." My polished accent did the trick and I saw him glancing at my left hand to see if it wore the knight's gold ring.

"I've been in the city seeing my goldsmith," I drawled with mild boredom, "and thought I'd look into a few shops while I was here."

The shop-keeper was convinced, I'm sure, that I was a wealthy gentleman, if not an *equites*, who dwelt in a country villa. Either that or he was the better actor. In any case, he bowed in servility. "Sir, your presence honors my humble emporium. Titus Cosconius Scaurus at your service, sir."

A freedman, no doubt; so proud of bearing three names that he'll employ them whenever he can. A born freeman would probably have introduced himself simply as Titus.

"Yes. Well then, ah, Scaurus," I said languidly, using

his *cognomen* which would have been his slave name, "what have we here, eh?" I held up a plaster bust, a wretched looking thing about five inches high.

"Ah, sir, that's the renowned Vitalis Hesper, sir. The famous charioteer as how was murdered recently. In fact, sir, the *praeco* was in the street out front not half an hour ago announcing the arrest of his killers. Yes, sir."

Feigning indifference, I turned the bust this way and that, examining it without enthusiasm. "Indeed? I fear the news of this Caspar fellow's death hadn't reached Noricum before I left there. We had other things to occupy us."

"Other things, sir?" he said, wringing his hands in deference.

"Um, yes. The Fifteenth Apollinaris has been busy of late...teaching manners to some recalcitrant, square-head tribesmen for the greater glory of Rome and Caesar who is its embodiment." Two *sesterces* says he'll be calling me "tribune" next, I thought to myself.

"Ah, tribune, yes, sir, of course if you've been campaigning in the north you'll not have heard of the Vitalis Hesper matter. A terrible business," he sighed, shaking his head in lugubrious solemnity.

As Scaurus the shop-keeper talked, I studied the bust of Vitalis. I haven't the faintest idea of what the late hero looked like, but I'd willingly bet another two *sesterces* that he bore no resemblance to the bland features of this statuette. Some unknown craftsman—a description I use loosely in this instance—probably produced thousands of them a few years ago and they've been serving to promote public adulation of assorted major and minor heroes ever since. Six months from now, when Vitalis is forgotten, the same busts will be passed off as those of the current athletic celebrity, military hero or fashionable poet. Should any of these shoddy pieces survive the passage of time, future historians might well ponder why so many public figures of Rome bore such marked resemblance to one another.

I drifted idly about the shop, casually examining the wares while Scaurus chattered beside me, eagerly relating the glories of Vitalis and the details of his murder. Not the least discouraged by my indifference, he gave a vivid description of blood drenching the street while a cast of dozens of whores, assassins and the Urban Cohort rent the air with shrieks, curses and appropriate cacophony. His account was akin to that given by Horio the greengrocer's wife's cousin.

Now he happily described the apprehended killers, both escaped slaves—one Merdo, a pastry cook from Spain; and one Gracchus, a one-eyed dwarf juggler. By decree of Tiberius Caesar, may the gods always smile upon him, the killers were to be flayed alive and their hides publicly displayed for three days before the Temple of Hercules the Victor as an act of propitiation to that god of athletes for the foul murder of one of his most illustrious mortal adherents.

"I'm sure you agree, tribune," he said.

For the last few minutes I'd paid no attention to his endless cackle. "Sorry, my man. I was looking at this little chariot. You were saying?"

"I said, sir, that the dwarf Gracchus is said to be from Neapolis and we shouldn't permit foreigners like him in the city. Them Neapolitans are swarthy, unprincipled thugs. Whoever said that Neapolis is nothing more than Africa's northernmost port was absolutely right, sir. And may the gods protect us from them Sicilians, too."

He wagged his head in doleful resignation, reflecting upon the worthlessness of our southern neighbors. I thought of telling him that I was a Sicilian myself, just to see him waffle and squirm, but I'd wearied of his prattle.

The tacky bust of Vitalis I rejected, but I was taken by the little chariot I'd been looking at. Made of wood and metal, it was about four inches high and carefully detailed right down to the design on the axle bosses. Now, that showed craftsmanship.

Noting my interest, Scaurus waggled his head in admiration. "Ah, sir, I see that you're a gentleman of taste, indeed, sir, yes," he oozed. "Now, sir, that very piece you're holding is an exact replica of the chariot Vitalis Hesper drove when he won his five hundredth four-horse race. Right here in the Circus Maximus it was, sir, and Caesar himself, all glory to his name, wept like a child and embraced him publicly while the entire senatorial and equestrian sections arose as one man and removed their cloaks, waving them like banners in tribute to Vitalis."

I suppressed a knightly yawn. "And tell me, Scaurus, were you present on this great occasion?"

"Ah, sir, no. I wasn't, sir. I was here minding the shop."

Next he'll tell me that he heard all about it from his wife's cousin.

"But my wife's cousin was there, sir, and he told us all about it," said Scaurus.

By now I'd had my fill of his garrulous drivel and I interrupted as he embarked on a detailed description of Caesar's tearful embrace of the charioteer.

"I'll take this chariot, my man," I said. "How much?"

"Now then, sir, an excellent choice, tribune. Yes. Now, these here chariots—they're made by a former charioteer of the Blues, old Nilus, lost his leg in an eight chariot pile-up about twenty years ago, did old Nilus, yes, sir. His brother runs the wine shop three stalls from here—toward the starting gate end of the circus, you understand—Nilus, he works there on race days. Has a wooden leg, sir, you see…"

"How much?"

"Well, sir, the price of these little beauties is five sesterces."

I stared at him in silence.

"But, for a fine gentleman like yourself, tribune, four."

A fine gentleman like myself. Didn't Bato's friend, the

chestnut seller, call me that last week? Must be a stock-in-trade marketing ploy with the city's vendors.

"Two," I said.

We settled on three *sesterces* after much hand-wringing by Scaurus and imploring of the gods to witness that he was losing money on the sale. If the immortals heard his plea, they gave no sign.

I had no wish to carry the little chariot the rest of the day and told the shop-keeper that I'd pick it up later in the afternoon or the following day…or send a servant for it. I gave him my name, Julius Viator Anthus.

He followed me as I was leaving. "Now then, sir, the bust of Vitalis Hesper. Yes, sir, these here busts are priced at six *sesterces*, but just special for you, tribune…"

"No, I think not," I said. "Gifted artist that the sculptor is, he hasn't quite captured the soaring spirit of the late charioteer."

On the street I retraced my steps to the north end of the Circus. During his lurid account of the coming executions, the shop-keeper had mentioned the Temple of Hercules the Victor. I wanted to see it.

Appropriately, the temple of the god of strength and patron god of athletes is located only a few hundred yards north of the Circus Maximus, in the Forum Boarium, the site of a livestock market several centuries ago. There's another forum, the Holitorium, close by—a vegetable and fruit market and popular gathering place. In recent years, many of the market stalls have been squeezed out by the erection of temples. Now, I'm as pious as the next man, but it seems to me the gods are more than adequately honored by the number of temples in the city. There's more than a dozen dedicated to Hercules alone.

The paramount temple is that of Jupiter Best and Greatest on the Capitoline Hill, dedicated to him, his wife and sister, Juno; and his daughter, Minerva, goddess of wisdom. Minerva, now—she had a most interesting birth, emerging from her father's head, armed with a sword and spear. The ways of the gods are mysterious indeed, but it is not for we mortals to try to comprehend them.

I've mentioned that I'm as pious as the next man, though I'm not exactly a religious zealot, but when I stood before the Temple of Hercules I felt humble…was aware of my own mortality and unimportance. The temple is a rotunda, and I counted twelve pillars in its colonnade. It's one of the city's most ancient sanctuaries, the original said to have been erected by King Evander, son of Mercury, a thousand years ago…long before Romulus built Rome. The Hercules cult is one of the oldest. Looking at the temple, I remembered my old *magister* saying that Hercules was fathered by Jupiter of a mortal woman. And when he was just minutes out of his mother's womb, he strangled to death two huge snakes sent by the goddess Juno to kill her husband's mortal son. I'd say that act alone foretold his future divinity.

I stood near the low broad steps which lead to the circular portico surrounding the temple, and as I admired the snow-white fluted columns, I became aware of someone watching me from the portico. It was an *aedituus*, one of the temple sacristans. The temples of the premier gods have an attendant day and night.

Moving toward me, he stopped at the top of the steps, about fifteen feet away. He was a young man, stout, with a round, pink face beneath his shaven head. Our eyes met and I bowed courteously.

"You can't come in, you know," he called out in a high, cheery voice. "The temple is closed to visitors today. Tomorrow, too."

Again I inclined my head and turned to leave.

"Wait!" he cried. "Don't go away." He beckoned me with his index finger. I ascended the steps and stood before him, mildly perplexed at his summons.

"Look here, seeing that there's only you, I'll let you in.

The god won't mind. Actually, the divine Hercules was a rather gregarious chap when he was mortal, and I think he still enjoys having people around. On closing days I'm sure he's bored with only an attendant to keep him company," he said happily.

I followed him uncertainly into the central chamber which was illuminated by a dozen tall windows set high into the base of the cupola. To the left of the chamber stood a huge statue of the god, clad in a lion skin and bearing a stout club on his right shoulder. Hercules' bearded face wore a quiet, thoughtful expression and his head was capped with the head and jaws of a lion.

As I stood before his statue, I reflected with reverential awe that, when a mortal, Hercules had bedded each of the fifty daughters of King Thespius. And all on the same night. So it is said.

The sacristan, clearing his throat loudly, interrupted my contemplation. "You do wish to offer a *libamentum* to the god, of course?" he said.

"Oh. Oh, yes, indeed," I said, realizing that I was expected to pour a libation to Hercules. My problem was that I'd never before honored a god in his temple. My liturgical experience was limited to the rites attending the household gods of the house of Macro and of my first master, the grain merchant. A temple such as this was a far cry from a domestic *lararium*.

The affable sacristan sensed my consternation, for he led me gently by the elbow to an altar on the other side of the chamber. He gestured casually toward a wooden bowl on the altar. "Should you wish to make a votive offering to the temple fund..." he suggested as he poured wine into a silver cup.

How much? I wondered. Not an hour ago I was acting lordly with a shop-keeper but now I felt like an untutored provincial rustic. Taking out my purse, I mused that a cup of good vintage would cost a *sestertius*...perhaps I should double that? No. Seemed rather paltry.

I put a *denarius* in the bowl as the sacristan watched. Smiling with approval he gave me the cup.

"A generous *donatio*. It will please Hercules. Now I'll invoke the god and when I give you the sign, pour half of the wine into this basin," he said, indicating a pottery bowl on the altar. "When the invocation is done, drink what remains and place the cup on the altar."

I nodded, trying to appear more composed than I felt.

Now his cheery voice became sonorous as he began the invocation. "O great Hercules, son of Jupiter, husband of slender-ankled Hebe, divine Hercules whose mortal body was consumed by the power of Vulcan, leaving only the immortal aspect of Jupiter which then ascended to the place of the gods in a chariot drawn by four horses…O Hercules, god of strength, be pleased to accept an offering from this mortal petitioner…"

Here he nodded to me and I carefully poured half the wine into the basin.

"…and if it is your will, invest him with virtuous strength of purpose, taking the direct route from the gate of entry straight to the center of his quest."

Again the sacristan's nod, at which I drank the remainder of the wine and placed the cup on the altar as instructed.

"Well now, that's that," he said, back to his happy mode of speech. "I say, I don't suppose you have time for a game of checkers? It's rather boring here on closing days. I was quite pleased to see you stop by."

Intrigued as I was by this bubbly attendant, I declined his invitation with thanks, pleading other matters to see to. As he accompanied me to the portico, I asked him about his reference to the "gate of entry" and such, used in his invocation.

"Oh," he replied breezily, "it's just a way of saying don't shilly-shally around…Hercules always tackled his labors head on, you know…sized up the situation and got on with the job. Just think of any problem you have as a city to be taken, its wall to be breached. Once inside the gate, you should proceed immediately to that place where you believe the solution or starting point lies. No meandering about, no hesitation. That sort of thing, y'know."

I said goodbye, then as an afterthought asked why the temple was closed on some days.

"Oh, my dear fellow, absolutely no reason whatsoever," he answered. "It's merely policy."

As I departed, a man, woman and two small children were standing nearby, gaping at the temple. I heard the sacristan call out to them that the temple was closed. After I'd walked a dozen yards, I glanced back and saw the family following him inside. Smiling, I wondered if the next invocation of the god would necessitate four cups of wine or if just one for the *paterfamilias* would suffice.

The invocation! The city gate…the chief centurion… the knight!

People on the street stared as I smashed my fist into my hip and cried out, "The center of his quest!"

XXIII

The sub-prefect of the Thirteenth urban district police department sighed gustily and squirmed his ample frame into a more comfortable position in his chair. Leaning his elbows on the desk, he stared coldly at the slouching man who stood before him. He picked up a tablet from the desk, studied it briefly and laid it down again.

"Damn me, *decurio*," he said, "the Aventine isn't one of Rome's more desirable neighborhoods, is it? If anything, it's one of the worst. Its crime rate is without peer, rejoicing in the highest number of murders per capita in the city. Not to mention the excellent record of the district's thieves, rapists, arsonists, wife and child beaters, unregistered prostitutes and thugs in general."

The decurion shrugged indifferently and absently scratched his large abdomen.

"You appear bored by my remarks, *decurio*," the sub-prefect said in a low, even tone. "How long have you held your present rank?"

"Umm, six years."

"Six years WHAT?"

Another shrug. "Well, six years."

"Tell me," the officer asked softly, "do you ever call your officers 'sir' or as a Roman freeman do you consider such courtesy to be self-demeaning?"

"Uh, yessir."

"So then, how long have you been a decurion?"

"Six years. Sir."

"And how long have you been in the Urban Cohorts?"

"Fourteen years, sir."

"Six years to go for pension, then?"

"Yes, sir."

"You'll probably never get it. On the basis of your dirty tunic, unwaxed boots and belt, scruffy hair and lousy posture, I'm thinking of demoting you. And the next step will be release from service as unsuitable. Is that understood?"

The decurion stood at attention, sucking in his paunch. "Yes, sir," he replied shakily.

"Very well. Now, I have here a report from my adjutant's office," the officer said, pointing at the tablet on the desk. "It was prepared by yourself, Decurion Linus Boter of the Third Urban Cohort, Thirteenth Urban District. It informs me that there was a murder in the district. Is that right?"

"Yes, sir."

"It tells me that a man was found dead last night in his fourth floor room of an *insula* close by the Lavernalian Gate. Strangled, apparently. Interesting. However, the report fails to tell me his name, marital status, occupation, age, how he was strangled or what the neighbors might have said."

"Well, he was just an old bum who lived alone," the decurion stammered. "I didn't think it mattered. Sir."

The sub-prefect arose slowly, deliberately from his chair and looked upon the white-faced decurion from his six foot height. "Ah, I see. You didn't think it mattered. Let me tell you something. The prefect Sutorius Macro has sent me to this wretched district to shape up its slovenly police department, and after meeting you, I can see why. So I'll start by advising you that you have neither the brains nor wit to assess what does or doesn't matter. From now on you'll act on the presumption that *everything* matters, regardless of how insignificant it might appear to you. Got that?"

"Yes, sir."

"You'll make out a proper report on the murder, including all you can learn about the victim. Talk to the landlord, the neighbors, his friends, everyone. Bust your ass on it because if you don't, I'll bust it for you. And pass my sentiments along to your chums. From now on you'll all earn your salary or get out. You no longer have a sinecure; you have a job. If you can't do it, there's plenty who can."

"Yessir," the decurion gasped.

"Find out who killed this old bum, as you call him...and quickly," the officer snapped. "Let the thugs in this district know that their holiday is over!"

"I'll do my best, sir."

"Yes, indeed you will, *decurio*. Because as of this minute you're on probation. Now clear out!"

His gut still sucked in, the decurion saluted and turned away.

"Before you leave, however, may I inquire if you know who the murdered man was?"

"Ignatius Carbo, sir. An old one-armed fellow."

XXIV

"Anthus," I asked myself, "are you guilty of unwarranted assumption? Have you taken something for granted?"

As I walked away from the Temple of Hercules the Victor, the words of the friendly young sacristan were fixed in my mind. "Once inside the gate...proceed immediately...no meandering, no hesitation." And that's exactly the way the knight would have acted, from all I've heard about him. No "shilly-shallying" by the likes of him.

I was certain that the knight had killed Vitalis—everything pointed to it—especially Bato's testimony that the knight had been inside the brothel at the time of the murder. And there had *not* been two men who fled the house, as Jucunda and Dorcas had said. No argument; the knight did it.

But—and this is where I'd been swept along on the tide of my own self-confidence—I didn't truly *know* that the knight was the agent of Sejanus. I'd assumed such, chiefly because of the old senator's letter to Tiro which predicted that Sejanus would soon arrange the death of the charioteer.

The circumstances suggested that the senator was probably right, but the thought came to me that probability was not fact. And when I make my report to Macro on his return from Capreae, it'll be based on fact, not supposition.

Yes, I'm sure that the knight, after parting company from his escort, Priscus, would have proceeded directly to the person who'd summoned him to Rome…so I must follow that same route, to the best of my ability. I knew his starting place and the direction he'd gone. With luck and common sense, I thought that I could find the "center of his quest."

But it was the eighth hour by that time, approaching mid-afternoon; not enough time for me to follow the knight's path and be home before darkness fell. I decided to do it first thing in the morning. There was time, however, for me to call upon Jucunda and be home by sunset, if I moved swiftly. And swiftly I did, following the Tuscan Road back to the forum, turning left at the Temple of Castor and Pollux and heading north to Silversmith's Rise, the avenue by which I'd entered the forum earlier in the day.

Soon I was on the Flaminian Way, passing through the Fontinalis Gate, one of the original gates of the old city wall which they say dates back five hundred years. Rome has expanded in every direction since then…Jucunda's brothel is about a mile north of the wall and still well within the city limits.

Weaving my way through the crowded street, in less

than half an hour I arrived at the narrow lane which leads to Bato's pottery shop, Apio's *thermopolium* and the House of Jucunda. The chestnut vendor, Ignatius Carbo, wasn't at his corner location. Maybe he'd be there later. I hoped so. I wanted to chat with him again about his friend, the chief centurion, and the knight.

I was about to use the satyr's head knocker on the brothel door, then changed my mind. First I'd look in on Bato and see how the cheerful potter was. I crossed the lane and entered his shop. He wasn't in the front, so I called out, presuming he was in the rear workplace. He appeared in the doorway, answering my grin with a cold stare.

"How are you, Bato?" I asked, wondering at his dour look.

"Are you interested in pottery?" he replied, still unsmiling. "Or," he paused meaningfully, "is it information you want?"

Perplexed at this cold reception, I asked what he meant.

"Perhaps you've come to assess the estate to determine the size of your reward!" he hissed. He limped out of the doorway and stood before me, his eyes puffy and bloodshot.

"Bato, what is it?" I asked in confusion.

"I believe that an informer's reward is one quarter the value of a convicted criminal's estate," he said. "You should do well out of Jucunda's property!"

"Informer!" I shouted. "Bato, what's this all about? An informer? Me?"

"You, Anthus! A *delator majestatis*. Everything points to you as the one who accused Jucunda of treason. *Falsely* accused her!"

"I'm *not* an informer! Now tell me what's happened! I've come to see Jucunda. I stopped here first to say hello to you."

The potter stared at me intensely, tears running down his face. In a quieter voice he said, "If it wasn't you, then who did such a thing?"

"Bato, I don't know what you're talking about!" I was shouting again in frustration. "What's this about Jucunda?" He stepped back as I reached out to touch his arm.

"When you came here not many days ago I liked you and trusted you. I even commended you to Jucunda when I'd known you only a few hours." Bato wiped at his tears with the back of his hand, leaving a smear of brown clay on his cheek. "You were in her house for a couple of days, talking with her girls, asking questions, winning their confidence with money. Yes, I know about that. The girls told me. And, when you disappeared, Jucunda was arrested and also Dorcas and Emmachia. Charged under the *maiestis*, they were! Soldiers came late yesterday afternoon and took the three of them away. We didn't even know what they were accused of, not until today."

"Soldiers?" I asked. When a magistrate acts against a person, it's the Urban Cohorts who execute his orders.

"The emperor's men it was who came," Bato said. He meant the Praetorian Guard. Whose commander is Aelius Sejanus.

Bato began to sob. "As if Jucunda and those girls could commit an act of treason," he gulped.

Horrified, I seized him tightly by both arms. This time he didn't shake me off. "Bato, where are they? What's happened?"

"They were executed this morning," he croaked. "Hanged and dragged with hooks to the river."

Jucunda, little Dorcas and the bride-to-be, Emmachia...they'd been flung into the Tiber, the final ignominy for executed criminals.

It was now I who cried. Later, I recalled Bato holding me in his arms and patting my shoulder as though I were a child. Then he led me into his back room and gave me wine.

Sodden with misery, I sat quietly for some time, forcing myself to think logically. It was impossible that the deaths of the three women had anything to do with my investigation. I'd talked to nobody about it...not even to Macro. My conversation with the informer, Marcus Soter, hadn't betrayed my interest in the brothel. There was nobody who knew that I was in the employ of Macro and acting on his behalf in the murder investigation. Not true. I'd told the black steward, Tiro. But I trusted him as fully as he did me, a fact he'd demonstrated by giving me the letter written by his late master.

"I believe you, Anthus," Bato said. "But others believe that you were the informer. Consider the situation and you'll understand why. Someone must have set the magistrate upon the women, and it happened as soon as you'd left after spending a couple of days in their house."

"It puts me in a bad light," I agreed, "but I didn't inform on them."

I came close to telling him what my true position was and why I'd sought access to Jucunda's house. Prudence prevailed, and I said nothing.

"Bato, you told me that on the night of Vitalis Hesper's murder a cloaked man visited the house, and that you suspected him of being the killer."

Frowning, he scratched his head. "Yes. I remember. But what..."

"And that Jucunda had told the police that two men had fled the house. Yet, you were a witness and said that there were not two men."

"Yes," he said cautiously.

"And now two men have been arrested and convicted for the killing. Did you know?"

"I know," he moaned, eyes moist again. "The herald announced it today, down at the corner of the Flaminian Way." His voice broke. "And then he announced the execution of Jucunda and her girls."

The realization came to me that the herald in the forum had made the same announcement but I'd not stayed to listen after he'd told of the conviction of the charioteer's killers.

"We both know that the condemned men didn't kill Vitalis and that the cloaked man probably did," I said.

Again, a cautious acknowledgment from Bato.

"And Jucunda, Dorcas and Emmachia probably knew that the cloaked man was the murderer, although they didn't know his identity."

He pondered this, trying to follow my reasoning. "Are you saying that the cloaked man had the women arrested?"

"You knew her better than I did, Bato. Why did Jucunda lie, she and Dorcas, about seeing two men run off? I think it was because she was afraid to tell the truth. I think she was threatened by the killer."

"But she *didn't* tell the truth to the police," he protested. "So if the women were arrested because of the cloaked man, what reason did he have? He hadn't been betrayed by them!"

"Well, we don't know that for sure. She wouldn't be likely to tell anyone what she'd done. But, Bato, doesn't the arrest and conviction of two innocent men make you wonder? And add to that the deaths of the three women, the only witnesses to the cloaked man's presence in the house. What does it tell you?"

The potter knitted his brows but his honest, pedestrian mind, weighted with sorrow, wasn't able to sort the events into a meaningful pattern. "I'm sure the cloaked man would have talked to Jucunda. But how would the two girls have been involved?"

"The charioteer was killed in Dorcas' room," I said. "And Emmachia, about to be married, wasn't permitted by Jucunda to entertain the men. Her job was door porter and helping in the kitchen. It was Emmachia who opened the door to the cloaked man. She and Dorcas were the only girls who actually *saw* him, *spoke* to him. So, with two men about to be executed for the murder, the matter will be soon forgotten by the populace. And with the three women dead, there's no witnesses to give concern to the real killer."

"Even though he'd frightened them into lying, the killer arranged for them to be arrested and executed... innocent women who'd done no crime?" Bato's voice trembled. "Why?"

I didn't reply, but I knew the answer. The dead carry no tales.

I went into the front of the shop, Bato following. We stood together at the doorway, looking across the lane at the House of Jucunda. Until a couple of days ago, a happy establishment of well-treated young women, loyal to their protective, benevolent mistress. But now a shattered remnant of grieving, confused women unable to comprehend the horror that had enveloped them.

"I'll leave now, Bato. Will you tell the girls that it wasn't me who informed? Please?"

He nodded. "I'll tell them."

"I hoped to see your old friend Ignatius today, but he wasn't on his corner when I went by. I wanted to find out where his army comrade, the chief centurion, lives. Now that he's retired and eligible to enter the knightly order, he may have need of my services."

Carbo hadn't been at his location for a couple of days, Bato told me. But that wasn't unusual, in view of his poor health. He told me where Carbo lived, giving an address in the Thirteenth City district, the Aventine, south of the Circus Maximus.

When I returned home, I told Petronia I wasn't feeling well and didn't wish to be disturbed by anyone. I laid on my bed thinking of Jucunda, Dorcas and Emmachia...of Senator Valerius Aviola and his steward Tiro...of Vitalis Hesper...of the Praetorian Prefect, Aelius Sejanus and of the knight, the man in the cloak.

It was dark when Petronia brought me a tray of food. I

hadn't eaten since breakfast but I wasn't hungry. To please her, I nibbled at a piece of bread before she left. After a night of fretful dreaming I was awakened by Giton, the night watchman. He glanced at the tray and I told him that I'd had an upset stomach and couldn't eat.

• • •

Cold, gray mist shrouded the city when I set out soon after daybreak the next morning. I headed north toward the Viminal Gate, a half hour walk distant. The arches of the Marcian aqueduct were silhouetted in the fog a couple of hundred feet to my right.

There were two things I intended to do. I wished to call upon Ignatius Carbo. Trying not to arouse suspicion in him, I'd see if I could learn more about his former legion officer talking to him, the night of the murder. Also, Carbo might be able to tell me where I could find the retired chief centurion, Priscus.

But first I'd go to the Viminal Gate where the knight had passed through the city wall. Then I'd follow his route to see if I could find any obvious indication of his journey's end.

By the time I arrived at the gate, the mist was fast dissipating, clinging only to occasional patches of low lying ground. A pale sun now shone through the weak overcast. Looking through the gate, I could just make out the wall of the Praetorian Guards' camp about a quarter of a mile to the west on the Old Tibertine Way.

The Viminal Road leads westward into the city, meeting the north-south Vicus Longus about half a mile further along. But only a few hundred feet from the gate, the Vicus Patricius branches off to the left, in a southwesterly direction. Ignatius Carbo had said, I recalled, that the chief centurion had observed the knight walking his horse into the Vicus Patricius.

After I'd proceeded a few minutes into the Vicus Patricius, I envied the knight his horse. Although a main thoroughfare, the street was a quagmire of mud, garbage and assorted debris discarded by the householders and shop-keepers on each side of the road. Need I mention again that Romans have built roads from Spain to Syria but can't keep their own city streets orderly?

Walking at a leisurely pace, I was constantly dodging to avoid collision with assorted loads carried by porters and contractors' wagons piled high with lumber and stone. The one exception to the rule that vehicles may only use the streets at night is that contractors employed on public buildings are permitted to transport their materials during daylight hours.

One minute I was darting nimbly out of the path of an ornate, curtained litter carried shoulder height by eight huge bearers, probably Ligurians; the next, I was pressing against the wall of a baker's shop to make way for a detachment of guardsmen whose hob-nailed boots I didn't need crunching into my sandals.

I kept one eye peeled for traffic hazards, while the other watched the buildings that lined the route—not that I expected the knight to have been concerned with a neighborhood consisting mostly of shabby shops and low class residences jammed in cheek by jowl. A neat phrase that, "cheek by jowl."

When I'd walked about a mile, I arrived where the Vicus Patricius intersects with the Vicus Longus. I remained on the former street and a thousand feet later came to the Sacred Way. My route had brought me into the heart of the city.

Which way should I go now? Turning right, onto the Sacred Way, would take me into the forum, with its law courts and temples. It was possible that the knight had business in the forum, but he'd traveled a long way by horseback and would have been tired and dust covered, in need of bathing before keeping his appointment, if I'm any judge of the noble and knightly classes. Which, of course, I am. Another thing—horses aren't permitted in the forum area except during ceremonial occasions. The knight was hardly likely to have secured his steed's reins to a handy statue of some ancient consul and entered the forum on foot.

Had he turned left onto the Sacred Way, it would have led him southeast toward the Tuscolana Way, which leads out of the city. Not likely.

So, presuming he'd remained on the Vicus Patricius, I passed the intersection. A thousand feet further on, the street ended at a cross road which fronted a high wall.

I had no need to proceed further. I was sure that I'd arrived at the knight's destination.

And I knew at that moment that in a few more days I had no choice but to inform Macro that Vitalis Hesper had been murdered by order of Lucius Aelius Sejanus, Prefect…and that the deed had been carried out by a knight of Rome.

• • •

For several minutes I stood gazing at the wall on the far side of the street and the upper stories of the building behind it. Then I turned away, and walked south toward the Aventine district where the chestnut vendor lived. His address was a mile or so distant and the most expedient route took me along the east side of the Circus Maximus. As it was my intention to return directly to the Macro household when I'd finished my visit with Carbo, it seemed a good opportunity to pick up the little chariot I'd purchased yesterday.

At the emporium of the unctuous Scaurus I entered with a swagger and acknowledged his greeting with my most affected accent. He "sirred" and "tribuned" me in his oily fashion and tried again to sell me one of his sleazy busts, calling on the gods to bear witness that he was losing money at such prices, and deploring his fate as a poor shopkeeper who, were he in his right senses, would pursue some other calling wherein he might improve his lot.

To assist him in fending off bankruptcy, I purchased a cloth drawstring bag in which to carry the little chariot. For this I paid two *sesterces*, a third of the price stated by Scaurus who again invoked the gods to pity his wretched state.

The little bag would make a nice present for Petronia.

Fifteen minutes later I stood in the street where Ignatius Carbo lived. The address given me by Bato was a six story *insula* that had known better days. Even the poor quarters in which Marcus Soter lived were an improvement on this. As in Soter's building, the stairwell walls were filthy and covered with crude *graffiti*, and the air was foul with the musk of stale cooking and urine. A dried puddle of fly encrusted vomit adorned the third floor landing.

I only knew that Carbo lived on the fourth floor, and when I got there I could see in the gloom that I had eight doors to try. At my knock, the first door on the right was opened by an old, toothless woman who peered at me sullenly. When asked if she could tell me which room was Carbo's, she muttered to herself and closed the door in my face. There was no response at the next two doors but the fourth was opened by a ragged boy. Before he could answer my question a sour-faced woman appeared, peevishly demanding to know my business. When I told her, she snarled, "I've already told them that I don't know nothing, so just leave us alone."

Apparently confusing me with someone else she nattered on about honest citizens being harassed. Eventually I prevailed upon her to direct me to Carbo's door. Last one on the left. As I walked away she hollered, "I don't know nothing!" and slammed the door.

Carbo's door was ajar an inch and inside I heard voices.

He was at home but seemed to have company. I had wanted to talk with him privately. Well, I could arrange to meet with him later, I thought.

The conversation behind the door stopped when I knocked. The door was opened, not by Carbo but by a pock-marked, paunchy individual wearing the uniform of the Urban Cohorts.

"And just who might you be?" he snarled, folding his arms over his chest. "And what's your business here, eh?"

Something wrong here, I thought. What are the police doing in Carbo's room? "I'm looking for Ignatius Carbo," I said cautiously. "Is he home?"

"I asked who you are, didn't I?"

A second policeman materialized, a tall, rangy brute. "Answer the decurion," he barked, "or I'll bend your face."

"Anthus," I said. Did my voice shake a little? I've been beaten by Greek schoolmasters, raged at by Macro and castigated by his wife and physically attacked by drunken cooks. But this was my first encounter with genuine bully boys, and ones who wore the mantle of civic authority. They could pulp me and then swear that I'd assaulted them resisting arrest.

"Anthus," sneered the paunchy one. "Is that your only name, then?"

"Yes." This was no time to play the fine gentleman.

"Slave, are you?" the taller one gibed.

"Yes."

"Who's your master, slave?" the paunch demanded.

"I'm the household steward and scribe of the prefect Quintus Sutorius Macro," I replied respectfully, hoping this would effect a less hostile attitude from them. I was wrong.

"Are you now?" jeered the fat one. "And I'm the governor of Africa." He grinned with rotting teeth at his colleague. "Ain't that right, hey Didius?" Before that worthy could reply, the decurion turned to me, seized my upper arm and yanked me into the room, then slammed the door shut.

"Look, slave bastard, you have two seconds to tell us what you're doing here."

"I've come to see Ignatius Carbo. A woman down the hall told me this was his room." My heart was pounding. "It is, isn't it?"

"I reckon you bloody well know it is, slave Anthus. Not your first visit either, is it? Why'd you come back, hey? To see if you'd overlooked any loot the first time?"

"They always come back to the scene of the crime," the tall one observed sagely.

"I've never been here before," I protested. "Carbo will tell you that. Where is he?"

"You know where he is, slave," the decurion said. "If he had a coin to pay the ferryman, he's looking around for his niche in the underworld. If not, I guess he's floating around in limbo, isn't he?"

Carbo dead? And why did he say that I knew about it? His next question answered that.

"What did you strangle him with, slave?"

I gaped at him, confused and frightened. My ears rang and silver sparks exploded as the tall one's fist smashed into the left side of my face.

"Answer the decurion!"

"I didn't strangle him!" I gasped through the pain. The sudden punch had triggered anger in me, replacing my fear. "I haven't seen him for several days. And this is the first time I've been here!"

"Don't shout at the decurion." This time his fist drove into the right side of my face and I was knocked sideways onto a narrow cot.

They didn't expect that I'd fight back and both stood grinning sadistically as I hauled myself from the cot. The drawstring of my bag was in my right hand and I swung the bag with full force into the tall one's leering face. It caught him on the bridge of his large nose with an audible thunk and crack. In times of extreme stress we tend to have frivolous thoughts and my immediate reaction to the sound of the impact was "Now I've broken my little chariot."

I hadn't expected my impromptu weapon would do much damage but, to my surprise, the tall policeman staggered backward and dropped to his knees, blood streaming from his nose. He felt it gingerly and, still kneeling, whispered thickly, "I thig by dode id broken."

When I'd swung at his assistant, the decurion had yanked out his short sword and its point was pricking my rib cage. He snatched the bag from me.

"You're under arrest, slave. For murdering Ignatius Carbo, assaulting a member of the Urban Cohorts, break and entry and resisting arrest," he snarled.

"I'm not resisting arrest," I said foolishly.

"Open your mouth one more time and you're dead."

I opened my mouth, then shut it again judiciously.

"Get on your feet, Didius. You lead the way back to the precinct office. Our friend, slave Anthus here, will follow and I'll be right behind him, egging him on with the point of my sword."

"By dode id bleedig," Didius bubbled.

"So it is. But don't worry, the citizens will take you for some kind of hero. Let's go. You'll get your reward later listening to slave Anthus gabbling like a chicken in the torture room."

The bloodied and snuffling Didius leading, we walked for six or seven minutes along the crowded street, the decurion's sword pricking into the small of my back. People stood aside as we approached, but their stares were more for the blood-smeared policeman than for me. A miscreant being hustled along the street isn't an unusual sight.

I was pushed into a tiny cell, unlit save for a sliver of light from a narrow slit near the top of the door. When my eyes adapted to the darkness, I saw that the cell was about four feet wide and six deep. The only furnishing was a wooden bucket.

My anger had turned to apprehension. Apprehension be damned. I was on the borderline of sheer terror. And the decurion had mentioned torture. The judicial torture of slaves is routine—on almost any pretext.

Disorganized thoughts raced through my mind as I stood numbly in the tiny cell, looking up at the crack of light. Petronia. Would I see her ever again? My old master, the grain merchant; the black man, Tiro; Marcus Soter's small child kicking me, the beautiful statue in the senator's courtyard. I thought of the small boy-slave Rufinus, my mother, King Tincommius, the cheerful attendant in the Temple of Hercules…of the Greek magister who welted my backside, the horse races which Macro had enabled me to see. I thought of Bato the potter and of Madame Jucunda and her girls.

Jucunda, Dorcas, Emmachia, executed for crimes they'd never committed, just as the two wrongfully condemned killers of Vitalis Hesper were about to be. Was I to join them, crucified for a murder of which I was innocent? Petronia won't get her drawstring bag now. I wonder what she's making for supper tonight? She has such beautiful brown eyes. My Petronia, my little *sucula*…

I squinted in the sudden light as the decurion snapped, "Out you come, slave. The sub-prefect's waiting to have a chat with you."

A policeman on either side gripping my upper arms, I was marched behind the decurion up a flight of stairs and halted outside a closed door. "Speak only when you're spoken to, slave," the decurion growled. "And call the officer 'sir.' Got that?"

He knocked once on the door, opened it and entered, followed by me and my escorts. The sub-prefect, a man about my own age, looked at us without expression, then said, "You two men leave." The escorts saluted and marched out.

"Hello, Anthus," the sub-prefect said genially in Greek. "Looking a little the worse for wear, aren't you?"

"My respects, sir," I bowed my head, answering in the same language. "It's always a pleasure to see the noble Aulus Caelius Ballista."

"Even under such unfavorable circumstances, eh? But we'll get to the bottom of that shortly." He turned to the decurion, saying in Latin, "Decurion, it's unbecoming for a member of the Urban Cohorts to gape with an open mouth. Close it."

"Now then, Anthus," the officer spoke in Greek again, "Decurion Linus Boter tells me that you're the murderer of Ignatius Carbo, which he's convinced you'll readily confirm after a spot of judicial torture. He also charges you with assaulting a member of the Urban Cohorts, resisting arrest, break and entry, theft...and damn me, if he doesn't suspect that you're an escaped slave. Tell me, Anthus, have you *really* fled the Macro household to seek fame and fortune in the teeming streets of Rome?"

Grinning as best I could through my bruised, aching face, I said, "No, sir. I'm still the steward of Sutorius Macro. Unless my mistress has sold me in the last couple of hours, which she's threatened to do from time to time."

"Yes," he smiled back, "we all know the lady Ennia."

I should explain that the officer before whom I'd been haled is a close friend of my master and was often a guest in the Macro household since his release from military service in Syria three or four years ago. The youngest son of a senatorial family, he holds the rank of knight but in time, if he inherits enough money, he'll be appointed a senator most likely. I don't approve of all of Macro's friends, but I've always liked Caelius Ballista.

"So tell me how you're mixed up in this."

I wasn't about to betray the details of my investigation,

but I gave him a credible account of my involvement with the dead chestnut vendor; its honesty was bent only a little by my not revealing why I'd wanted to see Carbo.

I told him I'd met Carbo through a mutual friend and I'd heard that the old fellow hadn't been seen at his place of business the past few days. Because I was in the city on household errands while Macro was away in Capreae, I'd called at Carbo's residence to see if he was ill. I gave a truthful description of my reception by the decurion and his assistant.

"But what theft am I accused of, sir?"

"Oh, that's the toy chariot," he replied, picking up the bag which was resting on his desk. He removed the remains of the chariot. Both wheels had broken off, the metal axle was badly bent and one side of the body was smashed.

"You see, Anthus, the decurion figures that if a hardened case such as yourself is carrying something around, you must have stolen it. A member in good standing of the Thieves Guild, are you, eh?"

He touched the bent axle. "I imagine this is the piece that broke that idiot's nose. You truly hammered him."

He turned to the decurion, speaking again in Latin. "Decurion, this man is the household steward of the prefect Sutorius Macro. He has been engaged this day carrying out duties on behalf of the prefect."

He paused, raising his eyebrows at the nonplused decurion. "You *have* heard of the prefect Sutorius Macro, I take it?"

"Yes, sir."

"Good, good. It's heartening to know that you keep abreast of things. Yes. Well, this man was considering pressing charges of false arrest, police brutality, public humiliation and the destruction of his personal property, namely this miniature chariot which your colleague caused to be broken beyond repair—Boter, I've already mentioned that it ill behooves members of the Urban Cohorts to let their lower jaws sag in public—however, I've been able to convince the prefect's household chief of staff that it would be unfair to discredit the entire Thirteenth district police division because of the stupidity of two of its members. Accordingly, he has most graciously consented to drop all charges but, reasonably enough, he wishes to be reimbursed for his broken property in the amount of two *denarii*."

Here, Ballista took two coins from his purse and handed them to me.

"A *denarius* each will be deducted from your salary and that of your colleague. You are dismissed, Boter."

The crestfallen decurion saluted and left the room. Ballista heaved out of his chair and settled his large frame on the edge of the desk. "I've got a lot of deadwood to cut out around here," he said. "Now you can see why Macro was given the job by the emperor. Poor old Calpurnius Piso's too old and tired for the job. So the Urban Cohorts have degenerated to the level of the two clowns you encountered today. Not that everyone's as bad as they are, but there's enough of them."

Looking at me directly, he asked, "Forgetting the charade we've just gone through, Anthus, do you have any idea at all why this Carbo fellow was murdered?"

I thought of the hooded man, the knight; I saw the faces of Jucunda, Dorcas and Emmachia. I heard Carbo's voice. "Gave me a gold piece, he did. Yes, sir, he was one of the men that helped the surgeon when my arm was taken off." And I had asked, "What is his name?" And Carbo had told me.

Then I thought of my *dominus*, Macro.

I returned Ballista's gaze. "No, sir," I lied. "I don't have any idea."

XXV

Macro returned last night just after sunset, in a grumpy mood after riding through steady drizzle for the last two days. I had a hot supper prepared for him and told his valet to take a jug of hot, unwatered wine to his chamber after he'd dined.

This morning, after a good sleep, he was his old bumptious self. The first daylight hour hadn't ended when he sent for me. In fact I was still eating breakfast while making a pretense of listening to our chef denouncing the vile merchant who'd foisted off low grade eggs at top price in our last order, proof further of the collective depravity of Rome's merchants.

"So, Anthus," Macro boomed, "still squandering my

money on your friends and driving me into bankruptcy?"

I thought fleetingly of telling him that I'd become more judicious in the disbursement of his coin, thinking of my donative to the Temple of Hercules the Victor.

"You'll be pleased when I give you an accounting of the expenses, sir," I said soothingly. I'd have said that even if I'd run riot with his money, however I felt justified in this instance. Of the two hundred *denarii* Macro had advanced me, I'd spent only forty-nine *sesterces*. So, what with the two *denarii* the sub-prefect Ballista had given me for "destruction of property," my net expenditure was a little over ten *denarii*, only one-twentieth of the funds.

"Yes, yes, Anthus, I'm sure," he said. "We'll go into all that later. I'm meeting with Caesar during the fourth hour this morning. Giving him a preliminary report on my trip to Capreae. Nice piece of country, that area around Neapolis. Mount Vesuvius is quite a sight. That's where that Spartacus fellow and his rebels holed up a hundred years ago. Took eight legions to take the bastard! Quite a man. Pannonian, I believe."

"Thracian, sir," I murmured.

"Thracian, then. If you say so. What was I talking about?"

"You mentioned the countryside there, sir."

"Yes. Very pretty. Excellent vineyards everywhere. One thing wrong with the place, though. Full of damned Greeks and Africans. Scurvy bunch."

"Well, sir, the Greeks did colonize that area more than six hundred years ago..."

"Yes, yes, Anthus. Damn your alien hide, let's have no history lessons. Bring me up to date on your investigation into whatshisname, Hastor's killing."

"Hesper, sir. Albino Vitalis Hesper, a charioteer of the Blue Stable..."

"Damn me, Anthus, I *know* he was a chariot driver...just get on with the story, eh?"

"I have a report for you, sir, but it's rather involved and will take some time. Observing that you're attending the imperial palace in less than two hours, may I suggest that I brief you later in the day or tomorrow? In the meantime, you may wish to advise Caesar that your staff have learned that a senior official compelled Senator Aviola to take his own life—and that the same person undoubtedly arranged the charioteer's murder."

He stared at me, lips pursed and head cocked in an attitude of doubt. "You're serious? You *really* think you know who was behind it?"

"I am, sir. And after I've given you the details, I'm sure that you'll agree." I didn't mention the senator's letter to his son. I'll save that for the right moment.

"Well, by Pollux, you *have* been working! Very well, Anthus, after the evening meal I'll send for you and we'll talk about it."

"While you were away, two men were arrested for the murder and are awaiting execution. As you told me before you left."

"Yes, yes. I heard in Capreae. Doesn't take long for such news to travel. Couple of runaway gladiators, were they?"

"A freedman and an escaped slave, sir," I said.

"Whatever. I left it with my deputy to select a couple of choice thugs. Plenty to choose from, eh? So now the populace is happy, Caesar's happy, everybody's happy except the two brigands, but I daresay they're both well deserving of execution, anyway."

He stood up. "Time I left for the palace. Tell that useless wretch Zosimus to bring my best cloak." He paused. "Oh, and send that young lad, Rufio, in. I'm told that he smashed all of our crockery while I was away."

"Rufinus, sir. He did break one small piece but it was an accident. I've already had a word with him."

"Yes. Well send him in anyway."

Concerned over Macro's order, I passed the word to Zosimus about the cloak and then, apprehensively, led little Rufinus to Macro's chamber door. I instructed him to knock gently, enter when called and be very, very polite and attentive. Looking at me with round, frightened eyes, he knocked and entered at Macro's bidding. I waited a few feet from the door and without being able to catch the words, could hear Macro's deep voice, pausing now and then as the child answered, I suppose. It wasn't fair and it wasn't like Macro to intimidate a small child. I willed myself to contain my anger as I waited for Rufinus to come out.

A moment later the door opened and Rufinus piped, "Thank you, master" in his thin treble. He gently closed the door and turned toward me as I went to him. Before I could speak he blurted happily, "Oh, look what *dominus* gave me! Isn't it beautiful? He bought it for me in a little shop in Neap…Neap…"

"Neapolis," I said.

"Yes. In Neapolis. He told me that I could play with it every day after my work is done."

The child hugged the little blue chariot to his chest, his eyes shining with joy. It was an exact copy of the chariot that I'd savaged on the big policeman's nose.

"And the master told me to be sure to show you the axle on my chariot, to let you see how straight it is," Rufinus said, holding up his treasure to me.

Now how in the name of Romulus did Macro learn about all *that* so quickly?

• • •

That evening I gave Macro a thorough briefing on everything I'd learned during the past two weeks. Well, *most* of everything I'd learned. His usual effusive manner set aside, he listened quietly and said little. And when I presented him with what I considered my crowning accomplishment—the copy of senator Aviola's letter to his son—he read it stony-faced, showing no reaction. An hour earlier I'd been bursting with confidence that Macro would be well pleased with my report. Now, I wasn't at all sure.

He stared absently at the letter on the table before him. I waited with some apprehension while he, presumably, reflected on my narrative.

"Very well, Anthus," he said at last, "the senator's letter is straightforward enough and it certainly implicates the Praetorian Prefect. There's absolutely no doubt in my mind that Sejanus saw to the charioteer's murder...but," he added after a pause, "we still don't know who actually killed Vitalis, do we? You can only say that it was an unidentified knight."

"Sir, he *was* a knight," I replied. "Everything that the prostitutes and the chestnut vendor told me points to it—his dress, bearing, manner of speech—and he wore the *annulus aureus*."

Macro raised his left hand and we both regarded the knight's gold ring that was on his little finger. "So he wore a gold ring," he said, "but that doesn't prove that he was a knight. The gold ring may be the privilege of the equestrian order, but I'd think that anybody who wanted one could acquire it without much trouble."

"Indeed, sir, and I also agree that the description of the man doesn't prove anything, either. But the old fellow, Carbo, was certain that the man had been one of his officers in Germany, a young tribune, and that clearly indicates a member of either the patrician or equestrian class."

"Yes, Anthus, if indeed this man had been an officer in his legion. What if Carbo was mistaken?"

"I'm convinced that he wasn't, sir. And he recalled their conversation in detail...about such things as the legion's emblem and the name of the legate in command. He was absolutely positive."

Macro considered this for a few moments, then sighed.

"Well then, that seems to be that. We can't put a name to the unknown murderer and probably never will...pity...otherwise, Anthus, you've done an excellent job."

I know his name, I said to myself. It's Pontius Pilate. But for your own sake, Macro, I can't tell you.

"As I told you earlier, sir, all of the people who talked to the knight on the evening of the murder are now dead. The women in the brothel—not that they'd have known his identity—and Ignatius Carbo. I went to see him, hoping I could glean more information, but..." I shrugged. "Well, sir, you know all about that. Nobody's left who can identify the killer. Most convenient, isn't it, sir?"

Macro grunted, then fell into another silence, his eyes fixed on mine. Then he said, "Anthus, I shall give the senator's letter to Caesar and advise him of your findings. Then we shall let him draw his own conclusions. I have no doubt that he'll consider that the Praetorian Prefect was the author of the charioteer's murder as well as Aviola's suicide. I'll tell Caesar that I believe the murder was done by an unidentified member of the equestrian order—or one passing himself off as such. And I'll tell him that I believe this on the basis of a thorough investigation carried out by a trusted member of my staff. Now, what have you to say to that?"

Flustered at this turn of events, I was about to respond with a flowery statement about the honor I felt at his faith in me and so on, but he preempted me. "And don't go on about how honored you feel, damn your alien hide. Instead, tell that boy Rufus to bring in a jug of wine. Not the plonk, the good stuff. Not that there's been any decent wine since the consulship of Plancus."

Good. My master was back to his old self again.

"Rufinus, sir. I'll tell him to bring the new Campanian red. It has a certain beguiling piquancy which blends furtively with..."

"Yes, yes, Quintipor—just get on with it, will you? And tell Rufio to bring two cups. We'll have a nightcap, you and I, and drink to the good work you've done in this affair. Then I'm off to bed. I have business with Caesar first thing in the morning, don't I?"

• • •

"Do you know what Sejanus had the gall to tell me when I asked why his troops had been picketed outside Aviola's house?"

"What, Caesar?"

"He said that Aviola had requested that his house be guarded!" Tiberius spluttered. "That Aviola, in his senility, feared assassins!"

"Never, Caesar!" Macro snorted. "The senator was an eccentric old bird, we all know that. But senile? No, he had his full wits about him. As for asking for a guard at his house—even if he had wanted such an unlikely thing—surely he'd have approached me and not the Praetorian Prefect. You well know the high regard in which he was held by the *vigiles* and *cohortes*."

"Exactly. I was sure that Sejanus lied when he told me such nonsense. And this," Tiberius stabbed his forefinger at the document that lay before him on the table, "proves that he lied."

"Also," Macro said, "the letter clearly suggests that the charioteer's death would follow soon after. We can be sure that whoever killed him was an agent of Sejanus."

Tiberius pondered this, his large hands clasped before him on the table. Seated across from him, Macro waited patiently, knowing that the emperor's silent moods could last for minutes.

Then Tiberius leaned forward and spoke in a low, conspiratorial manner. "Macro, you have no doubt whatsoever that the charioteer's murderer can't be identified?

That all those who saw him and talked to him are now dead?"

"No doubt, Caesar."

"And you believe that the deaths of the others—the prostitutes and the street vendor—were arranged by Sejanus?"

"Who else, Caesar? It stands to reason."

"Yes. Who else?" Tiberius murmured. Another brief silence, then again he leaned toward Macro.

"Sutorius Macro, what I am going to tell you is confidential. Swear to me as an equestrian and a prefect of Rome that you will honor my confidence."

Macro arose and held his clenched right hand to his breast. "I, Quintus Naevius Cordus Sutorius Macro, knight and Prefect of the City Watch swear by Jupiter, earth and sun, by all the gods and goddesses that I will be loyal to Tiberius Claudius Nero Caesar all my life in thought, word and deed."

Tiberius acknowledged this with a formal inclination of his head. "Be seated and hear me, then. I am convinced by the evidence you've shown me and by your report on the unknown murderer that Sejanus is guilty of both Aviola's and the charioteer's deaths. I also believe now that the death of my son Drusus may have been contrived by his wife Livilla and Sejanus. I shall investigate further into that matter in my own way.

"It's apparent now that I must get rid of Sejanus. The question is how and when? I realize that I've allowed him too much authority and through bribery and intimidation he's become a powerful figure. Powerful enough that if I were to impeach him now it would surely lead to an uprising and possibly civil war. Rome couldn't survive such a thing, in my opinion. The provincial legions would probably be divided in loyalty and in the resulting chaos the Germanic and eastern tribes would almost certainly seize their chance to attack our outposts, if not Rome itself."

Macro started to speak but the emperor stopped him.

"The Praetorian Guard is loyal to Sejanus. He's made sure of that by the privileges he's given them. He controls the city militarily and has much of the senate in thrall to him."

"Caesar," Macro interrupted again, "the City Watch and Urban Cohorts well outnumber the Praetorians. And I can rely on their loyalty. To be blunt about it, there's little love between my men and the guards."

"Perhaps one day we shall need them, but I hope not. I don't want Roman fighting Roman. There's been far too much of that in the past. I was no admirer of my step-father, Augustus—but I respect his memory for one thing. He began the reconsolidation of Rome when it had been broken by years of civil unrest and military intimidation, caused largely by such egomaniacs as Gaius Marius and Cornelius Sulla and others of their ilk. Yes, yes, Macro—I know that I'm digressing, but you take my point, I'm sure. What Augustus started, I must continue, if Rome is to survive. It's still a time when Rome must consolidate, not divide. So, Macro, I'll unseat Sejanus in my own way. Without violence. It'll take time, I realize, but I'll give him enough rope to hang himself...yes, it'll take time, a year or more, but it will happen."

"Observing that this is a privileged conversation, Caesar," Macro said, "I'll tell you that there's been unfavorable comment about the statues of Sejanus throughout the city. Their number is beginning to rival those of the gods. And every corner shop sells busts of the Praetorian Prefect. My own household steward found one in the servants' quarters. He confiscated it and informed the staff that the only busts permitted were those of Tiberius Caesar, the divine Julius, the divine Augustus and myself." Macro shrugged deprecatingly. "Since no such bust of myself exists, that leaves 'em a choice of three."

"What?" Tiberius cried in mock disbelief. "My world

is shattered! A Roman knight who hasn't commissioned a bust of himself?"

Macro grinned. "My steward hints in his cheeky fashion that I'm too parsimonious to pay for such work. Well, maybe one day…"

"Yes," Caesar said, his tone serious again. "One day. Most certainly when you are Praetorian Prefect."

"Caesar?" Macro said cautiously.

"When I have dealt with Sejanus, you will replace him. Have patience, Macro."

"I am honored, Caesar," Macro said, adding, "And I shall be patient."

"Another thing—you are sworn to secrecy in this matter but what about your man? The one who unearthed this information. Can he be trusted?"

"I vouch for him, Caesar. He is loyal."

Another thoughtful silence, then Tiberius said, "Very well, if you say so. The way I see it, there are only two ways to go—silence him forever or reward him. Therefore I'll give you fifty gold pieces for him. Tell him it's a gift from Caesar, who considers discretion to be a worthy trait."

"I shall, Caesar. I intend to reward him myself for his service."

Tiberius chuckled. "That story about your steward banishing the bust of Sejanus reminds me of another one. Sejanus recently had his statues consecrated in the temple of Mars and sent them to the four legions in Syria with instructions that they were to be placed among the standards in the legion shrines. All four legions returned the statues to him. The legate of the Twelfth Fulminata replied to him that his legionary and manipular standards shared their shrine with two statues and two only—those of the divine Julius Caesar who founded their legion and of the bull which is their emblem."

Taking his cue from Tiberius, Macro chuckled also.

"I've already sent a *donatio* of one month's pay for every

man in the Syrian forts," Tiberius continued. "They won't be told why they're receiving it but they'll know by it that Caesar is well aware of the Third Gallica, the Sixth Ferrata, the Tenth Fretensis and the Twelfth Fulminata."

"They will, Caesar," Macro agreed.

"And because your steward, in his small way, has done the same thing I reckon he deserves a reward also. So I'll give you five gold pieces for him. Don't tell him where it came from. Come up with a reason of your own."

Well now, thought Macro, the gods are indeed benevolent toward Anthus this day, damn his alien hide. Fifty-five hundred *sesterces*! He'll be able to treat his friends to hot sausages out of his own purse now without pushing me to the brink of poverty.

XXVI

Tiberius Caesar has left Rome and established his imperial court in Capreae. From the sound of it, he intends to stay a good while. Macro says that hundreds of artisans and laborers have been despatched to erect an imperial residence in addition to those already there. Administrative and household staff accompanied Caesar, also a cohort of Praetorians. He didn't take any of his family with him, though.

In the meantime, Sejanus is still as large as life and his position as emperor's chief of staff stronger than ever, with Caesar being absent.

Prior to his departure, Caesar hosted a gala dinner party for some three hundred guests—all "quality"; not an athlete or physician in the crowd. I was there myself, rubbing elbows with the gentry. Yes, I rather like that phrase "rubbing elbows." I must note it for my forthcoming textbook.

I was employed at the imperial dinner, actually, as a *triclinarium*, in charge of a section of the immense dining hall, ensuring that the dozen or so attendants assigned to me were doing their job properly. The preparation and serving of a dozen courses from eggs to apples for three hundred guests taxes the resources of even the imperial household and some of the wealthy houses were requested to loan staff for the event. So it was that I led a detachment consisting of our chef, Cerdo; Petronia, Zosimus and three of the junior slaves to "work" the emperor's farewell dinner.

I ensured that my Petronia was included because I knew she'd long savor the experience of working the palace. Years from now, she'll be telling our grandchildren about the time she cooked for Caesar. Did I mention that she and I are to be married? I'll tell you about it later as I don't want to lose the thread of my story.

Someone else was present that night—our mysterious knight, the focus of my recent investigation. He was, in fact, Caesar's guest of honor. But because I'd never seen him, I didn't know of his presence until the emperor called out his name.

Before the first course of eggs was served, and before some of the guests had imbibed too freely, Tiberius Caesar announced his imminent departure for Capreae. It wasn't really news to the assembly, observing that the emperor had made a formal statement to the senate a few days before. But the gathering gasped dutifully in dismay and gave loud cries of "No, Caesar!" and other such protestations of despair.

Gesturing for silence, Caesar continued. "Before departing, I have several honors and awards to bestow. Some of the recipients are present tonight, but others are not. I will speak firstly of those who aren't here."

His strong, rich voice, inherited through his Claudian descent, they say, carried to every corner of the immense dining hall as he announced the promotion of three legates to command legions in Spain, the Rhineland and Africa; two appointments to pontifex in the priesthoods of the temples of Mars and Ceres; and the elevation of several freemen to the equestrian order.

I was standing some thirty feet from Caesar and my attention quickened when he named one of those to be raised to the rank of knight. I noted that the emperor's eye caught that of one of the guests who was placed at the imperial table. The other man nodded his head almost imperceptibly in acknowledgment.

"For loyal service and exemplary leadership in the army of Rome, ten times decorated for bravery, Titus Serapio Priscus, son of Verecundus of the Quirine tribe, is invested in the rank of *equester* and is appointed as an assistant to the procurator of the Morning Games."

Interesting. I daresay that Priscus deserves his knighthood as much as anyone. But the glance that passed between the emperor and the other man suggested to me that the retired chief centurion had a friend at court.

Caesar next addressed those of his honors list who were in attendance—a decoration for a retiring general, two or three sub-prefectures for rising young aristocrats, and a number of other awards. My attention wandered and from behind my impassive servant's face I idly contemplated the splendid scrollwork and beautiful upholstery of the palace's *triclinium* couches. My eyes strayed to the shapely lower limbs of a noble lady who was reclining only six or seven feet from where I stood. I watched surreptitiously as she scratched languorously the sole of her left foot with the toes of her right...

"Pontius Pilate!"

That jolted me out of my errant observations! Caesar had called out the name of my hitherto unseen quarry, the knight. At last I meet him. Well, not meet exactly, but you know what I mean.

"Stand here beside me, Pilate," the emperor said. My pulse raced as I watched the man with whom Caesar had exchanged glances earlier arise from his couch. He smiled at the handsome woman who reclined beside him and walked toward the emperor.

I had pictured him as a tall, lean man, sharp featured with stern mouth and humorless eyes. I suppose my vision was colored by the vague descriptions given me by Bato and the girls and poor old Carbo. And after all, he was a murderer.

But the man standing beside Caesar was little more than average height, tending toward middle-aged stockiness, with thinning hair, gray at the temples. It was his face that fascinated me—not at all the crafty, grim countenance of my mind's eye. Instead, Pontius Pilate had rosy, rounded features with a firm chin, an amiable set to his mouth and eyes that suggested good humor. The overall impression was one of good-natured intelligence. He looked more avuncular than murderous.

An excited murmur ran through the assembly, the guests wondering what the emperor's last announcement of the evening would reveal. Caesar waited patiently for the hum to subside, his left hand resting lightly upon Pilate's shoulder.

"I am now in the thirteenth year of holding the tribunician power. This responsibility I did not seek but having assumed it I have tried to exercise it in the best interests of the senate and people of Rome. I know full well that there is an undercurrent of republican sentiment which survives in the breasts of many men from the rank of senator to the lowest stable attendant. What such men forget is that we live today, and that the Roman republic died half a century ago. Many of you lived, as I did, in its final years and you can remember the anarchy and civil wars which sapped the strength of Rome and left a divided senate and army. In contrast, today Rome and the provinces over which it holds dominion enjoy peace and a sound economy. This is so—but it is not the accomplishment of Caesar. It is the product of many dedicated, loyal Romans over many years, men who have left the comforts of Rome to dwell in distant garrisons and to administer Roman law and government throughout the empire."

Tiberius paused, as though reflecting on his own words.

"There are many such men as these and the loyal wives who stand at their sides. And their deeds are a rebuke to those who can only complain and find fault, those who render nothing of themselves to the state. Pontius Pilate is one of those who have served Rome faithfully over many years as a soldier and administrator. In recognition of his proven loyalty and demonstrated ability I appoint him *Praefectus Iudaeae* in the imperial province of Syria."

Tiberius turned to Pilate and embraced him. The Praetorian Prefect, Aelius Sejanus, arose from his couch, crying "*Macte virtute, Pilate!*" Instantly every male in the hall stood and echoed his words. "Well done! Bravo, Pilate!"

So, my elusive knight is to be governor of Judea. From all I've heard of the Jews, he'll have his hands full.

• • •

The circumstances of my becoming a freedman were most worthy of Macro's *modus operandi*. On the day after he'd reported to Caesar on the charioteer's murder investigation he sent for me in the early evening.

"Very well, Anthus," he began without preamble, "the emperor has accepted your account of the assassination of whatshisname, the charioteer."

"Hesper, sir. Albino Vitalis Hesper."

"Whatever. Sounds like a damn Greek. Greek, was he, eh?"

"From Corinthus, yes, sir."

"Bad lot, those Greeks. At best, nothing but a crowd of prattling lawyers and philosophers."

"Indeed, sir." It didn't seem an appropriate time to mention Alexander of Macedon and other such luminaries, nor the fact that at that moment Macro and I were discoursing in Greek.

"Anyway, Caesar was pleased with the result of your investigation. He doesn't know who you are, by the way. Didn't ask. I simply told him that you were a member of my staff. I understand the emperor well enough but I'm not quite sure how he'd take to the news that a slave had been the key figure in the thing."

Now his jocular tone turned serious. "Anthus, you're well aware of the grave implications of this matter. What it comes down to is that only three people know about it— Caesar, myself and you. I've sworn an oath of secrecy to the emperor and I've told him on my honor that you are to be trusted. Tomorrow I will ask you to take an oath before our household shrine and swear by Jupiter and the gods that protect this house that the entire matter remains secret."

I assured him that I'd willingly do so, but wondered at his request. A slave has no civil rights and his oath has no validity in law.

Macro dwelt a while longer on the subject of the old senator and the charioteer while I paid sober attention. Then he reverted to his mock brusque manner.

"So then, Anthus," he said, "now that this business is at an end, let's have an accounting of the expense money I gave you. I trust there may be a coin or two remaining after your profligate disbursements."

Would he ever forget about poor old Bato and the hot lunch I treated him to? "Sir, I'll bring the account and the balance of the money from my office."

"Do that, Anthus, do that. And while you're out, tell that lad Rufio to fetch us a jug and two cups. We'll probably be here awhile yet."

"Rufinus, sir. Yes, I'll tell him."

After Macro's past commentary on my extravagant dissipation of the expense money, jesting as it was, I thought I'd torment him a little and give him real cause to complain.

Sighing heavily, I studied the account page, holding it so Macro couldn't see the entries. "Sir, you'll appreciate, I'm sure, that I encountered many people during the course of the investigation. Yes, many people."

"Yes, yes. And all of whom you treated to hot sausage, I daresay. Just get on with it, Anthus."

"Um, well, not all, sir. No. But of course each one in his or her way had to be...encouraged, one might say. Their good will had to be, um..."

"Bought, Anthus, bought," he said wearily. "Dammit, just tell me how much you spent, eh?"

"Bought. Yes, sir. Although myself, I prefer a less direct description—gaining their confidence, perhaps? There were the girls in the brothel to start with, although the few *denarii* dispensed to them is a negligible item. No, sir, it was the others who required more substantial largesse."

"What others, dammit?"

"They're all noted, sir. Yes. There were the three tavern keepers, such avaricious, grasping men those people are, sir. Then there were the priest, the porter at the magistrate's office and the orderly room decurion in the Urban Cohorts' Fifth district headquarters. To name a few, sir, to name a few. There were several others, of course."

"Oh, of course!" Macro cried. "Pray, tell me more, Anthus!"

"Then, needless to say, I had a few other expenses, quite

unforeseen. But that's the way things go, isn't it, sir?" I gave another despairing sigh over the perversity of life. "You see, sir, while you were away in Capreae the weather here was most inclement. Oh, it rained ceaselessly, sir. And I walked many miles daily and unfortunately ruined my best sandals."

"Your best sandals, indeed!" he interrupted. "And just *why*, if I may presume to inquire, did you have to wear your best sandals, eh? Which, I suspect you're about to tell me, you replaced, no doubt graciously extending your custom to one of the city's more expensive *emporia*."

"Ah, sir," I said admiringly, "you're away ahead of me. As always, sir. Yes, you're right. But it was then I realized that with the excessive walking necessitated by my investigation in such foul weather...well, sir, in short, for the last few days I made my way about the city in a litter."

"You WHAT?" Macro stared in disbelief. "You hired a litter to cart you about your business! A litter! Damn your alien hide, tell me outright how much you spent!"

"Very well, sir. Now, you advanced me two hundred *denarii*...oh, did I mention the weaver's assistant? The one who..."

"Anthus!"

"Yes, sir. Here is a detailed list of my expenses." I passed it to him. "You will note, sir, that of the two hundred *denarii*, I'm returning to you one hundred and ninety-one." I withdrew a purse from my tunic and placed it before him.

He stared with raised eyebrows at the purse, then at me. "What? You spent only nine *denarii*? Only *nine*?"

"Nine, sir." Actually I'd spent a little more than that, but my devious mind wouldn't permit me to include the donative to the temple of Hercules or the cost of the little blue chariot. Besides, I'd actually made a small profit on the latter purchase, hadn't I?

He waggled his forefinger at me. "You were having fun with me, damn you," he grinned. "For a while there I was beginning to wonder."

Macro slid the purse back toward me. "It's yours. You've earned it." Taken aback, I stuttered some appropriate words of appreciation.

He poured two cups of wine, passing one to me. His manner was serious again. What other matters had he to talk about?

"What's a fair price, would you say, for a slave of your age and skills, Anthus?" Macro asked.

Startled, I quipped, "Thinking of selling me, sir?"

"Ump. If I had my wits about me, I would. Well?"

I mused a moment. "I believe, sir, a fair price for one of my age, health and training would be between forty and fifty thousand *denarii*." *What's all this about?*

"And the dark-eyed girl, Plautilla, the cook's assistant—what price would she bring, eh?"

"Petronia, sir. She's not fully trained yet, but shows good promise. Between twenty and twenty-five thousand, sir."

"Say forty-five for you and twenty-five for her—that's seventy thousand. Tell me, Anthus, have you got any money tucked away? I know damn well you must have, what with the gratuities my clients pass along to you...which I'm not supposed to know anything about. And only the gods know what graft and corruption goes on between you and the butcher and greengrocer. So then, how much?"

"I have a little more than sixteen hundred, sir..." I glanced at the purse on the table. "And this."

"A trifle short of seventy thousand."

"A trifle, sir. Indeed."

Macro raised his cup and took a long drink, followed by an exaggerated grimace. "The damn merchant who sold you this should be publicly flogged and you along with him. Getting a little kickback from him, are you?"

I refrained from telling him that this was the wine which he'd purchased himself in Neapolis a few weeks ago at a price which made me flinch when he told me. I'd have paid one-third as much.

"So, Anthus, you think you're worth around fifty thousand? Well, damn your alien hide, I'll tell you what you're worth. Fifty-five hundred *sesterces*. Probably less than that, truth be known."

I gaped. I must have, because he then said, "Don't sit there gaping. Just trot away to your office or wherever you keep your hoard and bring me fifty-five hundred *sesterces*. Or have you invested your wealth with some wretched grain broker in the forum?"

"Sir?" I squeaked, still dazed.

Macro sighed. "Anthus, you may purchase your freedom for the amount stipulated. Now hurry along before I change my mind."

I hurried along and returned in less time than it takes to cook asparagus. I placed the coins, wrapped in a small piece of cloth, in front of him. My heart thumped as I watched him count them slowly.

"Ump. Well, it's all there." He looked at me levelly. "Very well, Anthus, you're a freedman. Well, not yet of course. But you will be tomorrow when we have a statement of manumission prepared and witnessed. And Anthus…"

"Sir?" I whispered, trying to stay my tears.

"As a freedman, you may purchase the freedom of the woman Petronia. I was thinking of asking one hundred and ninety-one *denarii* for her. You wouldn't happen to have that amount handy, I suppose?"

Unable to speak, I picked up the expense money purse which still rested on the table and placed it before him. Now I couldn't hold my tears and, embarrassed, buried my face in my hands. I felt Macro's hand on my shoulder and after a moment I looked up. Macro, the crusty, profane, bullying old bastard, was weeping also.

"You're supposed to be happy, dammit," he croaked,

"so stop your snuffling. It's me who has the right to cry. I've got to start paying you a damn salary now—and your wench. Oh, yes, you'll force me into poverty yet."

"Salary, sir?" I said.

"Salary. Yes. Unless you're prepared to stay on as steward without remuneration. Quintipor, as a freedman, you may do what you wish, but I'm asking you to remain as household steward. Will you?"

"After twelve years in your house, I have no wish to serve elsewhere," I replied in all truth.

Three jugs of wine later and well into the sixth night hour we ended our evening. "G'night, Quintipor," Macro said. "Guess I can't call you that any more...you're not my boy now, are you? Rufus will be my "Quintipor" from now on. Nice little fellow." He belched loudly. "And one of your first jobs as a freedman will be to find a teacher for him. Gotta get Rufio educated, learn how to talk polished like Anthus, eh?"

"I'll find a good *magister* for your consideration, sir. Rufinus will prove an apt student, I'm sure."

"Do that, old Anthus, damn your alien hide. Do that. No, can't say that any more, either. Not right to curse my new freedman. But, dammit, Anthus, you know I never really meant it."

"I'd rather have my alien hide damned by Sutorius Macro than praised by Tiberius Caesar," I said. The wine had made me maudlin, perhaps, but I meant what I said.

"That reminds me, before you leave, I have a gift for you from Caesar." Macro took a purse from his table drawer and passed it to me. "The emperor said that he appreciated the job you did, and that he also appreciates a discreet man. He said to tell you that the assassination of Vitalis Hesper is to be chiseled from your memory."

"Caesar's trust will not be abused, sir," I told him.

He nodded, then after a brief hesitation said, "Anthus, when you are freed tomorrow, you will have the privilege of assuming two more names. I want you to know that should you follow convention and take my family name and given name, I shall be pleased."

"Sir, tomorrow I shall assume the *tria nomina* Quintus Sutorius Anthus. I will wear it with pride."

"Then goodnight, my Quintipor." He smiled. "I thank you for your loyal service, Quintus Sutorius Anthus."

"Goodnight, Quintus Naevius Cordus Sutorius Macro," I said. "And it is I who thank you."

In my room I spilled out the gold and silver coins from Caesar's purse onto my bed. There were exactly fifty-five hundred *sesterces*. Damn my alien hide—the exact amount Macro had named as my freedom price.

Epilogue

Today is the Ides of March, the day on which the senate never meets. It is the "Day of Parricide," the seventieth anniversary of the assassination of Gaius Julius Caesar.

After his death, Rome was plagued by civil wars until Caesar's sister's grandson, Octavianus, at age thirty-six became master of Rome and, therefore, of the world. He became the first emperor, Augustus Caesar, and ruled for forty years.

Caesar assassinated? Why not state more honestly that he was murdered? Ah well, the equivocators would explain, murder is evil and wicked whereas assassination implies dedication to some higher purpose. They could add that it also implies the use of a hired killer, whose employer would shrink personally from such a deed.

Julius Caesar, *dictator perpetuus* of Rome, was assassinated. Vitalis Hesper, charioteer, was murdered. Caesar was stabbed twenty-three times by a group of his friends in the senate house. Vitalis Hesper, lying drunk on a whorehouse bed, was beheaded by an unknown killer.

The settings of the two events exemplify the difference between assassination and murder—one, a public statement in defense of a noble cause; the other, plain butchery.

But when Macro told me of his conversation with Caesar he referred to the charioteer's death as "assassination." He hadn't done so previously. I believe I know why. Caesar probably used the term and Macro, without giving thought to it, echoed what the emperor had stated.

Was this a *lapsus linguae* on Caesar's part, saying assassination instead of murder? He should have been more cautious. His slip of the tongue confirmed what I'd believed since the day I'd followed the knight's path along the Vicus Patricius. For on that day, my route had led me directly to the main gate of the palace of Tiberius Caesar.

It was then I knew that Vitalis Hesper had been condemned by Tiberius Caesar and executed by Pontius Pilate. And, in the rarefied atmosphere of Caesar's perception, the charioteer's death was not the sordid slaughter of a provincial upstart, but the assassination of one who had profaned Roman morality.

Julius Caesar was assassinated by his erstwhile friends because they considered him a threat to the republican structure of Rome and, therefore, a threat to their social position in the system.

The charioteer was assassinated because he was a threat to the imperial family. He'd dared to sleep with the emperor's niece who was also his daughter-in-law. And he'd violated the law of treason by impugning the honor of the imperial family with his story of the murder of the emperor's son.

Vitalis Hesper was a fool. Like so many who achieve wealth and fame without the benefit of having been eased into them from birth, he lost his perspective. He mistakenly equated the mindless, screaming adulation of the vulgar mob with the amused tolerance of the upper classes. The awe-struck shoemaker's apprentice worshipped him as a hero but the nobility admired him as they would a handsome, well-trained horse.

I believe, therefore, that the charioteer of the Blue Stable died because he was a stupidly injudicious man whose indiscretions were brought to the attention of the two most powerful men in Rome, Caesar and Sejanus.

It was Caesar, not Sejanus, who closed the mouth of Vitalis forever. Why not Sejanus? I suggest that Caesar beat him to it by only a day or two. Sejanus had contrived the death of the senator in less than a day, so why not the charioteer also? The reason seems obvious to me. The death of a nobleman is of passing interest to the populace. The cruel ones say "good riddance"; the more humane merely shrug and say "it comes to us all."

But the death of a hero is a different matter. The people have lost a living symbol of their own fantasies. With overcharged emotion they cry "We shall not see his like again" and such bombast. But they mean it, truly convinced that an era has passed. If their hero was killed in a racing accident, then at least he died in a fitting manner, with glory and honor, and the shock of his loss is softened accordingly.

Should their idol be murdered, there is little that may soften their outrage. An enraged Roman mob means violence. Nor would the mob heed the fine distinction between assassination and murder, if indeed they were aware that such existed.

Both Caesar and Sejanus understood the temperament of the populace but Caesar acted while Sejanus held back. Sejanus had more to lose, I suppose. He hadn't achieved his goal and needed to proceed with discretion. I was given a purse of gold and silver coins for my discretion. What reward will Sejanus receive when his time comes?

You understand now why I couldn't tell Macro the name of the killer. When Macro gave the copy of the senator's letter to Caesar, the emperor was no doubt elated by such a windfall—the deathbed testimony of a patrician, clearly implicating Sejanus in the deaths of both senator and charioteer. His elation would have turned into something less, though, if Macro had then informed him that the name of the killer was one Pontius Pilatus, knight and one-time administrative officer in the imperial palace. Pleased with himself, Macro would have awaited an expression of satisfaction from Caesar.

Caesar would outwardly have praised Macro for his diligence and zeal. But to himself he would have said, "Macro is right, the assassin was Pilate; but Macro is wrong, Pilate was *my* agent, not that of Sejanus. Macro, excellent fellow that he is, has cut too closely to the bone—therefore, Macro must leave us."

No, I was right to have done things as I did. And matters have turned out well, for the most part. The two thugs who were selected as Vitalis Hesper's killers were crucified and burnt before cheering spectators during the Plebian games last November. The mob was satisfied and they've all but forgotten Vitalis now. New heroes are acclaimed on every hand—a Samnite gladiator and a rising young charioteer of the Red Stable.

Petronia and I are freed and receiving salaries for doing the jobs we both enjoy. Tiro remains as steward in the House of Aviola and seems contented with his new master, Felix Aviola, who has taken his place in the senate.

Little Rufinus—Macro calls him 'Quintipor' now—is doing well in school. He complains that his *magister* is a strict disciplinarian. Hah! These children today don't know what discipline is! Now, when *I* was in school...but that's getting away from the subject.

Caesar has been in Capreae for several months and if the marketplace chatter is to be believed, enjoying perverse sexual extravagances with a large assortment of slaves—men, women and small children. Sejanus remains in Rome as the emperor's regent. That puzzles me. Perhaps it means that Caesar didn't consider Sejanus's treatment of the old senator to be of much importance, and that he doesn't believe the story that his son Drusus was murdered by Sejanus and Livilla.

Sejanus is the most powerful man in Rome but the most powerful woman is Antonia. She's probably the only person that doesn't fear Sejanus. On the other hand, Sejanus probably fears her. She's the daughter of the republican hero, Marcus Antonius and her great-great uncle was Julius Caesar. She's the sister-in-law of the present emperor, she's richer than Croesus—and the entire population of Rome adores her. With these credentials, the noble lady Antonia isn't likely to be trifled with by anyone, including Sejanus. But even the exalted have their disappointments and Antonia's, so I hear, are in her children. She considers her son Claudius a buffoon and she knows her daughter Livilla is a wanton.

Young Gaius, Caligula, is a popular figure in the city. Wherever he goes the crowds applaud and call out such endearments as "baby" and "little chick." Like his grandmother Antonia, his credentials are impeccable, being descended from both the Julian and the Claudian families. Macro continues to cultivate him. I said before that my master considers him a rising star in the Roman sky. I'm a bit leery of the boy myself, and yet he's acted decently enough to me in recent months when he's been Macro's guest. He even gave Petronia and me ten gold pieces when Macro told him of our wedding, so perhaps I'm too critical of the lad. By the time Caligula assumes the *toga* of manhood he may have shaped up. Time will tell. A rather good expression, that—time will tell. I'll note it, with my other clever utterances.

Five months and five days have passed since I suggested to Macro that I investigate the charioteer's murder. I wonder now at my brashness and wonder even more at Macro's approval, reluctant as it was. At the outset I was highly pleased with my rapid progress. I thought I was such a clever fellow. But in less than a week Parcae, goddess of fate, tapped me on the shoulder and reminded me that I was but a tiny pebble on the beach, not a boulder.

It was, of course, the senator's letter with its damning statements about Sejanus that convinced me I'd found my man. I already knew who had killed Vitalis in the brothel— Pontius Pilate. That's all that I'd set out to do: find out who had slain the charioteer. My task was completed. But I then realized there was a more important question to be answered. *Why* would he have done it?

Apart from the high-minded idea of assassination, a member of the upper classes isn't likely to shove a blade into a lowly plebian, much less remove his head. Your average patrician might well have the desire to despatch a member of the lower orders but he'd be likely to hire a thug to do the deed.

Yet, here we had a gentleman of rank doing the job in person and in a whorehouse, of all places. If he wanted Vitalis dead, all he had to do was walk into the nearest tavern and make a few guarded inquiries. The city abounds with thugs who'd knife their own brother for the price of a jug of Falernian. But he didn't. He did it himself. And in a professional manner. By that I don't mean just the killing, which was professionally done from the description I've had—the objective report by the Urban Cohort, that is; not the lurid scene of mayhem as reported by such reliable citizens as Horio the greengrocer's wife's cousin.

I refer more to the manner in which the knight carried out his task. It was organized administratively, with premeditation and planning. The man knew where Vitalis would be at what time. He had the cooperation of Madame Jucunda and little Dorcas. There's no doubt that their cooperation was coerced by their awareness of his rank and intimidation by a no-nonsense manner, but the fact is he had their assistance. And he recompensed them for their trouble. Well, Dorcas for certain and in all probability Jucunda received a handsome gratuity for her discretion.

He killed the charioteer, and after washing his hands—the Cohort's report stated that there was a bloodied bowl of water and a soiled towel in the room—he walked away from the house. What a tragedy that he stopped to exchange a few words with old Carbo. If he'd ignored the chestnut vendor, Carbo would still be alive. I wouldn't have learned the knight's name, true; but what matter? I couldn't divulge it in any case.

It became apparent from what I'd learned from the brothel women and from Bato that this was not a personal vindictive murder. The indifferent efficiency of the act, the rank of the killer, his method of operation—it all added up to him being another's agent.

A man of his position would have been the agent of someone with influence, a man with *auctoritas*. Someone who could summon him to the city, employing a chief centurion as messenger.

The charioteer was beheaded with an officer's bone-handled, double-edged short sword—known as a "Spanish" sword—with the insignia of the Praetorian Guard on its pommel. The weapon had been left with the body intentionally. It was found lying parallel to Vitalis' right leg, his hand resting on the hilt. Was the knight making a statement? Such as "those who live by the sword die by the sword"? In this case it would have been more like "Behold what happens to plebians who tread on patrician toes."

Macro's sudden departure for Capreae was providential. If it hadn't been for that, I'd have informed him that

Pilate was the murderer and named the people who could testify on various aspects of the matter—the ladies in the brothel, Bato, Carbo and the chief centurion.

Pleased with myself at having learned the killer's identity so quickly, self-admiration had blinded me to what later became obvious—this was not a simple crime of passion, temper or drunkenness. The very nature of the crime should have alerted me to walk with caution. Yes, the extra time given me by Macro's absence was a blessing.

When Macro was away and I obtained the senator's letter from Tiro, I was still cocksure. Was I not now able to prove to Macro that Sejanus was the author of both the senator's and the charioteer's deaths and that Pilate was beyond doubt his agent in the murder of Vitalis?

It was the happy-go-lucky attendant in the Temple of Hercules who had jolted me out of my self-satisfaction and set me to reconsidering. While I walked away from the temple, musing on his explanation of his invocation to the god, I suddenly thought of Carbo telling me that his friend, the chief centurion, had accompanied the knight through the Viminal Gate. From there, the knight had proceeded alone, and with no "shilly-shallying," followed the Vicus Patricius into the heart of Rome, to the imperial palace.

When I realized that it had been the emperor and not Sejanus who had arranged the killing, it began to make sense. Vitalis had violated *maiestas*, the law against treason, by virtue of having repeated a scandalous tale involving members of the imperial family. Anyone other than a popular hero who did such a thing would have been publicly executed or at the least banished for life to a remote island. But a public idol had to be dealt with discreetly, without involving the state.

I believe that Sejanus would have handled the matter in such manner as sending for the president of the Traveling Athletes Guild Dedicated to Hercules and telling him, "I'm recommending to the emperor that you be elevated to the knightly order. In the meantime, please see that the charioteer Vitalis Hesper has a fatal accident during the games in Neapolis. And here's half a million *denarii* for your trouble." The president would have been created a knight and Vitalis would have had a glorious death on the racetrack.

So it was Caesar who ordered the deaths of Jucunda and her girls and of Carbo. Pilate undoubtedly told him later of the handful of people he'd encountered that evening. If Pilate had been a professional assassin he'd have slain the women, leaving no witnesses; nor would he have paused to talk with Carbo. But he saw no threat in them.

Caesar, however, took no chances. And Caesar has paid me for my discretion, mistakenly believing that my discretion concerns only the contents of the senator's letter. And I will honor my oath of discretion. But not for honor's sake—for the sake of my own life.

I am going into the city now. Five months ago today the brothel women and Ignatius Carbo lost their lives. I have vowed to honor their memories on the fifteenth day of each month for one year.

I will go to the Temple of Venus and pour a libation to the goddess in the names of Jucunda, Dorcas and Emmachia—the radiant and bubbly Emmachia who never had the chance to buy her nuptial veil with my wedding gift of two *denarii*.

Then I will offer wine in the Temple of Mars on behalf of Ignatius Carbo, once of Legion Twenty Valeria, who gave an eye and an arm for Rome in a German forest.

Who will remember them when the likes of Bato the potter and myself are gone? Who will remember Petronia and me?

Who now remembers Vitalis Hesper? Worshipped by millions half a year ago; today forgotten. And thousands of years from now the world will rave in mindless adoration of the athletes of their time, and then forget them.

For that matter, with the passage of time, who will know the name of Tiberius Caesar, ruler of the world? Or of his prefects, Sutorius Macro and Aelius Sejanus? Or of Pontius Pilate?

Perhaps Caesar and his prefects will be inscribed briefly on the pages of history. But Pilate is merely the governor of a small, remote Jewish province.

Who will know the name of Pontius Pilate fifty years from now?

Postscript

Tiberius Caesar spent the last eleven years of his rule on the island of Capreae, now known as the Isle of Capri in Naples harbor.

Aelius Sejanus remained Praetorian Prefect until A.D. 31 when he and his family were executed by Tiberius.

Sutorius Macro succeeded Sejanus as Praetorian Prefect. Promoted to the prefecture of Egypt in A.D. 38, he was executed by Caligula before assuming the position.

Pontius Pilatus was governor of Judea from A.D. 26 to 36, an unusually long term of office at that time. Removed on grounds on having exceeded his authority, he allegedly committed suicide. Pilate's final days are disputed by historians. He may have become a Christian. He has been canonized in the Abyssinian Church and his wife Procula in the Greek.

Gaius Caesar, "Caligula," succeeded Tiberius in A.D. 37 at age 24 and was murdered in A.D. 41 by officers of the Praetorian Guard.

Claudius—Tiberius Claudius Nero Germanicus succeeded his nephew Caligula as emperor in A.D. 41, dying in A.D. 54 at age 63.

Livilla, Claudius' sister, was starved to death in A.D. 31, allegedly, by her mother Antonia for her complicity with Sejanus in the murder of her husband Drusus, son of Tiberius.

Antonia, mother of Claudius and Livilla, committed suicide in A.D. 37 at age 72.

Julia Augusta Livia, mother of Tiberius and widow of Augustus Caesar died in A.D. 29 aged 86.

Titus Calpurnius Siculus, whose birth and death dates are unknown, flourished as a poet during the emperorship of Nero, who succeeded Claudius in A.D. 54. He may or may not have been a slave but he was certainly of humble origin. His poetic style was similar to that of Publius Vergilius Maro, known as 'Vergil.'

•••

Glossary

Arval Brethren An elite priestly college of 12 men dedicated to the worship of the agricultural god, Dea Dia. Its origins pre-date the Roman republic and its liturgy was almost meaningless to its members by the first century A.D.

Centurion, primus pilus The most junior ranking officers in the Roman army, centurions were, in most cases, promoted from the ranks and were "career" soldiers. A centurion commanded a "century"—80 men, plus 20 non-combatant logistic staff. There were up to 66 centurions in a legion, the senior one being the *primus pilus*, chief centurion, a figure of great prestige. In comparison with modern ranks, a junior centurion would be a lieutenant or captain, and the chief centurion a lieutenant colonel.

Conscript Father The formal term for senator. Originally, senators were from the patrician families, the *patres*, and were appointed or "conscripted" to the senate. Later, most senators were of plebian birth, but the name Conscript Father remained.

Equestrian Members of the *ordo equester*, the *equites*—knights—were originally a middle class between the patricians and the lower levels of plebians. By early empire, they had achieved considerable influence through their wealth. Financial qualification for the order was 400,000 *sesterces* in assets; admission was by birthright or appointment by the emperor. The knights eventually occupied most of the empire's administrative posts and dominated the senate.

Guilds By the first century A.D., there were more than 150 artisan and trade guilds in Rome. The ancestors of today's unions, Roman guild corporations had little or no political or economic clout by modern standards. They provided various services to their membership, such as schooling for children, social events and funeral services. The latter were very important to the Romans; they had a morbid fascination with death and the after-life and wanted a good send-off when their time came.

Hours of the day The Roman day had 24 hours, divided into 12 day and 12 night hours. The day hours began at sunrise and ended at sunset. This meant that the hours shortened and lengthened over the year. To illustrate, using modern time designation: the tenth day hour extended from 2:13 to 2:58 P.M. on December 21, but from 3:46 to 5:02 P.M. on June 21. Time, to the Romans, was elastic.

Ides of March Each of the 12 Roman months had three reference dates, the Kalends, Nones and Ides. The Kalends were the first day of each month and the Nones were the fifth day of some months, but the seventh day for others. The Ides were the thirteenth day of the month except for March, May, July and October, which were the fifteenth day. Roman time reference was "backward" from these monthly designations—instead of saying "the twelfth of October," they would say "three days before the Ides of October."

Insula A relatively small area, ancient Rome was a city of high rises by necessity; its one million population expanded vertically rather than horizontally, living for the most part in *insulae* (islands), apartment buildings. Some of these rose 100 feet or more, but the average *insula* was about five stories, half that height.

Jupiter The premier god of the Roman pantheon and patron god of the City of Rome. He was referred to by his full appellation, *Jupiter Optimus Maximus*, Jupiter Best and Greatest.

Lar, lararium The *lares* were the gods of the home and of crossroads. They were not anthropomorphic deities, but a spiritual presence, having no form, sex or mythology. The *lararium*, the household's personal family shrine, was a wall niche, usually with doors like a small cupboard. It often held statuettes of family ancestors.

Legions At the time of this story, A.D. 26, there were 25 legions posted throughout the empire, supported by a large number of auxiliary cohorts recruited locally from the indigenous population, but officered by Romans. A legion's strength was from five to six thousand men—spear and sword equipped infantry, supported by small cavalry and artillery units, and a large body of supply, finance and administration staff. Legions were identified by a number and, in most cases, a name, e.g. Legion XII Fulminata. A gold eagle was the standard for all legions, but each had its own emblem as well—bull, goat, horse, boar, etc.

Mile The Roman *mille passuum* (from which we take our name "mile") translates literally as "a thousand paces." It was a distance of 4,854 feet, roughly equivalent to our mile.

Money Roman money was minted in ten coins but the only ones worth mentioning here are the *as*, *sestertius*, *denarius* and *aureus*. The imperial gold *aureus* had the value of 25 silver *denarii*. The *denarius* equaled four bronze *sesterces*; the *sestertius* equaled 12 bronze *asses*. The standard Roman money reference was the *sestertius*, as the dollar is today in the U.S.A. It's misleading to define the value of Roman currency in terms of modern equivalents, but as a comparison guide, the average daily wage of a semi-skilled Roman worker was two *denarii*.

Names The three names, the *tria nomina*, indicated Roman citizenship. Its components were the *praenomen*, the given name; the *nomen*, the clan or gentilical name; and the *cognomen*, a family name within the clan. Thus, the name Tiberius Claudius Nero indicates that Tiberius (a first name like John or Peter) belonged to the Nero family branch of the larger clan, Claudius. A very few Romans used only the given and clan names, such as Marcus Antonius (anglicized to Marc Antony) and some took additional names to the *tria nomina*, such as Quintus Naevius Cordus Sutorius Macro.

Nobles Not to be confused with a patrician, a noble, *nobilis*, was one descended from a consul of Rome. The nobility included both patricians and plebians. By mid-fifth century

B.C., the earlier Roman kings had been replaced by two consuls, each elected for a one year term. These were the joint chief magistrates of Rome during the republic and held vast power. Although their authority waned under the empire, their political and social status remained the highest next to that of the emperor.

Paterfamilias The "father of the family," the formal head of a family unit, who literally held the power of life and death over family members. His extreme authority was probably an inheritance of the republican belief in the sanctity of the family and the lack of regular courts and policing.

Patrician By 500 B.C., Roman society had evolved into two socio-political classes, the patricians and the plebians. The patricians were the aristocracy, the oldest and wealthiest families, which dominated senate, priesthood and public office. During the 500 odd years of the Roman republic, the equestrians, the "knights," emerged from the plebian class and became a minor aristocracy to the patricians. By the time of the first emperor (Augustus Caesar, 27 B.C.), the patrician families had been depleted in numbers, wealth and political influence.

Roman year date Romans numbered their years from the founding of Rome in 753 B.C. by the legendary king, Romulus. The Roman year was designated by the suffix "A.U.C.," an abbreviation of *ab urbe condita*—"since the founding of the city." Sometimes this was given as *anno urbis conditae*, "in the year of the founding of the city." Tiberius Caesar was born, to us, in 42 B.C.; but, to him, it was 712 A.U.C.

Senate, senators The *senatus* was originally comprised of 300 patricians but by early empire, had swollen to about three times that many, more plebian than patrician. Augustus Caesar reduced its size to 600 and established a property requirement of one million *sesterces*. Although the senate lost much of its authority under the empire, it remained a semi-hereditary aristocracy with important duties and prestigious social position. Senators served for life. Their badge of distinction was a broad purple stripe running vertically on their tunic.

A final note The sayings and maxims used in this story are not anachronisms—the ancient Romans were using them two millenia ago. As they would have said, "Nil novi sub sole"—"There's nothing new under the sun."

Lovers are out of their minds. (Love is blind.)—*Amantes sunt amentes.*

Like father, like son. (A chip off the old block.)—*Qualis pater talis filius.*

Fortune goes to the bold. (Nothing ventured, nothing gained.)—*Audaces fortuna iuvat.*

The end justifies the means.—*Exitus acta probat.*

Let my will stand as a reason. (Don't argue; just do as I say.)—*Stet pro ratione voluntas.*

It will not be summer forever. (Everything comes to an end.)—*Non semper erat aestas.*

Let arms yield to the gown. (The army must be a servant of the state.)—*Cedant arma togae.*

Fight fire with fire.—*Similia similibus curantor*. Literally, "Similar things cure similar things."

Well done. Bravo!—*Macte virtute*! Literally, "May your merit increase."

The cobbler should not judge above the sandal. (Cobbler, stick to your last.)—*Ne supra crepidam sutor iudicaret*.

More people die partying than in war.—*Plures crapula quam gladius*. Literally, "Drunkenness kills more than the sword."

In the consulship of Plancus.—*Consule Planco*. (Today we'd say, "Back in the good old days!") This expression comes from the Odes of Quintus Horatius Flaccus (Horace) in which he refers to the happy days of his youth during the consulship of Munatius Plancus in 41 B.C.

A word to the wise is sufficient.—*Intelligenti pauca*. Literally, "To the intelligent, few words."

Soon it will be night; let's attend to business.—*Mox nox in rem*. Figuratively, "Let's get the show on the road."

To hold a wolf by the ears.—*Tenere lupum auribus*. The implication is getting on with a job, difficult as it may be. Today, we'd "take the bull by the horns."

Enjoy today; put little trust in tomorrow.—*Carpe diem, quam minimum credula postero*. Another quotation from Horace. Today we say, "Make hay while the sun shines."